Suit on the Run

An Ad Man's Odyssey into the Fourth Dimension

Suit on the Run

An Ad Man's Odyssey into the Fourth Dimension

by

Stephen Adams

Published by
Dreamstate Publishing Company
Toronto, Canada

Editor: Donaleen Saul
Book Design: Tracey Hway & Stephen Adams
Book Layout: Stephen Adams
Cover Illustration: Tracey Hway
Author Photo: Tim Leyes

Library and Archives Canada Cataloguing in Publication

Adams, Stephen, 1960- Suit on the run : --an ad man's odyssey into the fourth dimension / by Stephen Adams.

1. New Age movement--Fiction. 2. Spiritual life--Fiction. I. Title.

PS8601.D457S84 2007 C813'.6 C2007-902142-5

ISBN 978-0-9783357-0-0

For more information about Stephen Adams and his writings:

www.steveadams.tv

www.suitontherun.com

www.dreamstatepublishing.ca

Special thanks to my family, friends and all those who continue to make this journey a special One.

"You've got to be what you are...or end up in the bug house"
Golden Boy by Clifford Odets

~ 1 ~

"I don't know, Jack, is it necessary?" I said, not believing that the vice-president of the Ad agency was about to commit yet another unconscionable act.

"Look it, Peter, I wouldn't be where I am today if I sat around trying to decide what was the morally correct thing to do now would I?"

"Yeah, but Jack, you're talking about a multi-million dollar account selling beef for a corporation who just got a ten-thousand dollar fine for putting addictive chemicals in their cows. Don't you see the inanity of it all? I mean, do we really want to continue to do business with these kind of people?"

Jack slowly leaned over my desk, giving his usual sardonic smile and with one quick blurb, reminded me of what my years of loyalty to the company really meant.

"Listen, Peter, until you become vice-president of this company, keep your mouth shut! Got it? GET IT!"

And thus set the tone for my long weekend.

I couldn't believe that once again I was about to rack my brains for a company with no scruples. With no heart. That my job was on the line if I didn't come up with the best slogan for selling a slab of meat pumped full of addictive and deadly drugs. I'm not naive in the least - I'll play hardball with the next guy - but when it comes to selling out to the system and fooling the public, my shelf life was about to expire.

These thoughts and more raced through my mind as I sat in my high-backed leather chair looking out the window of my 21st floor office. My train of thought was broken when I noticed an elderly man in the building across from me smacking his computer with a nerf bat.

The sudden ringing of my phone spared me deep reflection on the man's feeble ways.

I picked up the receiver hoping it wasn't who I hoped it wasn't. I was starting to get paranoid. Slogans for recycled condoms were just around the corner, I was sure of it. Jack, my morally depleted boss, had a sixth sense for spotting guys looking for an escape route out of the corporate hand-basket.

"Peter here."

"Hi Sweetie!"

At least it wasn't Jack.

"How's your day going?" Sally asked with her usual enthusiasm.

How I ever got hooked up with a chirpy yoga teacher was another item on my list of things to solve as I poked away at the stuffed alien that sat on my desk. Sally gave it to me on our first date. She thought it was cute. Huh.

"Well, we've, ah, we've taken on that, uh, cow campaign."

"But Peter, I told you what those corporations are doing to consumers!"

"I know, I know, Sally. It probably would have been better if you'd explained it to Jack. He likes you. Although, quite frankly, I don't trust his motives. He looks at me as if I'm a warmed-over throwback from the sixties."

"Oh, I'm so sorry to hear that, Sweetie. Maybe I'll throw a bit of white light around his office and see if that changes his mind."

At least the sex was good.

"Maybe you could throw a bit of white light around my lottery ticket so I can go on a permanent holiday," I said, with my usual sarcasm.

I knew she didn't like to be teased about her New Age antics, so as the silence wore on, I surrendered.

"OK, I'm sorry. I'm just having a hard time at work. There's all this pressure to perform and I couldn't give a rat's arse about anything I'm doing here anymore. I'm bored. Disillusioned. Dysfunctional. There's no purpose to any of this crap."

I could hear Sally's wheels turning.

"Peter, I realize that you have, um, reservations, about some of the things that I'm into."

I knew where this was going.

"But why don't you come to the retreat this weekend? It'll be perfect. It's a long weekend and it will give you enough time to relax and clear your head. Think about your future."

I marvelled at her persistence to get me to that "sacred" retreat of hers.

"Honey, you know I respect what you're doing with all that…stuff, but the thought of having to be some place with a bunch of strangers chanting mantras and walking around talking about some guru or god doesn't do it for me right now, OK? Besides, I have a serious deadline with this big chem-, um, cow campaign."

Sally began to speak calmly and precisely. A sure sign I was about to be flattened with a dose of her integrity.

"I would much prefer if you told me the truth rather than lie."

"I am!" But even I could hear that my voice was at a defensive high pitch.

"Peter, you and I both know that you're going to sleep in tomorrow morning, meet the boys for brunch, watch the football game and-"

"OK, OK, OK. So what? It helps me relax."

"You won't even *try* to meet me halfway, will you?"

And with that, I heard the oh-so-familiar dial tone that punctuated every conversation I had with Sally about what to do on the weekend.

I'd been single most my life, well, except for one short marriage when I was too young and an even shorter one when *she* was too young. Routine had always been my best friend. Even though Sally had been good for me, in a calming and distracting kind of way, if there was one thing I didn't want to give up - *for any relationship* - it was my weekend routine with the boys.

I'm not sure I understood why I needed these male bonding activities but I had been doing them for so long, I didn't think about it.

Maybe the primitive pow-wow to watch sports was like an ancient male ritual, handed down over the centuries - a lineage of genetics, bonding of the highest order…or just pure lazy guy stuff. I was open to any of those theories. But bonding with a woman was another story. One that I had yet to comprehend.

I'd actually considered joining a men's group to figure out some of this male mythology stuff but the thought of having to beat on drums and scream at imaginary fathers didn't quite do it for me. It reminded me of - *"Peter!"*

I turned from my mythological reflections and the ever-persistent nerf-batting gent across the way to a red-faced, hyperventilating Jack. I was beginning to understand the guy with the nerf bat.

"Peter? I said, *Peter!*"

"Yes Jack. I hear ya. I'm the only Peter in the room."

"What are you doing?!" His apoplectic display of "I'm the boss and you're just the employee" was getting tiresome.

"I'm, I'm, thinking of new slogans for dead cows, Jack."

He walked over to me, threw down a folder, and headed toward the door.

"Forget the cow account, you're off it. I don't like your attitude."

The long weekend was looking better by the minute.

Then Jack about-faced, stopped, turned back, and gave me the cunning smile that I'd become all too familiar with over the years.

"Look over your new account. It's a small company that I just took on. They want to sell wash-and-wear, recyclable condoms. They tell me you can get up to ten uses out of them before they expire. I think that's a very interesting idea, don't you, Peter? Ecologically correct too! Right up your alley."

My mouth was in shock like the rest of me and couldn't find its muscles to mutter a response.

"I want a complete proposal by Tuesday morning. *Fresh ideas!* Enjoy your long weekend."

And with that, he departed, leaving the stench of conquest in his wake.

I looked at the nerf batter across the way and then the stuffed alien on my desk. I picked up the phone. Paused. Then I pressed the numbers.

"I'll pick you up at seven."

~ 2 ~

My sweaty palms firmly gripping the steering wheel belied my trust in the superior craftsmanship of my BMW. It was nearing midnight, my eyes were getting heavy, and the winding road ahead was looking for its next victim.

The last hour or so on this snaky road was beginning to wear me down. Only my curiosity about what lay ahead kept me awake. I feathered the gas pedal and gently tapped the brakes, cautiously avoiding the serpent's bite. Thankfully it was a clear fall night.

"So what you're really saying is that some guy walks around and pretends he's God?"

Sally laughed.

"That's open for interpretation. But don't worry, I'll be around to protect you from The Almighty."

"Hey, I'm supposed to be the gallant one around here, OK?" I said, defending my male honor.

"Even knights in shining armor need some down time."

Fair enough.

As we drove on, I began to get that uneasy feeling of being lost. Not having been on this road before, I was relying on Sally's memory which, when it came to directions, was not a good thing. We could just as easily end up at a sleazy motel in Tijuana. Sure, it only happened once, but that's a story for another time. I looked over to Sally, her eyes were closed.

"Excuse me? Sally? I need your eyes for directions here, OK? Sally?"

No response.

Then Sally suddenly opened her eyes and said, "Turn left in or about two miles."

"Oy! Sally. Why don't you have a map to this place?"

She laughed and reached for my hand on the armrest.

"The directions are in the mind's eye."

Ah geez, not that New Age crap again.

"Trust," she said, before closing her eyes again.

Just then, I felt a little tingle surf my back. Grandma always said that meant that somebody had walked over my grave. A disconcerting thought to be popping into my head right now.

"Uh, OK. Whatever. As long as you can get us there."

Oh man, and the Giants were the odds-on favorite this weekend.

We continued driving. In silence. Alone. Together.

Sally sat there in her usual poised calm, eyes still closed.

"Are you tired or am I boring you?"

Nothing. No response. I hate it when she does that alpha-state stuff on me.

I had an ominous feeling, driving on a dark and hidden road not knowing where I was going or even where I was *and* with a woman I didn't really know all that well. We could be driving to a place that, for all I knew, was a carwash for brain matter.

I reached over to turn on the radio. Sally stopped me, her eyes still closed. How did she do that? I caved. Sally resumed her alpha silence.

A fork in the road was fast approaching. Just as I was about to ask Sally, once again, for the next bit of direction…

"Go right, my friend," I heard her say.

"Thank you," I replied with what I hoped was a tinge of sarcasm.

She opened her eyes and looked at me. "For what?"

"For telling me to go right," I said, as I dutifully veered right at the fork in the road.

"I didn't say anything," she replied. She *looked* innocent.

"What are you talking about? You just said 'Go right, my friend.'"

"No, I didn't. But you're right, we did have to go right at the fork in the road. Good for you, Peter."

"Sally, you told me to go right."

Sally chuckled. "That was just your inner voice telling you where to go next on the journey. I didn't say anything. Honest."

Holy Mackerel, this chick's a loony tune. This was going to be one loooonnng weekend. They always say, travel with your intended before you get serious and settle down with her. That way, you get to see her, warts and all. I had just found a big fat wart!

"You OK?" she asked.

"Yeah. Sure. Swell."

This was already turning into a bad idea.

On top of it all, this was only Friday and I had three more days left in the middle of nowhere with my wacky yogi girlfriend. Now I know why they call northern Ontario "God's country." Even a global positioning system couldn't guide me back to my boys' weekend. I could feel my stress level rising.

Sally was not one to lie, nor was she one to pull my leg. But flaky? That was another story. Not to be judgmental, but there was a part of her who lived in another world, and she'd be the first to admit it! But she wasn't too crazy about the word "flaky." I learned that the hard way. But that takes us back to the Tijuana story.

OK, giving her the benefit of the doubt, maybe it was because we'd been driving for a few hours and she was tired? Perhaps even a tad delusional? I know I heard what I heard but I was way too tired to get into a major discussion over it.

I surrendered on this one. I learned long ago that whether it was dealing with women or bonehead advertising clients, choose your ditch to die in. Yeah, so I'd hardened over the years. Who hadn't?

As we continued down the endless winding road, a small, low-flying aircraft caught my attention. There were more lights blinking on it than Jack's house at Christmas. I couldn't keep my eyes off them as they reflected their bright colors off the dew-spread wheat field. They were flashing from the front of the aircraft to the back in an inconsistent, alternating pattern.

Fascinating, I thought. I'd never seen anything like it. The aircraft appeared to stop racing forward and was hovering above the glistening wheat field.

When I was a kid, I had taken pride in being able to guess what types of airplanes were flying overhead. Even at night, I could identify them. I had wanted to be an airline pilot when I grew up, and had spent my teens working at the local airport just to be close to my obsession. Although life had taken me in other directions, I had never lost my passion for flying.

This one had me puzzled though. Between its erratic flashing light patterns that were now lighting up the sky and its hovering in one spot, it could only be one thing. A helicopter. Not like any I'd seen before though.

"That's odd, Honey."

"What is?"

"That helicopter, plane, or whatever it is, over there. Look at the way the lights are flashing. Weird, huh? Maybe it's an army helicopter or one of those zeppelins? But then it was zipping around way too fast for it to be a zeppelin, so, huh."

"I don't know," she said, as she leaned over and looked out my side window.

"You think there's an airport around here? It seems to be hovering rather low."

Sally undid her seatbelt and leaned over even more as I noticed the wheat field being illuminated by the elongated aircraft's light show. For some reason, I could feel my spine-chill-o-meter rising.

"Not that I know of. Maybe it's a sign for us to turn left at the next crossroads?" she said.

My arm gently moved her over to her side of the car.

"Sally, buy a map, OK? Next time we go somewhere, buy a friggin' map! Getting lost does not help my blood pressure. It only makes me aggravated and miserable."

Sally squeezed my hand. "No, I'm serious. I feel it's a sign to turn left at the next intersection."

I lost it.

"*Sally! You go to this retreat practically every weekend. How come you don't know where it is? Is it so private that it moves around once a week? I mean, COME ON! This is getting to be ridiculous!*"

My little tantrum affected her angelic presence. Sometimes I felt like a fallen angel who was always struggling to stay on a puffy cloud in the Heavens just to keep at her level.

Her eyes became misty but she still managed to give me a loving smile. I hated it when she got quiet and more loving toward me because of my failings. It was a reverse Catholic guilt trick or something, I was sure of it. Very effective though. Very effective indeed!

"Hey, I'm sorry. Look, the plane, helicopter or whatever the heck that is, is over there on the left. Look, here comes an intersection, so I'll turn left, OK?"

Silence from my passenger. When she shuts me out, she really shuts me out.

I turned left and then noticed the flying object quickly move across the sky to stay parallel with us. Suddenly, its colorful array stretched like an elastic band and doubled its size. And then, just as quickly, the object slingshot itself into the darkness of the night.

My spine-chill-o-meter hit the red line.

Maybe it was one of those jets that can hover and turn on its afterburner. But I'd never seen anything move so quickly out of sight like that before. I stopped the car.

"Did you see that?!" I said. No response. Relationships took so much work sometimes. It's no wonder that, except for the two before-mentioned blips on the marital screen, I'd chosen to be single for so long.

"Honey, I said I was sorry. I guess I'm still carrying work with me. I didn't mean to take it out on you."

I raised her hand and gave it a soft kiss of apology. She looked over and gave me that gentle smile of hers.

I was lost in her soulful eyes.

"I know where it's coming from, but you can't expect me not to take abuse personally. I'm not that good yet."

Ouch!

"Hon, I-"

She leaned over and gave me a softer kiss of acceptance on the cheek.

"Shhh."

When she kissed me, I couldn't help but melt.

After a moment of peace between us, I got back to the task at hand. I put the Beamer back into gear and drove on, completely forgetting about her flaky directions and the unidentified flying object that had so fascinated me only moments before.

~ 3 ~

"OK, so we've done the bit about getting lost in the jungle with your prospective mate. Now where do we go?"

Sally smiled.

"Look, I don't mind being lost, just as long as I know where I am."

Sally laughed.

"We're never lost. It's just that sometimes it is difficult to remember where to go."

She pointed her forefinger to the middle of her forehead and moved it in a circular motion. "This initiates our visionary capabilities."

I played along and copied her actions.

"Right. Oh I see it now. We *are* lost."

"We're not lost," she said, somewhat defensively, at least for her.

"Oh no?"

"No, the next turn will be at the upcoming intersection where a bat will swoop in front of our windshield, bounce off it, and fly away. We just need to turn in the direction it flies off in. It's very simple."

I lowered my finger and gave her a quick side-glance.

"You know, I'm beginning to see why you weird out most of my friends. You're just lucky that in some warped way I'm getting used to your strange slant on life. I think."

"That's why I enjoy being with you. It takes a lot to rattle you."

I must have been a better actor than I thought.

She softly stroked my hand while looking ahead at the fast-approaching intersection. I slowed the Beamer to a complete stop at the dimly-lit crossroad and began to laugh internally at the very thought of two adults waiting for a bat to give them guidance.

We sat there in silence except for the Beamer's mighty, smooth-running engine raring for quick acceleration in any direction.

A few minutes went by.

"I think Batman's making a sequel on some Hollywood back lot."

Sally gave me a look.

"But who knows, maybe he'll send Batgirl to give us directions."

No sooner had I finished my sentence than a live bat came swooping down, striking my side of the windshield, bouncing off and flying to the right. I was freaked. I choked the steering wheel with ice-cold hands.

"It's OK, Peter. It's OK. Breathe. We just have to turn right, that's all."

It took me a few moments to put my car into first gear and turn right. All the alarms were going off. Who was this woman anyway? Sure I'd known her for six months, but what did I *really* know about her? What were the odds of a bat hitting the windshield after someone had just predicted it? What were the odds that I was with a nut case and just didn't know it? What were the odds of me surviving the weekend?

"Peter? Hello? Earth to Peter." I heard Sally's voice echo in my head.

I snapped out of odds-making mode and looked at her with new, distrustful eyes before going off onto the shoulder of the road. I quickly recovered, if for no other reason than I didn't want to be stuck in the middle of nowhere with this person.

I casually placed my left hand on the power lock button, just in case I had to lock or unlock my door in a hurry.

OK, so cowardice was one of my issues.

"Peter, there are some things about this weekend that may be new to your way of thinking."

At this point, getting into a relationship with a woman was new to my way of thinking.

"I hope you can stay open-minded long enough to experience it all."

I didn't respond. It was my turn to be quiet in the game of silent romance. What had just transpired might have seemed small and insignificant to others but I was living it. To see Batman - OK, a flying mouse, coming straight at me was having its effect.

"Peter, come on. Some things just happen and some things are meant to happen. In the grand scheme of things, everything is aligned with the Divine Master Plan."

I looked over to her and spoke as calmly as I could. "You know how I feel when you go off on one of those spiritual tangents. Right now, I'm having a difficult time digesting what just happened. So if you could lay off the New Age lingo, *I would greatly appreciate it!* Thank! You!"

Now Sally became silent. Sometimes the game of silence between couples can be deafening.

"Sally, look, I don't want to get into this too much. I don't even want to hear an explanation. Let's just say, for the sake of peace and sanity - *mine* - that coincidence placed a hand in our direction for a moment and leave it at that. Deal?"

Sally looked over, smiled and said softly, "Deal."

I took in a deep breath.

"Now what are we looking for? I hear deer are in season. They have a good sense of direction. Maybe we should find one."

Sally tapped me on the hand playfully. "Just relax. The next sign will be coming along any moment."

"When you say 'sign,' you wouldn't happen to mean something written on a wooden board that says 'Evergreen Retreat,' would you?"

Sally stared at me blankly.

"I didn't think so."

I was going to have to go on a retreat just to recover from this retreat.

I slammed on the brakes as I saw two glowing eyes staring at us from the middle of the road. I thought it was a cat. The screeching of the tires wasn't enough to scare it away and, as I crept closer, slowing into first gear, I saw what it was - an owl.

"What's an owl doing standing in the middle of the road this late at night? Surely it has better ways of getting warmed up."

"That's our next sign. The dirt road to Evergreen Retreat is just to our right," Sally said, all excited.

"Sally, I know you must be enjoying this but don't push it!"

Sally laughed out loud.

"I'm serious! I know a few peculiar things have happened between us before, but these symbol and sign things are getting out of hand."

THUMP!

I looked at the hood of my car and there was the owl, staring straight at me.

I was getting this weird feeling that it was trying to communicate with me. No doubt if I ate the same kind of food as Sally, I would hear what it was saying.

"OK, we have to move on, quickly. It's a timing thing."

"Huh? A what?"

"A timing thing!" she said, in an urgent tone.

"Look it, when I bought this car, the owl wasn't a hood ornament, OK? Now I know this may happen to you all the time but it's really new to me, so, please, you *have* to explain this one to me."

Sally took in a breath before speaking. "The owl is a doctor of time and it's just letting us know that now is the right time to enter our portal of opportunity. We need to go through it now or we'll miss the retreat this weekend. The retreat operates on a different vibration than the rest of the planet. It's not seen by the average eye."

I doubt if my face had ever looked blanker.

"We just have to turn right, OK?"

"You can't be serious."

"I'm very serious."

"Sally, do your students know you're like this?"

"Sweetie, just go with the flow. As of now, take a breath, trust, and just go with the flow."

I looked at her and then at the owl, then back at her. They were both looking at me as if I was the strange one.

"You know, I always suspected that there was something very different about you. Ever since Richard forced me to take one of your yoga classes, I knew you were different. But I *never* thought I would end up as a sacrificial lamb on some obscure winding road, about to be slaughtered by a stranger and her owl."

Sally began to laugh in what seemed like a frighteningly evil pitch. Or maybe everything was starting to seem frighteningly evil to me in that moment.

"Oh Peter, you're so paranoid. You've got to learn to trust me a little. Nothing is going to happen to you. I promise."

Yeah. Sure. I've seen those movies too. Even the spoofs. And they all have the same ending.

Her smile that usually melted me was going nowhere with this iceberg. I could feel my walls being raised. I would only be able to continue if my defenses were intact.

"So, um, now what?" I asked, trying to remain calm.

"We just drive along, slowly, until we see the dirt road on the right leading to the retreat."

"What about the new hood ornament?"

"Don't worry, it will leave when it wants to."

That was reassuring.

I gently took her hand in mine. "I know this may sound kind of shallow to folks like you, but, I have six payments left on this car. Now, all I ask, *all I ask*, is that I live long enough to experience driving around in a car that I've fully paid for. For just once in my life, *please!* I would like that experience. No, I would *love* that experience. That's all I ask. Pretty please. Let me live long enough to *pay off my Beamer!*"

"Peter, nothing is going to happen to you."

She was looking away when she said that. Hmm.

I took a deep breath, engaged the car in first gear and began to slowly drive down the road, veering toward the right, with the owl on my hood. I was sure there was a potential ad campaign somewhere in this. Man, my work brain was always on.

We, and I mean the owl too, slowly drove along the road for a few minutes.

"Does any of this seem strange to you? *Any of this?* I mean, you know, here we are, driving five miles an hour on some dark back road leading God knows where, with an owl sitting on our hood, ready to give us the signal when to turn right so that we can go to some spiritual retreat that operates on 'a different vibration.' I mean, does this not strike any chord in you that might say, 'Gee Peter, this is an unusual moment in my life, how about yours?' Or am I so terminally superficial that I don't know what's going on in the 'real' world? Is this what's been happening in the 'real world' these days and I've been too busy writing brilliant ad copy to experience it? Or is this just *your* world? I'm curious, that's all."

Sally gave me a stern look.

The owl swiftly flew off the hood and into the blackness of the night, apparently not wanting to witness my futile attempts to reason with Sally.

"There it is, Peter!" Sally sent a piercing shriek through my right eardrum.

"There it is!" she continued, pointing to our immediate right.

Sure enough, there was a dirt road on our right with enormous, plush evergreens standing guard at the entrance, leading us to our destiny.

I was going to miss that owl, I thought, as we drove through the looming evergreen sentinels along the dirt road of potential doom.

~ 4 ~

We remained quiet for some time, traveling down the muddied pathway. Me because of my fear of Sally and her New Age world; Sally because…who knows why?

Unable to fight my true nature, I had to start processing out loud. It was my way of figuring things out, much to the annoyance of some. Well, many.

"Is there anything I should know about this place? Anything you might need or want me to be aware of?" I asked, trying to seem open.

"No Hon, you're a big boy. You'll be able to take care of yourself."

I looked at her olive-skinned face that now wore a mask of disappointment.

"Are you still glad you asked me to come on your sacred retreat?"

Sally looked over to me and then took my hand. "Of course I am. I just have a hard time with expectations. I guess a part of me expects you to be this super-conscious man and understand everything that's going on."

Based on what? I couldn't help wondering.

"I've always expected the men in my life to know everything that I do and yet, I'm beginning to realize that having expectations of men or anyone or anything, for that matter, is a trap for a major downfall."

"Hey, I'm here aren't I?"

"Oh, I know, I know. It's just, why is it so difficult for men to listen to what's going on inside them? Is it really that difficult to trust your instincts?"

"Slow down, Sally. I'm still in therapy over the small questions never mind the big ones, so go easy on me, will ya? Besides, I trust my instincts every day at work. In my business, you have to if you want to survive. You and I just don't hear the same things, that's all. One way is not better than the other. We just have different voices talking to us."

Sally sighed, "I guess." Her voice trailed off as she looked out the window into the darkness.

"It's that whole Mars and Jupiter thing-"

"Mars and Venus," Sally interrupted.

"Yeah. Anyway, same universe."

Sally spoke in a silent whisper, almost to herself.

"I once read in a poem that understanding man is like letting a flower blossom according to its own arrangement with Mother Nature. I just hope we don't run out of time. Mankind, I mean."

I could feel her overwhelming sadness, although, quite frankly, I didn't have a clue what she was talking about.

"I'm very lucky to have someone who cares so much about the world. Thank you, Sally."

I leaned over to give her a kiss while accidentally driving into a small pothole on the road. I ended up kissing her eyeball. But I guess I'd kissed worst places in the ad game.

"There! There it is!" Sally's rapture signaled an abrupt change of mood.

"What's all the excitement for? You're here practically every weekend."

"You have to understand that part of the journey to this retreat is the process of getting here. Sometimes I've been so wrapped up in what you call 'drama' to get here, that I don't make it. If there is one thing I've learned about going on this sacred retreat is that it's always a privilege to walk with the

Masters. It takes a certain amount of trust to get to this portal of timelessness. Not to mention a few initiations."

"I'm glad you're happy," I said, trying to be sincere.

I turned up a narrow driveway, leading to what looked like the House of Usher. OK, maybe not quite that bad. But close.

We slowly drove toward the one-hundred-year-old, dilapidated house with a single porch light on.

"Oh, I remember this joint. Didn't the auto club give it a five-star rating?"

Sally laughed.

"Remember that old saying about not judging a book by its cover? Well, that aptly applies here."

"You know I'm not cheap but I hope we're not paying a lot of money for these, uh, accommodations."

Sally shook her head. "I don't want you to worry about anything; this weekend is on me. And no, it's not expensive. However, there is a price to pay."

"Hey! I don't mind paying-" I began, in full male honor mode, before Sally cut me off.

"It's not about the money, so relax. I'm thrilled you've taken the chance to come this far in your journey."

Uh-oh. The language was starting to change back to that jive-talking New Age lingo. Just when I thought it was getting safe.

I brought the car to a halt in the empty parking lot.

"Are we the first ones here or are we the only ones here?" I asked.

"Oh no, there's other people here. Not everybody drives to this retreat."

"Let me guess. They use flying carpets?"

Sally just smiled as she opened the car door.

"Come on, phase two of our weekend journey together begins now."

I reached down to my left, beside the seat, popped up the trunk latch and got out of the car. It felt eerie being in the middle of nowhere with a flaky, um, unique yoga teacher in front of an old, broken-down house. I noticed that there were no crickets or other nature sounds in the background. I found that a tad unnerving too.

I went to the back of the car and saw Sally smiling, looking in the trunk, shaking her head.

"What?"

"What's with all the luggage?" She laughed, gently gliding her arm beneath mine.

"Well, I didn't know what kind of retreat it was. I thought there might be some tennis courts and a nice place to eat in town. I didn't think I was going to end up in a haunted house on a hill, in the middle of nowhere. Why? What did you bring?"

She held up a large single cloth bag that was sitting with her. I knew it carried the contents of a health food supermarket and *maybe* her yoga outfit.

"Just this. Loose clothing and the usual supplements."

"Uh-huh. I take it there's no tennis court, swimming pool, hot tub, or any sort of amenities here?"

Sally's smirk told me that my bag with just jeans, shirts, underwear, and socks would suffice.

I closed the trunk and pulled Sally to my chest. Moonlight bounced off her olive skin, and sparkles of light from her baby blues pierced through my heart.

"You're one crazy chick, you know that?"

She smiled.

"I'm so happy you're here."

I then became the recipient of one of the most sensual kisses that I'd ever experienced. Ever. Sally broke away, laughing. I followed her like a puppy in heat.

We approached the haunted house. It wasn't as bad as it had seemed at first. There was a slight charm to the old red brick, even for an art deco man like myself. From what I could make out in the dark, it had three floors, a widow's peak, a slightly decrepit wrap-around wooden porch, windows with shutters that needed some work. But otherwise, it looked in pretty good shape.

Sally stood on the rickety porch and motioned me to follow. The kiss having worn off, I was thinking that this could really be it for me if I went through that doorway. What if I got brainwashed to do yoga everyday? I'd have no friends left.

I heard an owl hoot behind us. We both turned and, sure enough, there was our feathery friend sitting on the hood of my car. Sally and I just looked at each other and laughed. I glided up to Sally and took her hand.

The door opened.

Standing before us at about five feet, was an elderly, grey-haired East Indian man dressed in a long, white, two-piece pajama outfit. I might have known. All the gurus came from India, didn't they? No, really. No?

It suddenly dawned on me that he looked just like the nerf batter I saw earlier from my office window.

"Welcome, welcome," was the whispered, joyful greeting he gave us both. He spoke perfect English.

"Hi! Ohhh, it's so good to be here again," Sally said, running into his arms.

Sally gave this old, brittle man one of her "special" hugs.

I call her hugs the "New Age Squeeze." You squeeze each other as hard as possible and feel all the "energy" transfer back and forth. Then you let each other go and pretend that all you were doing was saying hello or good-bye, when basically you were having sex. At least that's what it was like for me with the hugs I got from some of Sally's friends. It was an embarrassment that was sometimes hard to hide, if you know what I mean and I think you do.

Sally and I have had a few disagreements over this issue because of all the men in her life that she was constantly hugging. But I digress.

"This is my friend Peter that I've told you so much about. Peter, this is Surrender."

"Excuse me?" I said, leaning closer toward them.

"This is Surrender," she repeated.

"That's your real name? Surrender? I mean, it's a nice name, I, I've, I've just never heard it used as a name before. I mean, uh-"

"Very nice to be with you again, Peter." He spoke in a soft whisper, leaning toward me.

"Again? What do you mean, again? Oh wait, do you work downtown? There's a guy across from my office who looks- "

"I never leave this place." he interrupted as he stretched out his arm, leading us through the doorway.

"Let's go and get your sleeping arrangements in alignment," he continued.

I looked at Sally and she just shrugged her shoulders. She then coaxed me into the house of unknown origins and perplexing destinations.

~ 5 ~

I dragged my travel-weary body through the dark front hallway. About every three feet were white candles in copper holders protruding from the walls, giving off a dim light. There weren't any sounds, as in sounds of other humans. Maybe they got smart and turned back when Batman showed up.

Still, the house had a calming quality.

For a brief moment, I started to think that it wasn't a bad idea that I'd come. I was even thinking that maybe I could learn something from all this. It had been several hours since we'd left the city and I hadn't once thought about the condom campaign.

As we rounded a corner, I accidentally bumped into a piece of downtrodden furniture.

"Maybe they should increase their rates. That way they could pay for their hydro and get better furniture," I whispered.

Sally whispered back, "They don't use hydro. It's mostly solar power. It's just the basics around here. For cooking and heating, they use only wood-burning stoves or fireplaces."

"Maybe they should increase their rates so that they could get hydro," I persisted.

I got the proverbial "Oh Peter" look.

We rounded a corner and walked down a hallway that had several doorways opening onto it. This Surrender guy stopped and turned toward Sally. He raised his left arm, indicating that she should enter the first doorway.

"Thank you, Surrender," Sally said, walking into the dark room.

I followed Sally. "Uh, yeah, for me too. Thank you, uh, Surrender."

I didn't know why but I was very intimidated by this small elderly man.

Sally quickly turned around and stopped me.

"Peter! This is the women's dorm. Surrender will take you to the men's dorm."

Alarms went off in my head again.

"What do you mean 'women's' dorm? Men's dorm? What are you talking about? We're on this retreat *together*. I don't want to sleep in a room full of strange men. No offense, Surrender."

"I'm sorry, Hon. I thought you knew-"

"How would I know? I've never been here before. What, are you telling me there is no sex at this retreat too?" It was hard to shout and whisper at the same time.

Then I felt the gentle touch of Surrender's hand on my shoulder. A surge of energy shot through my body.

"It is OK, my friend. You two will have lots of time together. But for now, we must get you both to sleep so that you will awaken for the four a.m. meditation."

"Wait a minute. WAIT-A-MINUTE! *Four a.m. meditation*? It's after midnight! More importantly, it's Saturday. In my world, it's a universal law that everyone sleeps in on Saturdays. Come on, Sally, what's going on here?"

She hesitated.

"I could leave now and not think twice about it."

"I'm sorry, I meant to tell you about-"

"*Meant* to tell me? You *meant* to tell me? You deliberately didn't tell me. Why?"

She looked over at Surrender who wasn't showing support in one direction or the other.

"I, I didn't want to say anything, in case you backed out."

"Gee, I wonder what the odds of that would have been?"

"I'm sorry. I just wanted you to be here so badly. I guess I was blinded by its importance to me. I'm really sorry, Sweetie."

I looked over at Surrender and he just gave me his soon-to-be-familiar shrug and innocent-looking grin. I looked back to Sally and relaxed.

"Ahh, it's OK," I began, as I pulled her close, "I was looking for something different in my life anyway. Maybe this will shake a few things up. There is coffee here right? Don't answer. I don't want to know. I can only take so much bad news in one day."

Sally looked soulfully into my eyes and I was lost.

"There've been a lot of 'I'm sorry's' since we've left, haven't there?" she said, with a vulnerable smile.

"Think we're covering new ground?" I asked.

"Looks like it, Sweetie."

"Oh boy. Here we go."

Sally playfully snuggled the top of her head into my heart. Then we gave each other the "New Age Hug" and she went into her quarters like the angel she was. However, the devil in me was due for a cold shower.

"Please follow me," Surrender said.

"OK, fine. Looks like you're my boss this weekend," I answered. I vaguely noticed that something had shifted inside that helped calm my nerves.

I followed him as he turned the corner. He stopped and pointed me in the direction of the all-male sleeping quarters. I looked at him as he stood there staring at me. In that unusual moment of silence, I had the awkward feeling that something was hanging from my nose or he was waiting for me to tip him. I just said "good night."

His soft-spoken words stopped me. "At the edge of your cot, there are clothes for you to wear. We all wear the same clothing as a symbol of peace and unity."

"Must cut down on the cleaning bills," I said, trying to break the spiritual ice.

Nothing. Not even a hint of a smile. He just stared at me as if I was from another planet. He then put his hands in prayer position and bowed toward me. I didn't reciprocate.

He came up from his bow and looked me in the eye. Geez, he so looked like that guy I saw earlier with the nerf bat.

"You have traveled long and hard, my friend. I'm happy that you have had the courage to make the journey this far."

I nodded in agreement.

"Yeah. I know. Traffic was a bitch. But once we got out of the city, we were OK. Anyway, thanks. Nighty night."

And through the doorway I went. As I entered the dark room that was lit only by a sliver of light from the hallway candles, I glanced over my shoulder. Surrender gave a slight nod and walked away. I didn't know what to make of this man of demure but charismatic presence.

There were at least four other men in the room sleeping soundly in their cots. In the darkness, I couldn't make out if they were the usual New Age retreat types, or if I had entered a cult initiation for unsuspecting suits.

I made my way to the only empty cot. Humble sleeping accommodations indeed. I wouldn't have been surprised if the cot and blankets had come from the First World War.

I took off my clothes and quietly slipped on my new, white two-piece outfit. If the boys could see me now, I thought, laughing to myself.

They had all tried to warn me about Sally but I was thick-headed when it came to affairs of the heart. There was my way and then there was my way. Nothing in between. I often confused integrity with stupidity. I just hoped coming on this retreat with Sally wasn't the latter.

I put my city clothes on the chair beside the head of the cot and slid my traveling bag to the opposite end. Lying down on the ancient bed, I tried to be as quiet as possible but a few creaks were unavoidable.

Unfortunately for me, the noises prompted the man in the next cot over to give me a sermon via his nose. He began snoring. Loudly. This was going to be a long four hours.

And Sally was supposed to be a one-night stand.

~ 6 ~

The night was filled with dreams and mysterious murmurings. I was having a difficult time sleeping with unfamiliar thoughts racing through my mind. And besides, the man next to me was snoring like a toad

In a moment of silence, I heard a voice whisper, "It's time."

Uh-oh.

Now you have to understand, I absolutely did not go to horror flicks. Ever since I was a teenager and saw the one with the severed hand that let loose on a small town and nearly wiped it out. Nor did I stay in a room if any came on television. But I had seen enough horror movies in my time that when I heard, "It's time," coming out of the depths of darkness, *I knew it wasn't a good thing!*

I heard the creepy voice once again. "It's time, Peter."

Yep, I screamed. Loudly. Or at least I tried to. But nothing seemed to be coming out of my mouth.

Now it was one thing to be startled by a voice or a noise out of the blue and then think, well maybe it's the TV next door or, as in this case, the guy in the next cot babbling in his sleep. You screamed a bit, realized what it was about, laughed, and then you got on with life. But it was another thing when you screamed, couldn't hear your voice, and couldn't move your body.

I couldn't handle things that went bump in the night, but I'd take them on. I couldn't even handle things that went bump in the day, but I'd give them a whirl. But in a situation that caused me to freeze like a flank of dead cow in a meat locker and scream in mute terror, I wanted that big-bellied Buddha guy in the sky to bail me out and I didn't even believe in him.

I think that when they had been passing out nerves of steel, they had looked at me and thought, "Oh, genetic experiment. Let's infuse this guy's spine with jello, just for the hell of it."

Once again, I heard the voice, only louder. "It's time to begin the next step of your journey."

"Uh, no thanks. I would much prefer to stay here and listen to this guy snore like a freakin' chainsaw," I said in my mind, unable to move my frozen lips.

Despite my lame attempt at a witty defense, I felt a tingling sensation that started at my feet and moved up my body, toward my head. Soon, my whole body began pulsating with what I could only describe as electric currents.

It reminded me of when I was a kid and stuck a screwdriver in a wall socket. Except this didn't make me cry. This had me vibrating with aliveness. Like a very bizarre sexual experience I had once had with Sally, which she later explained was something called tantric sex. I had told her to never do that again, unless she warned me.

This was confusing because it was exciting yet completely terrifying. Never had I been in such a vulnerable situation, unable to comprehend what was happening, and therefore unable to resolve it. There was no allowance for comprehension. There was no allowance for resolution. There was only allowance for fear. And believe me, I was the major shareholder of fear in that room.

It got worse.

With all of this electric fear going on, I began to lift up out of my body, starting from the head. I could see and feel myself lifting into the vastness of space. There was an electric charge in the air. Soon I was floating above my physical body, looking down toward its stillness. And I had thought recovering from a double happy hour in Cancun was an out of body experience.

I vaguely remembered this happening to me before as a kid. But this time there was a voice present and I was very conscious of all that was happening. Feeling in the usual groove of life I was not!

I saw my physical body lying on the bed making absolutely no movement. Eerily lifeless. I could still hear the guy in the next cot snoring like an amphibian with a respiratory disorder.

All of a sudden, something began to change in the room. I was hearing less of my friendly neighbor's snoring and more of a sharp buzzing sound. Soon, it was drowning out all normal sounds in that room.

While floating around the ceiling like a birthday balloon, an unusual apparition appeared above me, adjacent to the ceiling. It looked like a whirlpool of swirling particles, similar to a bathtub being drained of water. Except, this wasn't water. It was like a diagram out of my high school physics textbook. A vortex of molecules swirling around on the ceiling.

This vortex of molecules and its unusual energy began sucking me in. Again, there was that double-edged feeling. Yes, I was scared, but another part of me was becoming fascinated with it all. Could this really be happening? If so, what part of me was floating and what part wasn't?

I felt real enough as I floated around, and yet I must have looked like a ghost or some other kind of apparition.

I heard the voice again.

"Will you please join me on the other side so that we may begin the next phase of the journey?"

Oy. The odds of me paying off the Beamer were diminishing.

I was pretty open-minded, but leaving my body, floating around the ceiling, observing a vortex of molecules swirling above me, and then hearing a voice asking me to take a journey to the far side, left me with one of two thoughts. I was either having an acid flashback or my addiction to Starbucks' one-percent, no-fat, double-foam, extra-hot lattes was becoming a problem.

Was this an experience that was necessary in order to take a progressive step in my life? Or was this *it* now? Was my life over? No enlightenment? No second chance? No universal understanding of mankind and its purpose? Just, "Hey bubba, it's over. Nice try. Time to step over to the other side for a little chat."

It seemed so unromantic - and I wasn't even a romantic!

No. No, I was not going through any hole in the ceiling to gain enlightenment. No, I was not going to continue floating around in any room with my real body lying there on the cot like a corpse. No, I wasn't going anywhere. But I could think what I wanted. My brain was doing one thing and my body, astral or whatever, was doing another. I *was* going through that vortex of molecules and I was going *now*, whether I wanted to or not.

Should have bought the convertible.

~ 7 ~

With the gentle pull of a guiding hand through the swirling molecules, I moved into the Mystery. Attached to the hand was none other than Surrender himself. He stood back and smiled. There seemed to be so much love emanating from him. I could do nothing but give him what was probably a confused smile in return.

We were both in what seemed to be our regular physical forms.

In my mind, I heard him say, "Would you like to speak using the mouth or telepathically?"

"The mouth would be good, thank you." I said, standing there, slightly stunned.

He smiled again and spoke with his mouth. "Very well."

I sensed such a calm about him and our surroundings. We stood in a meadow, enveloped by plush trees and vegetation. Everything was rich in color and form, as beautiful as a Japanese garden and similar in smell. The landscapers knew what they were doing. The sky was an endless blue, enriched by swift-moving, downy clouds. If I had died and gone to Heaven in that moment, this would do nicely.

"Everything is Heaven, even in the third dimension of planet Earth," said Surrender.

Uh-oh, a mind reader.

"It is not so much that I am a mind reader as that there is nothing to hide in this vibration. A thought is a thought, a word is a word. It's all taken as a positive manifestation of Truth."

Funny, I think my boss once said that about a cigarette campaign we were working on.

"You mean it doesn't matter if we think it or speak it, a thought is still going to be heard?"

"That is true."

"Then how come I can't hear what you're thinking about?"

"Because I'm not thinking about anything."

"Huh. You can do that?"

He smiled. "Shall we take a walk?"

"Sure. Why not get at the mystery of this?"

I was surprised at how calm I was, considering.

"No mystery," I heard him say in my mind. "It's just a walk in the meadow."

And that's exactly what we did. We took a walk in this heavenly-looking meadow from another dimension.

I'd never seen such an exquisite display of Nature's beauty. Exotic-looking birds were in flying formation, singing soft melodies of morning glory. Looming, rolling mountains were covered with long, flowing, green grass, protecting all of Creation.

I normally don't take notice of Nature, probably because I was always thinking.

"You're always in your head, Peter, never in your heart," had been a common refrain in relationships with women.

I had never understood how they expected men to think with their hearts. I was supposed to make a presentation to my clients, thinking with my heart? Uh sure, *feel* my point.

"Gentlemen, what you see before you is an ad campaign that will triple your sales. Now if you would please take the time right now to get into your heart space and chant the mantra, 'Om'." Yeah, right. There's the door, hippie.

"Peter, why is your mind always chattering?" asked Surrender.

"That's the way I've trained my mind, so that a fresh idea is always available when I need it."

"Do you know why you chose to grow on planet Earth?"

Oh great. Now there's a stimulating question.

"Yes it is, but it's seldom contemplated and rarely answered."

I forgot I was in mind reader's Heaven.

I deliberated on my reason for being on Earth. I wasn't sure I wanted to reveal that much of myself to an almost complete stranger. Then to my surprise, I did.

"I used to think it was to help others. That's how I got into the ad game, so that I could spread the good word, so to speak. And make lots of money!"

"Do you think you're spreading the good word?" asked Surrender.

"Perhaps. Well, sometimes. Actually, not very often. Well, to be honest, not at all. I would say that only a handful of the ad campaigns that I've handled were a definite contribution to the community. There isn't any money in public announcements or charity campaigns, so our firm politely declines any approaches from the needy. I guess it has just become a job. A game. Who is going to get what account? Who is going to win what award? I think the reason I got into the ad game has become lost over the last couple of years. It doesn't excite me like it did in the beginning. But I am making lots of money!"

I became silent. As if I had just revealed too much to someone I knew too little about, including myself.

It didn't take a genius to see that the feeling I had been experiencing in the last few months was boredom bordering on despair. I had become so uninspired and disillusioned, I had lost sight of why I had gotten into this profession. What did it matter if I'd graduated at the top of my class or had been a major player in top car campaigns? None of it meant anything. No wonder I was unproductive, uncreative, and unenthusiastic. This was a sad place to be as I approached my mid-forties. Or *any* age for that matter.

There had to be more to life than the way I'd been living it.

These unhappy thoughts brought me back full circle. Who was this person, spirit, or man that I was revealing all of this to? What was I doing walking down this garden path of so-called Heaven? If this was really a dream, why was I feeling a deep sadness swelling in my heart? Did we have emotions in the dream state? Or was I just imagining that I was experiencing this deep sadness?

We stopped walking simultaneously and I looked at Surrender, feeling hollow and lost. When I was in "the game," I was far too busy to feel anything. Now that I was outside "the game," I saw it for what it really was and how little I'd been enjoying it. I felt that wet trickle of salt water make its journey down my right cheek but quickly managed to stop it with my hand. No way was I exposing the boy inside the man.

"Why are you holding back, my son?" Surrender asked, with genuine compassion.

"Well, I've just left my body. I don't know if I'm dead or alive; if I'm a ghost or a human being. I'm in the middle of what looks like God's country, spilling my guts to a complete stranger, with tears rolling down my face. None of this is making any sense to me at all."

He put his arms around me and gave me a loving hug. I'd never felt so much love from one person in my life.

The dam broke and the tears took their natural course. I collapsed into Surrender's arms like I'd never allowed myself to do with anyone. I felt him open a space for me to let go.

Was this the "unconditional love" that people talk so much about? Holding a space for the other to just *be*? To let go? Honoring and respecting the moment? I didn't have any answers. A fog set in to stop the constant queries of my mind.

"All I have ever really wanted from life is to be comfortable in my skin," I said, pulling away, so I wouldn't be using him as a snot rag.

"The soul's comfort and the personality's comfort hit a fork in the road a long way back. Now it's time to come home."

Uh-oh, I didn't like what he was getting at.

"Does that mean I'm dead?" I asked, preparing myself for the worst.

"Partly," he said, with no hint of emotion.

"What do you mean, 'partly?' Half of me is dead and the other half is alive?"

"The part of you that is alive is constant. The part of you that is dead is man-made."

"Speak English, Teach."

He smiled, "You are at the stage of your journey where you are ready to remember why you came here."

I didn't have a clue what he was talking about.

"Do you know what multidimensional means? he asked.

"Something on many levels," I responded, before I even knew what I was saying.

"Yes, we are all multidimensional beings who operate on a frequency that is tuned to whatever our thought is at that moment, not unlike a radio. We operate on many different levels, and a single thought as a human entity on planet Earth affects all levels of our multidimensional being. Which is why in this world of dualities, positive and negative, a positive thought has so much power. As does a negative thought. Both have rippling effects on the multidimensional being."

"Oh, I see, that explains everything. I understand the Universe now. Can I please go back to my real body?"

He stood there looking at me patiently.

"You really don't want to remember, do you?"

I shook my head from side to side.

"Not if I have to learn another language, I don't."

"My dear friend, it is all very simple. Come, let's walk some more."

He led me along a path of silence. I could not digest being out of my body and having a conversation about the workings of the Universe with a complete etheric stranger.

Some time went by, as did a million thoughts. Mind you, I couldn't hold one coherent thought in my brain for any length of time anyway. What was it that I needed to experience in order to get through this muddled, dreamy confusion?

We continued down the dusty pathway.

Eventually I turned to Surrender.

"If I'm some sort of ghost in some alternate dimension, then why do I feel confusion? Why do I feel pain? Why do I have tears? For that matter, why do I feel at all? I mean, I've seen ghost movies. They don't cry. Other than in that Demi Moore flick. You know the one where-, well, probably not. Never mind. But you know what I'm getting at."

He smiled patiently at my ramblings. His short stature offset the volumes of wisdom he carried so gracefully.

"Tears, pain, and confusion are a manifestation of what you *think* you need to experience in order to enter this realm or others. Yet the very pain you experience is man-made. They are not real tears. You are not real."

"I'm not?"

"Neither am I. None of this around you is real. It's an illusion to help your soul evolve to a higher vibration, bringing you closer to the Source of what some people may term God. And please remember, from here on in, God is only a word. Don't get caught up in any word, especially that one.

By allowing yourself to experience this dimension, you come one step closer to the next, until you are once again a fully-realized, conscious aspect of God."

"Does that mean I have to give up burgers and fries?"

Surrender smiled, looked ahead and began walking along the path. I wasn't sure if he was upset about the wisecrack or if he just felt a good walk would help me understand. I quickly followed. No use being in another dimension by myself.

More time passed before Surrender interrupted the silence. "Did you ever consider why you met Sally?"

"Not really. It just sort of happened."

"Do you know why you chose to be here with me?" He continued asking, with relentless persistence and soul-piercing eyes. I glanced at the flowing grass as a warm breeze swept across my face.

"I really didn't feel I had a choice. As a matter of fact, I'm still not sure this isn't some weird dream."

I continued attempting to resolve my disorienting situation aloud. "Perhaps this is just a subconscious release from childhood repression. I mean, I do read books. Maybe not your kind…"

He was silent for a moment, taking in my words. But just for a moment. Then he spoke his incomprehensible utterances, yet again.

"First, like I've said before, it is important to realize that time is but an illusion. Second, you do contribute to the choices that are made in the Universe, immediate and otherwise, by projection of thought and action. And third, this is not some 'weird dream.' This is your new reality."

I became frustrated with his New Age prevaricating.

"Then just what is it that I am experiencing?"

He looked over to me and said in a matter-of-fact manner.

"You're experiencing the emergence of your soul into its other dimensional realities."

"Give it to me straight, Doc, I can take it. What are you trying to tell me?"

Surrender smiled. I think my confusion amused him.

"What I'm trying to communicate to you is that we are all One. That this planet Earth is one of many schools that help us evolve within the Source. The God Source, if you like. I am telling you that you chose Sally, as you did me, to assist you in your soul's growth as a multidimensional particle of the Source."

Oy. Have you ever noticed how these New Agers speak in some language that sounds like utter Trekian gibberish? There must be a New Age immersion school in the sky where they go to learn jargon that means absolutely nothing to the layman. And have you also noticed how these people talk as though they are saying something really meaningful to you? That they are smarter than you? That they know better? And of course, they all appear on Oprah. Not that I watch Oprah. OK, occasionally when I'm at home, uh, sick. But I digress.

"When did I make this choice? And please, keep it simple."

Surrender closed his eyes briefly and then began to speak, softly.

"Because the soul evolves from conscious particles of the Source, it becomes more aware of what is needed in order for its continued growth to resonate as a fully realized aspect of the Source. That is, if it hasn't been tainted in some way. In this case, part of the process for your soul's evolution has involved assuming the form of a human entity, which has been tainted through the course of its evolution on Earth.

"We never really leave the Source. Our goal is to realize ourselves within the Source and utilize our talents and abilities for the greater Whole, while still maintaining a sense of identity within it. Eventually, we all become One united with the Source. It's kind of like a universal game of Truth. We go away. We learn. We come back. All the while we are One. Understand?"

"*Are you serious?*" I shot back.

He smiled.

"I don't even think you answered my question."

"You made your choice in the beginning. We all did. We're all a natural pulsation of the Source. It's natural for us to expand and contract. To learn, grow, and contribute to our Oneness with the Source."

"You're not sounding any saner."

"You don't have to understand what I'm saying, just be open to the newness of it all for now."

Was he messing with my mind? Breaking me down to build me up into one of his devotees?

"This human entity you've chosen to embody is now desperately searching for other like-minded human entities with whom to merge in what we would call a soul group. Simply put, a group of particles of light work together and resonate for a greater awareness of the Truth, eventually merging back into the Oneness of All. Again, think of it as a game. *Like* attracts *like* for the betterment of mankind, Self and the Oneness of the Source.

"In giving yourself a stronger vibration of Truth, you will attract other strong vibrations in their aspects of Truth. Other soul groups. You will find that, eventually, the particles of light, now operating within a stronger vibration, will rediscover themselves as fully realized aspects of the Whole."

He couldn't possibly be talking to me.

"You see, my friend, increased chances for growth come to those who help themselves and others to fully realize the

Whole, or God, or however you choose to term it. Words matter little at that level of resonance.

"In previous lifetimes, you, Sally and I have all worked together to support our souls' evolutionary process. And now we, along with other people in their aspects of Truth, have come together at this point in linear time on Earth to help each other *remember* and live our true potential for the purpose of being One with Self and All That Is."

My thoughts had been drifting to my comfy couch and the football game that I was missing. I heard myself say, "Remember what?"

"That's something that patience will teach you," he said, grinning and giving me a little wink.

I'm not sure what he was up to with the playful gesture but I was relieved for the break it gave my brain.

"It is important for you to understand that time has no limitations."

Uh-oh, here we go again. This guy should do infomercials.

He continued, apparently oblivious of my obvious discomfort. "Time is always *now.* Past, present and future are all in the *now.* Your choices that you make *now* affect your soul's evolution *now* and in the future. That's why it's so important to make conscious choices as multidimensional beings."

"Do you ever watch football?" I asked, tired of the information overload.

Surrender let out a little chuckle. Laughs were hard to come by with this little guy.

"Just let the concept of man-made time being an illusion, and the past, present and future being in the *now*, rumble around in your head for awhile. It will grow on you."

I was now officially on overload.

We continued our never-ending walk.

I got out of my crowded head for a moment and began to observe what was surrounding me. Majestic mountains shadowing the pathway and protecting this hidden valley of peace. In their magnificent presence, we were but a speck. Each mountain was protected by a covering of lush greenery.

"Is this Heaven?" I asked again, "And please, tell me in simple terms."

"Yes, you might say this is Heaven - your version of Heaven."

"What do you mean 'my version'?" I asked, prepared for yet another onslaught of New Age gibberish.

"Each of us experiences God or Heaven in a variation of light that corresponds to how we *need* to experience it. You, for instance, will bring us to this place for our talks. Sally would take you or me to another place."

"Really? Like where?" I asked, thinking I might understand her a bit more in her own Garden of Eden.

"That's something you can ask Sally. Perhaps she'll bring you there. As you evolve, your perception of Heaven will also evolve. There are many doorways to Heaven. Man did not build the foundation for that mansion. So, beware of the person who offers you a key to Heaven. Chances are, they are trying to get through *your* doorway because they are not at peace with themselves. And always beware of anyone's concept of Heaven. Heaven is not a word. Heaven is something you experience. It's not above you, it's not below you, it's in you."

What do you say to an old man who thinks he's doing you a favor by telling you his philosophies of life? I said nothing and just found myself shutting down mentally and emotionally. Beautiful words maybe but did he walk the talk or talk the walk? Was he one of those charlatans that he'd been warning me about? Was I becoming his unwitting devotee?

We wandered over to a large rock and sat down. For the first time I noticed that I was wearing the same long flowing white robe and brown sandals as Surrender. How could I not have noticed I was wearing this get-up? Had I been so wrapped up with this experience with Surrender that I didn't even notice I was walking around in a Jesus suit? What was with these long flowing robes anyway? What was with this color white?

Once again, I was reminded that I was in mind reader's Heaven as Surrender interrupted my chattering thoughts.

"White is only a symbol of light. White is One. It is a symbol of remembrance of who we are and where we are from."

"You mean to tell me that white represents this so-called God?"

"Every color is embodied in the color white. White represents All That Is. We are all light beings. We wear white in honor of ourselves and the God that is within. But white is only a symbol of an abstract truth."

"Huh. Hate to be the one who does all the washing."

With all of the esoterica flying way over my head, a feeble wisecrack was all I could offer

"Oh now, that's good. I like that," he chuckled.

Somehow him laughing seemed weird to me.

"It's the washing, cleansing, and purifying throughout the constant evolution of the soul that raises the soul's vibration," he quickly added.

It was time to keep my mouth shut and my mind clear. However, as had often been observed by my friends, it didn't take long for my mouth to open again.

"I'm not really comprehending any of this. I mean, even if I were really here, which I don't know if I am, I'm not sure I would be comprehending any of this."

"That's OK, my son, you will get what you need this time around. The rest will stick later."

I could feel my eyes bulging out of their sockets. "You mean we're going to have another round of this?"

"Let me just leave you with one thought before you go back."

I braced myself against the rock we were sitting on. I didn't know how much more I could take and not have a brain explosion.

"It is important to listen to the silence of The Way, *your* way. For in that, you will find what it is you are seeking. For in that, you will find the Truth of the vast Universe. For in that, you will find the Truth about the illusions of your life and how you can become One again."

His words hit me with a heavy blow. I didn't know why but I felt their weight. Many times I had kept myself busy so that I wouldn't be alone with myself. An effective, if unconscious, way not to listen to the silence of The Way.

Silence was a fear of mine.

This was something that Sally pointed out to me right at the very beginning of our relationship. She often told me to meditate and listen to the "whispers in the wind." Yikes! Of course, I quickly blew off any notion of doing that. It was remarkable how one could resist something that seemed to be so basic. So inherently true. Listening. Silence.

I finally noticed that my head was in my hands as I tried to comprehend the preceding discourse. When I finally looked up, Surrender was nowhere to be seen. I quickly scanned the spectacular scenery. He was gone.

I felt so alone. Even if it was a dream, I could feel a deep longing inside my heart that told me something was missing. That there was something I needed to know about myself. Now! Something profound was gnawing away at my soul, but what was it? I was at a total loss. I couldn't grasp any of this.

There I was, sitting on this rock in paradise, not knowing if I was just having a psychedelic dream.

Suddenly, I felt a wave of energy rush through my body, not unlike a sugar rush after eating a piece of chocolate. Then I heard Surrender's "whisper in the wind."

"Choices are made in accordance with the overall Master Plan."

"Yeah, but who makes those choices?" I shouted in a desperate plea for understanding.

The wind became silent.

Time, as I knew it, passed.

I felt a peacefulness embrace me. Love filled me as the wonders of Heaven began to dissolve before my weary eyes. The last thought I remembered was that I never wanted to leave this place.

~ 8 ~

I sneezed.

My eyes opened in a dark room full of whispers. I heard a match striking the side of a box and soon the room was dimly lit by a single candle.

I felt sluggish to say the least. It seemed only a few short hours ago that I had laid my head down on this rock-hard pillow. I slowly began to recollect what had just happened. Was it in my dreams?

There were four other men slowly rising out of their cots. They all had a Jesus Christ thing going on with their long beards and straggly hair. It was clear that they didn't work for any corporations that I knew of.

Gentle greetings were mumbled by all.

My body was very slow to respond, the weight of it magnified by my short but eventful sleeping time.

Not having made up my mind as to whether I was going to meditate with the rest of them, I noticed all eyes turning toward the doorway. It was Surrender, greeting everyone with a clasping of his hands in the prayer position. The other four responded likewise. I felt the impulse to do the same but waited for the urge to go away. A very good habit I'd developed over many years spent in the bar scene. Did I really want to wake up next to her in the morning? Yeah OK, I know, rude. But those kind of reality checks had saved me a lot in the headache department.

Everyone got out of their beds in their near nakedness and proceeded to put on their white cotton shirts and pants that lay at the foot of their cots. They immediately filed out the door past Surrender. Looking like obedient sheep, I couldn't help thinking.

Surrender remained standing in the doorway with his usual "all knowing" smile, looking at me. I felt that warm rush in my body as in my dream state. Maybe I hadn't been dreaming? He walked over and placed a package before me, and then turned and left the room without saying a word.

I sat up, picked the package off the edge of the bed, and unraveled the plain brown wrapping to find a fresh outfit to replace the wrinkled one I had been wearing. I got out of my wrinkled gown and began to put on the fresh, two-piece, one-size-fits-all white uniform.

My first reaction had been to resist this retreat, but resistance slowly turned into why the heck not? My resistance was low when I was sleep-deprived. Wait a minute! Wasn't that a cult technique?

I thought about last night, or rather this morning. I thought about Surrender and his purpose here. I thought about having met and gotten together with Sally. Was it predestined or was it coincidence? All this was heavy stuff for what was usually my sports day with the boys.

Philosophy was a college course that I had left for the horn-rimmed ones. My objective was to get a degree, not try and change the world, or understand the workings of the Universe. I was a big believer in the K.I.S.S. principle – Keep It Simple Stupid!

What I had been hearing and experiencing at this retreat was all rather indigestible for first thing on a Saturday morning. As a matter of fact, *any morning!* Why I felt compelled to stay was as puzzling to me as why I wasn't feeling more of an urge to resist what I was being asked to do.

I was beginning to understand that there was something eerie yet exciting about exploring the Unknown. This was what I was coming to as I walked to the end of the hallway at a snail's pace.

I'd had more enjoyable hangovers. My spirit was willing but boy, my 40-ish body was ailing.

My recent "dream" reminded me of the hit of acid I took when I was 14, an experience that gave rise to a blend of abstract confusion and subtle pleasure. But not enough pleasure to ever take it again. One hit almost ruined a month of adolescence, not to mention the flashback at last year's office Christmas party. The rumor mill was still churning.

As I turned the corner, I observed my fellow students of life huddled in a sacred room that was about to swallow up this confused ad hack.

In the dim candlelight I could make out four men and five women, including Sally, who was obviously in her element. Looking at her made me think of the word goddess. In every way. Her movement, graceful presence, serenity, all emanated inner strength.

Sally spotted me at the doorway and motioned for me to come and sit beside her. I did, quietly excusing myself to the others, trying not to trip over them as they settled into a sitting yoga position.

Sally squeezed my hand as I sat down on a straw mat to her left.

She whispered something like, "Happy you made it."

"I was really just looking for the rest room and got lost," I said in a whisper.

She smiled, squeezed my hand again and folded her legs into what she once explained to me was the lotus position. As she often said in her classes, "It is one of the best ways to meditate because of the way it corrects your spine and allows the energy to flow freely up and down it."

I gamely tried the "lotus position," but my right foot would not stay on my lap. Instead it shot straight out, whacking the lady in front of me in the back as I fell backwards onto the lap of the man behind me.

They both were very polite, considering that I could have hospitalized either one of them. The man behind me offered his pillow to sit on.

"It will give you more leverage," he told me in a bellowing whisper.

The woman in front of me offered my foot back as she eased it out of her ribcage, smiling.

Sally leaned over and whispered, "Just try crossing your legs in a normal position for now. And don't forget to breathe."

I collected my wits, not to mention my extremities, sat on the pillow and began to breathe, as instructed by Sally. After a few minutes went by, I checked out the people around me. Everyone had their eyes closed and was facing the front of the room, where there was an altar of sorts. It stood about waist high and four feet long.

Sitting on it was one fresh-looking lily.

To my surprise, there was no guru in front of the room to lead the way, nor were there any pictures of Jesus, Buddha, Confucius, or even Bob Marley. Whoever was running this organization wanted to remain anonymous, unbiased, or maybe just unseen. If this *was* a cult, I would never know the face of the ringleader, the one who could be putting me in therapy for the rest of my life.

I continued to casually survey the room. There, sitting at the back, was Surrender. His eyes popped open just as I looked at him. He gave me a polite smile. I quickly turned away, feeling as if I was invading his privacy in some peculiar way.

The room was now silent despite the difficulty I was having relaxing. The candles gave off a low light and there was a peaceful ambience that made me want to lie back and sleep.

I tried to close my eyes but was afraid of what would happen next, so I continued spying on people's private moments.

Each woman in that room had a story to tell, I was sure. Each looked as if she had experienced life to the fullest. Not that any of them looked rough. On the contrary, wisdom seemed to emanate from each of them. It was that same kind of wisdom and presence that I saw in a colleague of mine at work. Even under extreme pressure she remained cool. You always knew that she would be able to solve any problem that would arise. How she remained in the game of lies for so long was beyond me. She was a Buddhist and a vegan. Enough said. I wasn't going to that dance.

But none of the women stood out the way Sally did. She was, like I said, a goddess. Albeit, I was a tad prejudiced.

The men were different, however. They looked like life had hit them hard and they were just hanging on, except for one guy who didn't seem as hard hit as the others, including me.

I would later get to know his name - Bobby. He seemed like a pussycat in a football player's body. There was such peace in his face but, as I found out later, he was the one who had been the hardest hit of all.

I looked back toward Sally. I found the polarities between Sally and me interesting. One always thought about God, and the other never gave God a single thought - until now. We were on opposite poles, and yet there we were in the same place doing the same thing. If it was true that God had no favorites then I was a "testament" to that fact, no pun intended.

I began to focus on my breathing, as Sally had shown me in her yoga classes. I kept my eyes open. Then I heard a humming sound. To my amazement, it was coming from an enormous crystal, sitting smack in the middle of the room. Where had that come from?

I couldn't believe how unobservant I'd become; how I seemed to miss things in plain sight.

I had been so preoccupied with getting a seat beside Sally that I hadn't bothered to take in the room. And maybe the people had been just a little too fascinating.

This tall, clear, octagon-shaped quartz crystal stood proudly, about three and a half feet high and two feet wide. It was a beautiful monument to the quartz family. I wasn't a specialist in crystals but I had seen enough of them at Sally's apartment to know that this was impressive by any standards. Must have cost a fortune too.

The candles on the side tables against the wall gave off enough light to allow me to see clearly through to the other side of the crystal, where the woman who looked like my co-worker appeared to be meditating. Suddenly, she turned toward me and opened her eyes. My eyes froze on hers as the crystal gateway diffused, only slightly, her intense glare.

I quickly broke the uncomfortable gaze, closed my eyes, and faced the front of the room. What was she doing here? Once again, I felt intimidated by yet another person who seemed to have the ability to penetrate my soul. A co-worker nonetheless!

The humming noise from the crystal became louder. My curiosity, once again, got the better of me as I did a little side glance to see if my co-worker was still staring into my soul.

It was then that I noticed a faint glow coming from the crystal; it increased and decreased with the fluctuation of the humming sound.

The crystal began giving off a brilliant fluorescence, as the humming sound deepened. I gazed at it in wonder. I couldn't help myself. Maybe spectators at the Wright brothers' first flight had the same feeling.

The humming intensified further, becoming a constant drone. The crystal lit up the entire room. Then, the people around me began to hum in the same tone as the crystal, including Sally.

I watched in utter amazement as they began to sway their upper bodies back and forth to the rhythm of the sound, matching their sway to the increasing humming noise.

"I'm going for Sushi," is what raced through my mind. "Anybody starts flying in this room and I'm out of here - *fast!* Levitating is for helicopters."

"Allow the Presence to be," I heard whispering in my head.

The whisper was coming from none other than Mr. Surrender himself. His mind-reading was becoming a tad annoying.

I looked over my left shoulder and there he sat with a slight smile and his eyes closed. This was a sure way to turn me into a mental patient.

"Please turn around and face the front of the room. Allow the sound to resonate throughout your whole body," he piped into my brain waves.

Oddly, I did this without delay, as though I'd been hypnotized. No longer could I be in that room with that humming noise and not be a part of it.

Why didn't I just get up and leave the room, or for that matter, leave the whole retreat? Was I that eager to please that I would remain here, completely vulnerable, just to make Sally happy? Being so mutable had sometimes put me in places I didn't want to be or with people I didn't want to be with. Too many pints were one thing, but this? I was out on a limb now.

I closed my eyes for the first time and faced the front. I couldn't resist the noise. I found my upper body rocking back and forth like the rest of the flock.

Once again, my body was pulsating with energy in and out of every pore. What was this surge of energy that was beginning to consume my body? Where had it come from? Why couldn't I resist it?

Before long, I was experiencing an incredible sense of peace. No longer did I remember anything in this world. No longer did I feel the need to prove myself to anyone. And no longer did I care about my fancy car and other toys. Entering this sweet oblivion erased all memories of what I had known to be my reality.

The humming became louder, the rocking faster, the bliss more eternal. Then I heard them say something like, "Ra-Me-Ra-Ma. Ra-Me-Ra-Ma." This chant quickly permeated the room and I was just as quick to come out of my tranquil trance-like state. No longer did I feel the bliss. Mr. Skepticism stepped back in and questioned this new reality.

"Uh, Sally, if you can hear me, what's going on here?" I said, in my mind.

I did want to understand, although where I got the courage to explore something so foreign was beyond me.

"We're only increasing the vibration of our frequency. It's OK," Sally said, telepathically of course.

I was beginning to feel like a radio transmitter.

"Not far off," I heard Sally interject.

"Wait a minute, does this mean that you have been able to read my mind ever since we met?" I shot back, telepathically.

"No, relax. The only reason we can relate to each other in this way is because when we're operating at this vibration, we tune into a higher frequency. We are more finely tuned and no longer need physical apparatus to communicate."

These people could build an airport in my head.

I finally gave in. I was too tired. It was too early in the morning. They were wearing me down. I relaxed "into the moment." I even found myself quietly mumbling, Ra-Me-Ra-Ma" as I slowly descended into another dream state. Everything around me became a soft, high-pitched, hissing sound.

And then there was nothing.

~ 9 ~

I stepped through the clouds, as though walking on air. I saw Sally sitting on a white rock, surrounded by white misty fog. I could smell the ocean. Waves pounded on the rocks below like two mighty forces battling for position.

I walked toward Sally and, in the blink of an eye, I was standing beside her. Again, nothing I could comprehend. Nothing I could relate to. I was just there, standing beside her, in awe of her radiant beauty.

"Whatever you think, you will attain," Sally said, noticing my face, which probably looked disoriented.

"Is this *your* Garden of Eden?" I asked, remembering what Surrender had told me.

"Yes it is," she replied, and then stood up and turned to face me.

"What are you reading?" I asked, slowly removing a large, aging leather-bound white book from her delicate hands.

"It's the Book of Nothing," she replied.

I opened this "Book of Nothing" and she was right, there was nothing on the pages.

"Whenever I look into those pages," she began, as she moved closer to me, placing her hand on my shoulder, "I can make up whatever I want. Tell any story I want. Paint any picture I want. Read any literature I want."

"I'm sure you could get a good price for this baby on Earth."

"It will never manifest on Earth until greed and misuse of ego disappear."

"Huh. I guess it won't be on the coffee table in the reception area at work any time soon."

Sally smiled.

"Speaking of which, a gal I work with is here. The dark haired one. Her name's Janice."

"Huh. Small worlds." Sally replied as she went back to her book.

I couldn't hold it back. "Why is all of this happening to me? Why now? Why not two years ago? Two months ago? Why am I here with you? For that matter, where are we?"

"First of all, you are here with me in the same dimensional frequency as you were with Surrender last night."

No secrets around here.

"That's for sure," she chuckled. "Anyway, this is a vibration where some of us go to learn about the Universe, digest new information, and frequently, just to be alone."

"Oh, excuse me, am I interrupting?" I said, thinking that we were going to get into our boundary issues, just like on Earth, wherever that may be at this point.

"Don't be silly," she said, giving me a playful slap. "This is all happening to you now because you chose to have it happen now. You're ready."

Once again, I wasn't sure I understood what she was talking about but just looking at her made me appreciate having her in my life. It would take an incredible amount of patience to teach this stuck doggy new tricks. It was nice to have someone to help me go through whatever it was that I was going through, even in this dreamy state.

Sally interrupted my thoughts. "Peter, don't you see? You're also helping me. It's not just me being here for you."

"How could I possibly be helping you? This is your territory."

Sally's right hand caressed my face, gently moving my head toward her so that our eyes met.

"The very fact that you are willing to stay and experience what you're experiencing helps me. Helps mankind. We all need to keep growing."

I broke away from the locked lovers' gaze and moved to the other side of the rock.

"How could I possibly be helping you or mankind? I feel like a rag doll in Ethiopia. No purpose, no knowledge, and no strength."

She laughed and then assumed her usual serious tone, "The very fact that the rag doll is present in some small Ethiopian child's life is allowing a space for love. It has a purpose."

"This is getting kind of weird. Forget the Ethiopian thing, OK? If I'm here helping you, why is it that you're the one telling me everything?"

She glided next to me, pulling me down so that we were sitting on the rock side by side. "Peter, I'm just helping you remember what you already know. Having you with me again helps to activate some of the things that I've forgotten as well. Believe it now or believe it later, you and I have spent many lifetimes together. We have helped each other grow to the point where we are able to remember our past lives in the present one."

I still didn't comprehend, but Sally was persistent. "You see, as the soul grows and evolves, it comes closer to the Source."

"Which is what? Everyone talks about the Source but no one seems to be able to explain it in layman's terms! The Source sounds like something the Nile River flows from."

She stared into me.

"The Source is All-"

"All what?!" I wanted to stop her before we went off on another New Age spin.

"All That Is. We are part of All."

"So, we are made up of this Source, this God thing and now we have to work our way back to God or the Source, as you call it?"

"Yes." Sally smiled, thinking that I was getting it.

But I wasn't buying any of it. "If we are from this so-called God Source, or whatever you want to call it, and have to work our way back to this God Source, then why in heck's name did we leave in the first place? It seems kind of silly, don't you think? We leave a good thing and then spend eons trying to get back to it? No wonder most of us are in therapy."

Sally leaned her head on my shoulder softly saying, "I can't answer that, Peter. I just don't know. I'm learning just the same as you are. That is one of the questions that I've been asking for a long time."

I detected a hint of melancholy in Sally's voice as she continued, "I truly miss my home, my people. There isn't a day that goes by that I don't wonder when I'll be home again."

A moment of silence fell between us as I absorbed Sally's sadness. I put my arm around her shoulders in what I knew was a futile gesture to ease her troubled soul.

We just sat there listening to the ocean waves below, staring at the infinite white clouds surrounding the lone rock and ourselves. My mind wouldn't let go of the idea that what she was trying to tell me was completely absurd. I had to break the ocean's muffled pounding to assuage my skeptical mind.

"You know, Sally, this God of yours has a warped sense of humor."

"How so?"

I took in a deep breath and exhaled. "If we were all One, some time ago-"

"We still are," Sally interjected.

"Yeah, whatever. So we're all One, then we get our severance papers from the big guy in the sky who is callously telling us that he, she, it or whatever *still loves us*, meanwhile kicking us out of the mansion. So then we find ourselves spiraling downward to planet Earth with our heads spinning in grand illusion. And finally when we land, the *Whatever* tells us to come home again and if we don't, the *Whatever* makes it difficult for us. Think about the logic, Sally. The *Whatever* was the one that served us the notice that sent us down here in the first place. I'm not sure I want to go back. This *Whatever* seems like a sick puppy, no?"

"No," Sally softly replied.

"Hmmm. I don't know about that. And when you say God Source? What are we talking about here? Is there an actual person up there, using a satellite phone, calling all the shots or what? I mean really, Sally, what the heck is going on here?"

She sat there quietly, holding my hand and whispered softly, as if I had just deflated her spirit.

"I really don't know, Peter. I don't know."

That's when I knew I was in trouble.

We held onto each other like two lovers lost at sea, not knowing if we'd ever survive.

I heard a buzzing sound. My scenery was changing around me as rapidly as my life.

Moments like these never last long.

~ 10 ~

What had seemed like minutes had been hours. By the time I opened my eyes again, everyone had left the room except for Sally and me. I turned to her as she slowly opened her eyes.

"That was a very interesting trip. I guess I should thank you," I said, again not fully comprehending what had just transpired.

Sally looked into my eyes for a moment, and then quickly snapped out of her dreamy state and said, "It's time to do our chores."

"Chores?" I was thinking about going straight back to bed.

"At six a.m. we always do chores, to help offset the work that is needed to operate this retreat."

"Work?"

"Yep," Sally responded, slowly getting up and stretching her long slender body.

"Six a.m.?" I asked, still in disbelief.

"Yep," was her instant cheerful reply. "You'll notice that time plays funny games around here, Peter." Smiling, she extended her hand to help me get up.

My male pride made me ignore her hand. I tried to get up by myself but my legs were locked in their folded position. Sally laughed. Pride is a luxury of youth.

"Just straighten out your left leg," she said.

I did, slowly, feeling like a founding member of a group of medieval torture chamber survivors.

"Now your right leg," she said. I felt needles of pain exploring all of my arteries and muscles. Meditation was not a sport I was going to take up any time soon.

"OK, now lie back for a moment and shake the pain out of your leg," she said, kneeling beside my aching tree stumps.

She watched me writhe in my performance art piece called *Pain!*

"Inhale deeply. Now exhale. Bring your breath all the way down to the bottom of your feet and back up again."

"Now what the heck does that mean? 'Bring your breath all the way down to your feet and back up again.' Air goes into my lungs and back out. That's it. End of story. Lose the airy-fairy lingo, please."

Sally stroked my forehead with a gentle sweep of her hand.

"Peter, the air that you inhale is energy, prana, life force. The more you breathe in, the more air you allow to circulate throughout your body, and the more alive you will feel."

"Sally, my legs are numb with pain. How the heck is breathing going to help the circulation in my body?"

Her angelic eyes locked onto mine. It was becoming a soulful, "breathless" situation every time we locked into a gaze. I know it sounds corny - is corny - but it was *true* corny. If there was such a thing.

"Sweetheart, just imagine a current of energy flowing through your body down to your feet on the inhalation, and then on the exhalation, have it flowing up through your body and out the top of your head."

I decided I wasn't the only one who had acid flashbacks.

"Why don't you just pass me a screwdriver and I'll plug myself into the wall. It would be a lot more efficient."

"Oh, Peter," she began, in a manner bordering on condescending.

"Just help me up, will you?!" I said, cutting off any further rescue attempts from this angel.

I was beginning to realize that having someone help me while I was in a vulnerable position pushed a lot of my buttons. Something to do with my ego and always wanting to prove to the world I could do it on my own. When I thought about it, even Napoleon had help. OK, maybe not a good example.

Sally pulled me to my feet. Strength she had, both physical and mental. She then gave me one of those warm, loving New Age hugs. I could feel her body heat. Entwined in love, I became.

"Now let's go get our job assignments," she whispered softly into my ear.

Job assignments were the furthest from my mind as Sally held my hand and escorted me out of the room. Stumbling through the doorway, I knew exactly how I would be walking when I was 80.

As we continued down the long, moody hallway, I noticed numerous pictures hanging on the wall, some almost recognizable.

"What's the story behind the pictures staring at us?"

"These are but a few of the spiritual Masters who have walked the Earth," Sally responded.

I stopped in front of that familiar old reproduction of Jesus Christ and called out to Sally as she forged on ahead of me.

"Do you think this guy really existed?" I asked. In high school, this was the guy I had always heard about from our religion teacher. Almost as much as that other guy they called God.

Sally walked back toward me.

"Of course." Sally stood in front of the picture, looking at it intently. "Jesus is an aspect of God and therefore an aspect of us all."

"Yeah right. Where's the coffee?"

"No, no listen. It's important that you understand the history without the religion. Jesus Christ is considered an Ascended Master. He landed on this planet about two thousand years ago to help man get back on course. Unfortunately, people would not take responsibility for their actions and persecuted him instead. Again, mainly because of a great denial of their own need for growth." She said all this in one breath and in a rather pat manner, which always made me suspicious.

"OK, I'll play. When you say 'to get man back on course,' were we as far off back then as we are now?" I asked.

"Definitely!" she answered sternly, reminding me of an old school teacher of mine.

"You see, Hon, the problem for many was that Jesus had achieved mastery over his actions. Sure, he was born a very special being, but like many who have been given the chance to ascend on this planet, he had to cultivate and nurture his being. Once he had fulfilled the initiations, he became a living Master. When one is confronted with a true Master, all of their inadequacies become magnified. In this case, rather than deal with their own 'issues,' they condemned the very person who had come to lead them into a greater understanding of Self."

I was beginning to understand what she was saying, but I wasn't sure if I wanted to believe it as the Truth. I had long given up on that guy called Jesus because I thought he belonged to just one religion. I hadn't considered the possibility that he was a universal Master.

Sally continued, loving every moment that she got to play preacher. This was a quality that crept into our conversations every once and a while. Sometimes it bothered me because I felt inadequate not knowing about this kind of stuff. Sometimes it didn't. I was usually too tired from work to resist. Whether or not her spiels were true or not, I didn't know, but there were times that the information was so fascinating that I could set my ego aside and just listen. This was one of those times.

"Like attracts like, light attracts light. Basically, people didn't want to hang with the light," she said.

"If Jesus were here right now, do you think he would do any better?"

"I don't know," she said, staring deeply into the portrait of Jesus. "I don't know if people are more receptive now."

I thought about it for a moment and I figured she was probably right. I couldn't imagine listening to some guy with a long beard telling me that if I did this, I would feel that. Then I thought about the four longhaired men I saw in the meditation room. Maybe this was some sort of Jesus boot camp? Maybe these men were being trained to go to different parts of the world and play the role of Jesus, telling everyone that they were the "second coming of Christ."

"Or maybe they are just on a retreat to learn about Self," I heard Sally's voice enter my mind to try to stop its panic-induced paranoia.

I just smiled at her intrusion. Although it had bothered me at first, I was beginning to like the idea of having telepathic conversations, especially at parties.

"Shall we go into the bathroom for a quickie?"

Sally nudged me, bringing me back to the room.

"I can't believe some of the things that run through your mind," she said, "Come on or we'll be late for our assignments."

"Whoa, hang on, I thought you couldn't read my mind on Earth?"

"We're now at the stage where the retreat is operating at a different vibration. We're on Earth but not in the usual sense."

"Does that mean my BMW is gone?"

"Don't be silly," she said, taking my hand.

"Six payments left, Sally. Six payments."

Sally laughed.

"And how come I can't read *your* mind?"

"Not yet. Now come on." Sally led me down the hall.

"Let me ask you something," my curiosity and desire to duck the chores continuing unabated, "do you think there will be a second coming of Christ?"

Sally squeezed my hand. "I think so, but I'm just not sure how it will look. That's one you could probably ask Surrender."

"It's nice to see that you don't know everything," I replied, in an unexpected blurting of the truth. "It helps me feel more comfortable when I'm with you."

Sally blushed.

Lately in our relationship, I have found that I only got together with Sally when I was feeling good about myself. Other times she had this uncanny ability to intimidate me. She didn't even have to open her mouth and I would feel intimidated. Which made me wonder why she was attracted to me. Like attracts like? On what basis in this instance?

Sally became very serious as she began to speak of things that had been told to her in past retreats.

"Some prophets have talked about the second coming taking the form of the mass consciousness being raised to a certain vibration, very much like that of Master Christ; that we'd all become Ascended Masters, as he is. Other prophets say that Jesus will come back and give us a second chance to understand his teachings so that we may experience Heaven on earth."

I was trying to digest what she was saying, while at the same time hearing my 40-something knees creak from the early morning meditation. My sporting years were catching up with me.

Sally sat down beside me as we both stared at a large picture of the Universe hanging on the opposite wall. Even though it was only a picture, it made me think. There were probably things going on out there in the vastness of the cosmos that even a genius would have a hard time comprehending.

I was reluctant to ask this next question, however my curiosity was getting the better of me.

"You talk as if this Jesus is still alive. So what's he doing? Riding around in some cloud-formed chariot, watching all of us, or better yet, sitting up there in a cloud-formed throne, passing judgment on who will go to Heaven and who will be left to the dogs?"

Sally remained silent for a moment, staring at the picture of the Universe.

"I know we've touched on this in the past, but the way I'm beginning to see the world is that there is no death, just different experiences of reality that we pass through in order to evolve into a higher frequency, eventually vibrating with the Oneness. So yes, in a way, I do think Master Christ is watching us and is in each of us, in some strange, inexplicable way."

I just marveled at the idealism of this woman and her incredible perceptions – or were they deceptions?

"Come on, let's go. And quit trying to stall," she said, standing up, facing me and extending her hand. I reciprocated and we both helped my yoga-challenged body stand up to its full six foot one.

We started to walk down the hall toward a doorway that was filled with light. Then Sally laid another one on me.

"There are some who believe that just before the so-called Armageddon or Judgment Day, there will be all sorts of beings helping those who choose to ascend to the Light. Some of these helpers live on Earth. In other cases, angels, extra-terrestrials, Ascended Masters, spirit guides, and others will assist those people who choose to evacuate before Mother Earth does some serious physical shifting to rid herself of the massive impurities resulting from mankind's lack of consciousness.

"They say we will be given great teachings 'in the skies' and then, when all has quieted down, we will be brought back to Earth to begin a New World at a different vibration - The Fourth Dimension. The Golden Age. One thousand years of peace. Those who choose not to raise their vibration will continue their lives in a parallel universe, still going through their everyday struggles in the third dimension. However, most people making that choice won't survive the vibrational shift and the third dimension will be a very lonely place. But entering the Fourth Dimension demands that we reconnect with our multidimensionality and strive for the light."

I stopped in my tracks. I had to sit down again. What she had just said sent a chill up my spine and a dagger in my gut. Of all the things that Sally had been saying, this affected me the most. Angels, Ascended Masters, spirit guides, extra-terrestrials??? Someone had been spending a lot of time watching Saturday morning cartoons!

It all sounded ridiculous. However, and this was beginning to scare me, there was something that rang true - sans slimy green aliens, of course. Something that made me fearful of the future. Something that made me distrust the future. A future I had taken for granted all my life was being challenged by this new perception of what we had been doing to this planet and to ourselves.

If I allowed any of this information to permeate my thoughts and feelings, which at this rate of accelerated growth was becoming more and more likely, I would have the beginnings of a belief system. Something that I had been lacking for years.

These recent revelations may have been real and true for those around me but they had not been real and true for me. But despite my resistance, I was slowly and surely waking up to a new way of seeing this world in which I had been living. It didn't make me feel any happier though.

It was the first time that I had given any thought as to whether mankind was destined for global destruction and disaster. Could we do something to change our future and save our world? I didn't know for sure but what was interesting was that I was asking the questions. This seemed like the beginning of new thought patterns. That intrigued me.

Can you imagine advertising oncoming global disasters? Now there's a commercial that wouldn't sell. From my experience in the ad business, too many people were preoccupied with the material things in life. "Don't put any food for thought on their plates. That will make them ask questions!" to quote an old boss of mine. Interestingly enough, he died of food poisoning at his favorite fast food joint. I think it was the fish burger with extra mayo. Maybe he should have ordered the food for thought.

"Honey, please get out of your head long enough to enter the common room." Sally's voice pierced through my thoughts.

"Oh yeah, right. The common room," I said to the mind reader as I held my overstuffed head up with my hands, rubbing my temples.

I raised my aching body and followed her through the doorway of light into yet another "self prescribed" phase of my journey.

~ 11 ~

The room was quiet, except for the occasional whisper. It appeared to be a meeting room of sorts. Not the kind that would pass muster in the ad biz, but it was obvious by the worn couches and chairs surrounding the huge stone fireplace that this was where people got together for fireside chats or, in this case, whispers.

There was a warm feeling in the room. Even though the fireplace was unlit, it radiated warmth.

The large cathedral windows were the only indication of any sort of organized religion. But the things that went on around here were a bit too "out there" for any organized religion that I was familiar with.

"Would you like a juice?" Sally asked, leading me to a chair by the window.

"No thanks, I'll wait for breakfast."

"That is breakfast," Sally said, before realizing that she had not warned me about yet another "feature" of life here at "Cosmo Ranch."

I stopped. "Oh no, no, no. This can't be happening. I don't care if that other stuff was real or not. This would be a nightmare."

Sally looked at me innocently. She knew how to utilize her little girl for effect. I tried hard not to let it work.

"Not having my sausages and eggs on a Saturday morning after a tough week is just not acceptable, Sally. *No way!*"

"I'm sorry, I forgot to tell you. We follow a special dietary program at this retreat. It's a form of fasting. It helps the body become lighter."

"What? Are you kidding? Of course the body is going to become lighter. It will be dead in three days if all we have is juice."

"Oh Peter, quit exaggerating. All of your nutritional needs will be met. We start our day with mixed organic fruit juice, and then we have different combinations of organic fruit later on in the morning. It helps clean the digestive system from the week before. Vegetable cocktail for lunch and then a wonderful mixture of basmati rice and organic vegetables for dinner."

She caressed my face and gave me a soft kiss on the cheek, and whispered, "You'll enjoy it. It will be good for you."

I love it when women tell me what they think is good for me. I think that women think that men wouldn't be able to survive without their help. OK, let's just not go there.

"We help each other, remember?" came the echoing of Sally's voice in my head. This mental telepathy did have its drawbacks.

I looked over at Sally and could see her incandescent grin as she stopped in front of the table, waiting to pour us some "breakfast." What logic could there be in intentionally starving yourself?

I could see the guys sitting around the table at our usual greasy spoon, getting a good chuckle out of this story while eating delicious, greasy, fried eggs with a large mound of even greasier bacon and home fries. Depriving a guy of a Saturday tradition *and* real food, it wasn't fair.

Sally walked back over and handed me a little eight-ounce glass of juice.

"That's it?! That's going to feed my body? Give me energy to continue this day of 'enlightenment?'" I shouted, in a whisper of course.

Some people were beginning to shoot side glances at me but I didn't care. This was outrageous. Sally sat down beside me holding a glass of juice in each hand.

"Peter, it's quality not quantity that our body asks for."

"How could this puny glass of juice possibly be enough food for my body first thing in the morning? How?"

"It's simple," Sally perked up. "This is freshly-squeezed organic fruit, its energy is still alive, therefore, we are feeding the body something that is still alive, directly from Nature - not man-made."

She would be perfect for an infomercial too.

"You see, Hon, our cells regenerate and respond to herbs, fruits, and juices that are not man-made or concocted by corporations that are feeding nutritional lies to consumers."

Again, a sermon I hadn't asked for, but in this case she had a point. I had done many an ad campaign for "health food" companies that I knew sold absolute garbage. It had become a fad. Billions were being made from the health-conscious consumer. They were going after the almighty dollar and it was my job to convince consumers that what they were buying would change their lives. I cringed at the thought of buying any of those foods that I helped con the public into buying.

"OK," I conceded, "Maybe you're right about man being conditioned to eat certain foods, but I still don't think this is enough for someone weighing in at 185 pounds. I need some real food first thing in the morning, especially Saturday morning. It's, it's, tradition."

Sally looked at me penetratingly. "I know this is difficult for you, but just give me this weekend. Be my partner for this weekend. That's all I'm asking. I don't want to change you, I just want to help you see the world through my eyes for a few days."

How could I not surrender to those luminous blue eyes? How could I not surrender to her sincerity?

"OK, OK, hand it over." She smiled and passed me the small glass of juice. In the back of my mind I knew I would pig out as soon as I got back from this retreat. *If* I survived.

I clinked her glass and chugged it down the old hatch. I didn't have time to taste it because there was so little of it and it went straight to my stomach, non-stop. I smiled and mumbled something about it not being too bad. I was lying.

"Have you always been like this and I just haven't noticed?" I asked.

"Well, let's just say, it's in me to be like this. I just find that I need to have more walls up when I'm in the outside world."

Sally paused for a moment and looked away from me.

"It scares me to show you this side of me."

"Why?" I asked, surprised that anything would scare Sally.

"I'm afraid that maybe you'll leave me, that I'll be too much to handle."

I moved my chair closer to hers.

"Sally, why would-" I could see her becoming emotional and I immediately felt protective of her vulnerability. I began to caress her long, flowing blonde hair as she slowly bowed her head.

"Why would you be afraid to reveal this part of yourself to me?"

Tears rolled down her cheeks. It was all I could do not to sweep her up in my arms and take her into another room, slowly wiping away her tears and caressing her body, sharing the love for her that was beginning to well up, deep in my heart.

"I'm afraid you'll leave me, like the other men. Every time I've exposed myself, I-" she sobbed and put her head onto my shoulder, "Never mind."

I brought her closer to my chest, feeling a dash of knight-in-shining-armor galloping into the scene.

"That's why I waited six months before I brought you into this part of my world. I wanted to have some sense of who you were and build a little trust before I revealed this part of myself."

I had often wondered what she saw in the retreats that she went to almost every weekend. I guess my curiosity, combined with what happened yesterday at work, finally got the better of me.

I was beginning to have strange feelings around my heart – warm, tingly sensations. I guess there was something to be said for a space that provided this kind of opportunity for sharing.

"I know in the big picture that we are all One and these feelings of abandonment and rejection aren't relevant, but I just can't stop these feelings from overcoming me every time I expose myself," she said, burying her head deeper into my shoulder.

I took her chin and softly lifted her head toward me so that our eyes met.

"Everything is relevant to the big picture, Sally. Even abandonment issues."

I could see in Sally's eyes that she couldn't believe what had just come out of my mouth. Neither could I for that matter.

"You're right, Sweetie. Thank you. Thank you for saying that," she whispered in a soft, sexy tone. Then she proceeded to kiss me on the lips, melting every part of my body except one.

She slowly pulled away, gently stroking my leg down toward my knee. Had it gone the other way, there could have been trouble. Then, Mr. Ego, my faithful companion in life and business, kicked in.

"Looks like I've got a few words of wisdom myself."

We both laughed.

It was good to see her smile again. She had a startlingly beautiful smile that could easily light up a room, no matter how bright it was already, or how dark it got.

Sally leaned back and sipped her juice slowly as our attention was brought back to the room. All the whispering had stopped. Surrender had arrived.

"Everyone is aware of their next place. Please begin accordingly," Surrender said, in his usual soft tone.

"I'll see you at lunch," Sally said, as she squeezed my hand and gave me a peck on the cheek.

She was about to leave, except that I wouldn't let go of her hand.

"Oh no, you're not leaving me alone with these people." I was beyond being too ashamed to beg.

"Don't be silly. These are wonderful people and besides, you won't be alone. You'll be with Surrender."

"Like that's supposed to comfort me?!"

"It's your first time here, Peter," Sally said, patiently, "Anyone who is new has to spend time with Surrender, to get acquainted."

"Sally, the guy's in my dreams and reads my mind. How much more acquainted do we need to get?"

"Peter, please, just relax. It's OK. He's not going to hurt you."

I hadn't even thought of that. Great!

"I'll see you at lunch. Bye."

I reluctantly unclenched my hand from hers as she filed out of the room with the rest of the sheep.

Except, of course, Surrender.

This was the man who was going to dissect my every thought and turn it into some "enlightenment" experience that would make me a better human being. I mean really, what did these people do for fun?

Maybe my regular life wasn't so bad after all. Other than the dead cow and used condom accounts, I usually got the ones that I wanted. Usually. The money I wanted. Usually. The toys I wanted. Usually. The women I wanted. Usually. So basically, I could leave this room right now and have a reasonably good life with a reasonable amount of happiness, but… That damn "but" came up again. Something was telling me that it was important to stay.

Maybe while I was asleep they had programmed me to stay. Maybe that wasn't fruit juice I had just had for "breakfast." Maybe it was a lethal concoction passed out to this community of innocent seekers to-

"Peter! Please! Do yourself a favor and get out of your head, it's driving you crazy." Somehow Surrender managed to enter my head from across the room.

This mind-reading stuff was too much. Where was the door?

Surrender smiled at me. "Relax, Peter, I'm not reading your mind. I said that out loud. You were so preoccupied with your thoughts that you didn't realize that you just dropped your glass onto the floor."

He was right! I looked down and there was shattered glass surrounding my bare feet. I had no idea what I had just done. I grabbed a magazine from the lamp table to clean up the mess.

"There is a broom behind the door, it will make the task a lot easier," I heard Surrender say out loud, as I looked down at the floor.

I could make out the silhouette of a broom and quickly snatched it from its dark quarters.

I turned to sweep up the broken glass, but it was gone! I felt a chill up my spine. In no way or manner could anyone

have cleaned up that mess without me hearing it. Besides, there was nobody else in the room except Surrender.

Which was even more heart-stopping because I was wide awake. Wasn't I?

I turned to Surrender and his familiar smile. I dropped the broom and made for the opened doorway. I hit an invisible wall. What was happening to me? There was nothing in front of me and yet something or someone was not letting me pass through that doorway.

I was frozen in fear. I felt very cold, barely able to breathe. And yet at the same time, my body was alive with electric pulsations. Did Surrender really have that kind of control over me?

"It is the intention of your Higher Being that you not leave this learning space," Surrender said. "I am merely an advocate for your Higher Self, helping to guide you toward reconnection with the Source, thus helping you embrace the multidimensional being that you have always been."

I saw a movie about these guys once. It took about a year to deprogram the unwilling participants. I wondered if I could do it in under a year. If so, who would I get to help me? My coworkers were my friends but I'm sure they would be more into stealing my accounts than telling me I was a wonderful human being. Okay, a tad negative on my part. I agree.

"Come back to the *now* and breathe, my friend. Just breathe."

Once again, Surrender's voice penetrated my thoughts. Despite myself, I took his advice and noticed an immediate change in my body. As I began paying attention to my breath, my body began to relax, and once again, warmth was my partner. The electric currents that had been pulsating throughout my body dissipated as the warm air filled my lungs.

I turned around, looking at Surrender, and sat down on the closest chair. Out of breath, out of control, out of interpretations, I broke down. I felt a deep swelling of uncontrollable emotion smash through the floodgates hidden deep inside my hardened body.

Yeah, I was crying.

But I didn't know why. Perhaps it was because I was caught in this unknown place of Self with no one to help me - including me. I felt very alone. Very afraid. Very tired.

~ 12 ~

I slouched at the edge of my chair with my head buried in my hands, bursting with uncontrollable sobs. Never had I cried so much in so little time. OK, there was the thing about little red wagon when I was eight, but doesn't everyone have a red wagon story?

I felt a hand touch the top of my head. A warm surge of energy coursed through my body. I knew it had to be Surrender. I didn't even look up. Any strength I had, any will power, had long since departed. I felt empty.

Suddenly, visions started to fill my head. They were startlingly vivid and appeared to come from an old Viking movie.

"Don't attack until I give the command!" shouted the enormously built Viking stepping off the wooden vessel.

"We need formations of ten on the left and ten on the right!" he bellowed, "You and you, come with me. We're going up the middle."

I could see two young warriors who weren't happy with their orders. Their eyes were familiar but I couldn't place them. "But sir," one of them spoke out, "If we go up the middle, we will surely die."

"If you don't go up the middle with me, I'll surely kill thee!" barked back the fierce-looking Viking. I saw both young men reluctantly go into battle, feeling defeat before they had even begun.

"The outspoken young Viking was you and the other young one was your brother," I heard Surrender whisper into my right ear.

"The loud and obnoxious Viking was me. Then, I had control over people's fates. Now I do not. Now my role is to assist fellow beings into the new world, provided these people want my assistance."

I began wiping away the tears and tried to suppress the snot running out of my nose. I wanted to hear what Surrender had to say. I looked up at him as he moved his hands away from the crown of my head and got on his knees in front of me.

"My child, it is your chosen destiny that you awaken to the true Being that you are. You made that choice long ago. I'm only one of many who will come into your life to help you remember your purpose."

I felt my body recoil with fear and excitement upon hearing these words. I knew, deep down, that what he was saying was true but couldn't take it in. I sensed the love that was coming from him and could almost reciprocate.

I knew I was holding back though. I wasn't sure who or what to trust any more. Words couldn't express what I was experiencing. Was this real? Did it matter?

Whatever was occurring was showing me something about myself. My fear of change was upon me once again. I had always disliked change and disruption in my life. I consciously tried to keep everything in my life routine and boring. I had developed the ability to sense imminent change and could usually head it off at the pass. I was getting that feeling again. But this time I didn't feel I had the strength to resist Surrender's faith in my ability to change; my ability to "remember."

"You have a great will and a burning desire deep in your being and that is a good start for the work we need to do together," he said.

He gently raised my head.

As I tried to look directly into the windows of his soul, I noticed that his eyes had a youthful vibrancy that belied his ancient wisdom. Even his face lacked the wrinkles of a person his age.

I became aware that this was not your average senior citizen. This was a man who was somehow able to maintain his youth despite life and the tricky games it throws at you. This was a man who truly cared about what was going on in this world.

But did he possess the true eye of the observer? If so, was I willing to learn from this teacher? Could I possibly ignore all that had transpired this weekend and live a "normal" life? Would I be in some sort of denial if I did? Who would I call upon for strength and courage to comprehend all of this? My friends? Not likely. Sally? Maybe.

Was it really up to me to grow and change? Didn't life just happen? I didn't know anything any more.

I just sat back, exhausted from what had been happening since my arrival. The only thing that I knew for sure was that I was having a difficult time understanding what was real.

"Come, my friend, let's go outside and say hello to Mother Nature," Surrender said, interrupting my thoughts.

"Fresh country air is always a soothing welcome to a recovering soul," he continued, as he rose from the floor.

I figured that he could at least be trusted for a bit of fresh air. I didn't know why but I still didn't trust him fully. Maybe he really was that Viking who had led me to my death. Maybe I just didn't trust people in general. For sure, mistrust was a survival strategy that I had needed in the ad game.

Surrender stood at the doorway, awaiting my next step.

"OK," I responded to his unspoken request, unable to say anything else.

I struggled as I got up from the chair. I observed my exhaustion as well as the peculiar noises coming from my knees. By now, Surrender had already left the room and was down the hallway, confident that I would soon follow.

I stood in the doorway and turned around to face the room I had just blubbered in. I felt its permeating peacefulness. For the first time in my life, I found myself bowing and thanking a room, just for being there for me.

I caught up to my teacher at the back door leading to the porch. He stretched out his arms, closed his eyes, took in a deep breath and then exhaled. "It's difficult to realize one's potential without harmonizing with Mother Nature," he said, without looking at me.

I stood there viewing the various shades of green. It was a rare day that I gave Nature full credit. It was a rare day that I gave Nature anything.

"Have you ever heard the term 'chop wood, carry water'?" he asked, as he slowly turned towards me.

"Noooo." Where was this leading?

"Today we are going to do just that, chop wood and carry water."

"When you say 'we' does that mean you and me? Or just me?" I asked. Never, ever, liking the idea of doing any physical labor.

"I'll carry the water, when necessary, and you'll be chopping the wood."

Why wasn't I surprised?

I followed Surrender as he stepped off the back porch and onto the wild and carefree grassy "lawn." Actually, the lawn was more like a meadow. It led to a thick forest that sloped down a rolling hill. It felt familiar somehow. It was like a flash of a memory that left as quickly as it came.

"What is a deja-vu?" I asked, having heard this expression before.

"A deja-vu is a subtle remembrance of All That You Are."

"Huh?"

"You remember the term multidimensional being and the notion that past, present and future converge in the *now*?"

"Yeeaah." I was faking it.

Surrender crossed his hands behind his back and continued as he led me down the dirt path to the forest.

"A deja-vu occurs when linear time, the time experience on Earth, allows the eternal to enter our earthly thought form patterns. When this occurs, we experience aspects of our Universal Self. It all occurs in one moment. We remember our future in the present."

"Okaaay."

Why did I even bother?

"Outside of this planet, in this universe and others, we don't experience linear time as we do on Earth. A deja-vu allows us to get a thorough glimpse of the multidimensional beings that we are. We all have the ability to see our past or future in the present. However, most people experience a deja-vu as a shock because of the lower vibration at which their physical body customarily operates. They need to be initiated and acclimatized before they can reawaken and realize the multidimensional beings that they are."

I had lost him somewhere after "A deja-vu occurs…" Actually, I had lost him somewhere in my dreams last night.

I tried to comprehend his theory of "no time" as we walked along the path. I distracted myself by taking in the looming evergreens surrounding us. They were obviously the protectors of anyone who walked this path. I turned and looked at Surrender's peaceful face as he too observed the evergreens.

"What would trigger a deja-vu?" I asked, always the glutton for knowledge, no matter how incomprehensible.

"Often a moment is so strong that it penetrates linear time. These are the moments to remember. They will help you break through the earthly time barrier and will carry you through a timeless continuum, thus reconnecting you with the Divine spark that you are. It's also a good way to know that you're on the right track."

"How so?"

"The more deja-vus you have, the more you are truly connecting with your multidimensional Being, and that's a good thing."

I stopped abruptly just as we were about to enter the forest. I stood there, watching him. He stopped, turned toward me and smiled.

"How could you possibly think that I believe or understand everything that you just said?" I asked, feeling totally exasperated.

Surrender took in a deep breath and exhaled. "I don't talk to just you, Peter, who walks on this path leading to the woods. I talk to all of you, including your Higher Self. The essence of you is far greater than who you think you are."

I stood there looking at him. Then at the crow flying above our heads. Then I looked back at him. "What do you mean, my 'Higher Self'? Is there a part of me sitting in outer space, holding a piece of wood with strings attached, moving me around like some puppet? Is that what you're trying to tell me here?"

He chuckled - a rare occurrence.

"Peter, quite simply, there is a part of you who governs all and is now asking your physical self to remember."

He bowed, turned away and entered the forest before I could question him further. Chicken.

I thought about what he had just said. Remember what? I swallowed that question just as quickly as it had popped into my head. I shrugged it off as more "New Age" talk.

I then followed him into the forest of the unknown.

~ 13 ~

Who was this Surrender? Where had he come from? Why was he so eager to teach me things? Was he trying to brainwash me into becoming another self-deluded messiah?

So much inner strength from such a fragile looking man. He was five feet tall at the most and slender as a blade of grass. His hunched-over walk had a vulnerable quality as he took his small, measured steps. His presence was dynamic though. He had the charisma of a movie star and the silence and wisdom of a Franciscan monk. I found him to be as present and focused in conversation as he was in silence. He only spoke when it was necessary and his mind appeared never to wander. Now I, on the other hand, had the city guy's version of A.D.D. Meaning, I was easily distracted by shiny things and new types of lattes.

"Where are you from?" I asked, trying to see if I could verbally dissect his mind. Words were my only power tool in this foreign environment.

"Perhaps some day I'll take you there," he said, with a wink and a smile. I wasn't sure I wanted to go. It could be another dimension, or worse, another planet.

"How long have you been here?" I asked.

"Oh, let's just say I've been here for a long, linear time," he answered wryly.

I was getting the feeling that information about him was on a need-to-know basis.

"Where are we going?" was the only question I could come up with without getting too personal.

"When we come to the end of this path, there will be a clearing. To the immediate right there will be a wooded shed on top of a little hill. There, you will proceed with the chopping of wood."

Oh yeah, the physical labor part.

We continued down the path and I began to take notice of Mother Nature. Living in a downtown condo did not offer Mother Nature's best scenery. The leaves in my part of town weren't the green they might have been at one time. Some said it was because of pollution from local factories, some said it was because of the increase in cars during rush hour, and some said they didn't remember the leaves ever being a true green. I wasn't sure who was right but the trees in my neighborhood were no match for my present lush surroundings.

I inhaled the fresh air and then exhaled. I savored the aroma of the surrounding trees, plants, and meadow. I began to realize that this was how fresh air should smell. Calling it "breathtaking" was not just another bad pun.

I stopped for a moment, letting Surrender continue the walk for both of us. I knelt down to feel the coarse texture of the wild grass mixed with rich, brown soil. How many people had walked this path, I wondered? How many people had reconnected with Nature? Was I the only rookie retreat-goer to experience this lushness and beauty? Why I had never taken the time to become acquainted with Mother Nature could only be explained by my obsession to be number one in the ad game. A pretty poor trade-off.

I caught myself before getting too melancholy, got off my knees, and stood beside Surrender.

By this time, we had come to another clearing. It was more expansive than the last meadow and was overshadowed by something bigger than the "hills" that he had been talking about earlier.

In awe of their sheer enormity, from a city folk perspective, I broke the silence.

"Surrender, in some parts of the world, people would consider those mountains."

He turned to me, his arms folded into his sleeves. "And in some parts of the world they would be considered hills. It all depends on what your reality is."

These people just didn't stop, did they?

He reminded me of an old geography teacher I had in high school. "Learn the lands, learn the lands," would be drilled into our thick, youthful heads. He had always included his geography teachings in his conversations outside the classroom too. Talking about landforms and tectonic shifts seemed a bit much when he was supposed to be coaching football. Mind you, if I was still talking about it, I must have learned something.

"Where's the wooden shack?" I was afraid it was on top of the highest "hill" that loomed to the right.

"On top of that hill," he said.

Guess which "hill" he meant.

He began to walk in that direction with his precise stride. It could be worse, I thought. I could be married to him.

"I know I'm repeating myself here," as I huffed away, "but some people would call this a mountain." We both stood there looking at this gigantic phenomenon of Nature. He smiled. "It's all about perspective, my friend."

"You mean to tell me that we have to climb this 'hill,' chop wood, then carry it back down to the house?"

Surrender smiled.

"How much wood am I going to chop? I can only carry three or four logs at best."

At a 45-degree angle, it looked like a rough climb. Fortunately, I was wearing my cross-trainers. Unlike my friend here, I was not into barefoot mountaineering.

"It is the process, not the result, that is important," he said as he turned and began his ascent up the "hill."

"The process and not the result." What the heck did that mean?

Did it mean I was going to chop one log or 50? There was no way I was going to chop 50 logs plus go up and down that mountain all day. I played squash three times a week, which was more than enough exercise for me, thank you very much.

Memo to self: *Must cut back on my whining.*

I took a deep breath and began my uphill journey. My knees were reminding me of how they had felt after that morning's meditation. Or maybe it was after all those years of hockey and football. Either way, a jacuzzi and a massage were in order after this weekend. *If* I survived.

About a quarter of the way up the "hill," I felt a strain in my calves. If my body could have said anything to me right then I was sure the words "naïve" and "stupid" would have entered the dialog.

I tried mightily to keep up with Surrender and his effortless gliding motion.

"Please don't slow down on my account!" I yelled, trying to bring some humor to the situation.

My hilarity fell on deaf ears because there was no response as he continued his swift upward movement.

It seemed as though a half an hour had gone by as I worked up an early morning sweat. Surrender had long been out of sight, which deflated my ego slightly, but I could see that the top was only a few minutes away.

I stopped for a moment because it was getting difficult to hear my thoughts through my heavy breathing. I turned around and viewed the stunning spectacle of Nature surrounding me. This was a Heaven I sure could hang my hat on.

I looked down, appreciating the climb thus far. I felt good about myself.

"Yes, it does feel good, doesn't it?" I heard Surrender say to me.

I turned around and there he was, standing at the crest of the "hill," only a few yards away. He was a stunning vision with his long white flowing robe. Behind him "the rays of Heaven reached out into the newborn sky," as Grandma used to say.

Surrender was definitely in his element.

I could see a glimpse of a smile as he turned away, allowing the sun to blind me. I climbed the last few steps of the "hill" and finally reached the top. From there, the view was even more breathtaking. More of what I would call mountains, surrounding us. More of Mother Nature's beauty.

Immediately in front of us was the old wooden shack, barely standing on its grassy foundation. Beside it stood Surrender, smiling, waiting for me to come forward.

"It ain't fancy but it's home," I quipped, wiping the sweat from my brow.

I walked toward it, noticing that it had been standing here for some time. It was hard to imagine how it could have withstood the storms that must assail this "hilly" range on a regular basis. But no doubt Surrender had a remote thermostat for this area and kept storms at a minimum.

"Let me guess, this is where you come to play video games?" I said, trying to make light of a situation that I was sure was about to become heavy – literally.

"No, this is the place for the sacrificial lamb," he said, looking me straight in the eye without a hint of a smile.

My body froze.

After what seemed like *forever*, he finally said, "Just kidding." He broke into laughter. "See? I too have a sense of humor."

"Don't ever do stand-up," I said, although I had to admit, at least to myself, that I was relieved that 25 devotees weren't going to jump out of the shack, slit my throat, and offer my blood to the gods in exchange for more rain.

"Let me know when you are ready to begin," he said. He turned and faced the sun. "This is my favorite spot on this planet."

"This *planet*?"

Ignoring me, he raised his arms toward the sky and started to mumble something in another language. A flash of deja-vu appeared in my mind and then disappeared before I could grasp it.

I could easily understand why someone would want to hang out in such a beautiful spot. The spectacular view alone was enough to make you climb the mountain, uh, hill. I closed my eyes and deeply inhaled the newly discovered fresh air. I started to wonder if it was possible to do what I did for a living *and* live out here. I was sure I could come up with even better ideas and snappier promotions. My whole being felt lighter up here. Whole "being?" Uh oh. My lingo was changing.

"Surrender, why do I feel so different here?" I felt layers of city life lifting off my shoulders.

I noticed that he was still enjoying the sun and I felt that perhaps I was selfishly interrupting him.

"Oh, sorry," I whispered.

"That's all right, my son," he whispered in turn. He took in a breath.

I braced myself for the next installment of wisdom.

"Matter is energy. Therefore, more condensed matter is comprised of more condensed energy. When one is in a city, matter is more compressed, or dense."

Kind of getting it, I tried relating it to my own experience. "You mean because of all the buildings, cars and people, I feel more closed in, as opposed to the infinite space surrounding us here?"

Yeah, I noticed the word "infinite." What about it?

"In a manner of speaking, yes. A denser situation, continuing with the example of a large city, will attract more pollution because of the lack of natural cleansing devices. Mother Nature has her own cleansing cycle. However, man and Nature have yet to discover a way to coexist harmoniously."

I thought about this for a moment, scanning the beautiful scenery that I was beginning to feel privileged to experience. In fact, I appreciated it more by the moment.

Surrender continued with his sermon on the "hill."

"Matter naturally expands and contracts when it is allowed to harmonize with Nature. Here before us we have the trees, hills, and plants, all living matter, living close together and in harmony with one another." He paused for a moment. "Do you know why?" He looked into my eyes, making sure I was paying attention.

I tried to hold his gaze, but found it difficult to look him straight in the eye. I had the feeling that he could see through all my lies. After all, he could read my mind. "No, I don't," I responded, like a little schoolboy whose mind has gone blank in the mere presence of a teacher. In a desperate bid for approval, I then blurted out, "Because they want to?"

"Yes," he responded, softly.

"Unfortunately, man has lost sight of the rhythm of Nature, her ebb and flow. The necessary cycles that are needed to cleanse, purify, and grow. Man has been taking a dangerous course that doesn't harmonize with Nature. Now Nature is about to begin a major cleansing, with or without man."

He seemed saddened by this thought and I felt compelled to probe, "What are you saying? What's going to happen?"

He bowed his head for a moment, then slowly looked up at me. I could see his eyes moistening. He just stared at me. I could feel his sadness envelop my heart.

Another memory appeared, this time staying long enough to decipher. When I was in high school, I had this hippie teacher who told us about this old guy named Nostradamus. Nostradamus, who lived in the 16th century, predicted our future. One of his major predictions was the end of the world. Could it be true? Had all of this been for nothing? Could we be facing total annihilation because of some nuclear weapon? Or man's greed for power? Or both?

These thoughts were entering my mind for the first time, and the weight of them began to affect me. Not so much because of my fear of dying, although that was an issue in itself, but in the bigger picture I felt sadness for all of mankind. A very unusual feeling for me indeed.

"Are we going to blow ourselves up?" I asked, at the risk of hearing a yes.

Surrender remained silent as he wiped a tear with his forefinger. "I can't answer that, for the final decision as to how and when has not been made in some respects, but has been made in other respects."

I stood up and approached him. "So are you saying that man's destruction is inevitable? How?"

He looked deep into me.

"For mankind as we know it, yes. There will be several continuing major disasters and catastrophes in order to help cleanse the Earth. Who will survive and who will ascend, will be left to each individual consciousness. How it will look for the mass consciousness, I cannot predict. It will be a different choice for everyone. But there will be changes in Earth's vibrational level. We will soon be entering a higher vibration - the Fourth Dimension."

I stood there, silenced and stunned. Was I supposed to believe this man? Could he really have this kind of knowledge or insight? Or was he just a fraud? Whatever he was, his words were affecting me greatly, almost profoundly. My head was spinning as Surrender took a step toward me.

"This is why it is so important for you to learn about silence. This is why it is so important for you to listen to what that little voice inside you is saying. For it is that little voice that will teach you the way when this time comes. For it will come."

I felt my body tremble all over, I couldn't stop it.

Surrender took another step toward me and put his hands on my shoulders. "Don't fear humanity, my friend, for mankind is only doing what his hardened nature asks. Fear only yourself if you do not listen to your own true nature."

Then he pulled me closer as I burst into uncontrollable tears. It must have been an interesting sight to see this five-foot man holding up a six-foot one child.

I was beginning to have a new understanding of the term "being humbled." But while my body was reacting to the words and to the presence of this wise man, my mind was busy doubting. Was I being programmed?

And yet I couldn't help but feel humbled in the presence of such majestic scenery. Maybe there was a God of some sort. Maybe there was a Master Plan involved. Maybe I had been contributing to the destruction of this planet. Knowing what was really going on, could I continue to do what I had been doing for a living? My foundation was shaking and I was truly lost, yet again.

Much of who I was and what I was about was being chipped away. It was having its effect. Had I been lying to myself all this time? Had I? I just didn't know any more.

~ 14 ~

Surrender gently guided me to a tree stump in front of the shack as I continued making a mess of my sleeve.

"Time to get you out of your head again," he whispered into my ear while pointing to an axe lying beside the stump. Somehow I hadn't noticed the axe before.

I slowly began to regain control over my faculties. I bent over to pick it up. It had the appearance of being brand new.

"The logs are at the side of the shack. We'll chop one at a time," he said, pointing to the right side of the shack.

"We," of course, meant "me." I got up, leaned the axe against the stump, and walked around the corner of the shack. I picked out one log for its ultimate dismemberment.

It had been some time since I had chopped wood. My fireplace at the condo was gas that I lit up with my spanky remote. The only time I worked up a sweat was looking for the darn thing.

But now I was at the stump and beginning my "chop wood" lesson. Setting the log so that it was perpendicular to the stump, I raised the shiny axe over my head.

"Don't forget to thank the wood for permitting us to use it in this way."

I turned to him, axe still above my head. "You've gotta be kidding."

Surrender sat down on a nearby stump. "It is important to honor and respect all aspects of Nature when we are using her for our benefit. It's give and take."

That was a bit much for a clump of wood. My hard core city self was returning.

"Uh, OK. Um. Thanks, log," I said, looking at the log and feeling a tad foolish.

THWACK!

I missed it completely. My axe slammed straight into the stump. The abrupt stop had my teeth vibrating like a bowl of swirling jelly beans. I could hear Surrender chuckling.

"You have to mean it," he said. "It too is an entity with feelings."

I looked down at Mr. Log.

"I want to thank you for letting me slice you into smithereens." This weird situation was giving 'dia*log*' new meaning. Couldn't resist.

I turned and looked at Surrender, sitting there with his eyes and mouth closed.

"Something like that?"

No response from the Master.

I thought I would give it another go but I couldn't pull the axe out of the stump for the life of me.

"Uh Surrender, did you hex this thing or what?"

Surrender barely opened one eye. "Remember, everything works in unison."

I didn't know what that meant but I knew I was going to have to thank the log and the stump with sincerity if I was going to get any action. Seeing me now, no one would guess that I had been in charge of million dollar ad accounts.

"I thank you for allowing me to use you in serving my needs," I said out loud, with both sincerity and embarrassment, if that's possible.

I looked over at Surrender once again, noticing how much he was at peace with himself as he sat there with his eyes closed. Although he had an early-morning shadow on the side of his face, I wasn't quite sure if his ear-to-ear grin was directed at me or at some pleasant thought of his.

I tried pulling the axe out of the stump. My sincerity seemed sufficient.

I lined myself up for the next swing.

THWACK!

Sliced in half – perfectly! Yes, pride was kicking in and it did feel good. I looked over to Surrender for his approval and got nothing. I looked down at the perfectly spliced log and said out loud, "I guess I'll do another one."

I laid the axe down beside the stump. Walking past the silent Surrender, I went to the side of the shack and picked up another log for yet another ceremonial cutting.

I wondered where these logs had come from and why the people who brought them here didn't just bring them straight to the house in the first place? I also wondered if any of the 'honoring' dialog was directed at the trees before they were sacrificed to the forestry industry? Not too likely.

Memo to self: *Note developing conscience.*

I walked around the corner, log in hand, only to find Surrender gone. I looked toward the crest of the mountain and there he stood, arms folded into opposing sleeves, about to begin his descent.

"Where are you going?"

"That's all we came here for today," he said, looking back at me.

"But, what about the wood for the house?" Was I *really* volunteering for physical labor?

"And carry it all the way down that hill and back to the house? Use your energy wisely, my dear friend."

"But-"

"And if you'll remember, I did not say that we were cutting wood for the house," he smiled mischievously. "Besides, there is enough wood at the house to last many lifetimes."

With that, he turned and began his descent down the 'hill', laughing out loud at his warped sense of humor, and perhaps at his feeble student.

OK, so if this was all I had come up here to learn, then what did I learn? That Mother Nature had feelings too? Geez, a lot of effort for such a small discovery. Had I been that unaware to realize this simple truth? I didn't know. I'd have to chew on that one a wee bit longer. This man had a peculiar way of teaching.

I put the log back onto the pile at the side of the shack. I came back to the stump where I had chopped the first log. There was nothing sitting on the stump except a whole log. The chopped log was nowhere in sight.

I looked around for the axe that had been lying there only a few moments ago. Nada. Had Surrender moved it or had it moved itself? I started to get that familiar tingly sensation that came easily and often hanging around with these people.

I looked up and saw a crow circling above me. Not quite an Apollo moment but I knew it was time to leave nonetheless. My graceful sprint down the side of the mountain quickly turned into slipping and sliding, along with a dash of panic, as I desperately tried to catch up to Surrender.

For some inexplicable reason, my mind started racing as fast as my legs and I whizzed past the old Master, thinking that maybe he was carrying that axe underneath his robe, preparing for the *real* ceremony. OK, so I could be a tad paranoid. But after the events of this weekend, I had good reason. I wasn't about to stop and chat until I was at least on a flat surface. Easier for me to run away and harder for him to catch me.

Memo to self: *Confine paranoia to workplace. Avoid indulging it in Mother Nature's lush surroundings.*

I continued my oh-so-graceful slip, slip, sliding down the side of the mountain, repeatedly falling on the knee-high grass. I thought this was just like me, always running from something. I must have been quite a sight.

I began to slow my descent as I realized that fear was a great motivator for injury. Plus, the closer I neared the bottom, the more confident I became, and the more I let go of my paranoia about Surrender.

As I reached the bottom, I turned around to see Surrender about three-quarters of the way down the hill. I collapsed onto the ground, laughing at myself for thinking that Surrender was going to pull out an axe from beneath his robe and start swinging at me in a demonic fury. My mind created wonderful horror film scenarios. Maybe I was in the wrong profession.

That's when I heard the clap of thunder.

I looked up and saw black clouds rolling in. I looked back to Surrender and he was just taking his time coming down the hill.

"Hurry, Surrender! We're about to get a nasty storm."

There was no response. He kept his impassive descent, head bowed, and watching his every step. Then I heard a deafening crackle in the sky. I felt drops of water landing softly on my face. Suddenly, there was a whizzing and a thump behind me. I turned and there was a huge chunk of what appeared to be a ball of hail on the grass.

THUMP!

Another one fell just in front of me.

THUMP!

Then another. Soon there was a deluge hailing down around me. I yelled to Surrender as he neared the bottom of the hill.

"Hurry, Surrender! This looks serious."

Still no response. Still focused on the immediate task at hand. Still walking.

The wind started to pick up as it began to hail harder and faster. My visibility extended only a few feet in front of me.

Surrender was out of sight. I was on my own. I started toward the bottom of the hill where I thought he would be. I could no longer see anything but my own two feet.

"Surrender! Where are you?" I screamed at the top of my lungs. "Say something! Think something!"

No answer. Nothing but howling wind and pelting hail.

The large balls of hail were starting to hurt. I was worried that my little friend was in trouble. Then I realized that I was the one in trouble. I didn't know where I was and Surrender wasn't anywhere to be seen or heard. I was becoming used to his guidance, even if most of it went over my head.

"Stop it!" I screamed to the imaginary Greek God of storms, "Stop! It!"

By this time the pelting had become harder and I was down on my knees with my head buried in my arms trying to shield the pain.

"Don't resist. Allow it to be. Give into Nature and you shall be free," I heard Surrender's welcome voice whisper inside my aching head.

"I can't, it's hurting me!" I screamed back, in my loudest silent voice.

"Don't resist. Allow it to be. Give into Nature and you shall be free," he echoed in my head once again.

I tried to crack the New Age code but I couldn't. I tried to pretend that it didn't hurt but failed. Then I felt a warm hand touch my shoulder and I knew who it was.

"Don't resist. Allow it to be. Give into Nature and you shall be free," I heard him say out loud.

"I repeated this three times so that you would receive it in body, mind and spirit."

The hail was still pounding my body. I didn't understand what he was trying to say and when I pulled my head out of my arms, there was a young man kneeling beside me. It was a younger version of Surrender. I recognized his soulful, penetrating, cat-green eyes.

"Surrender? What…are…you? Who are-?" I asked, momentarily forgetting my pain as I touched him for the sake of sanity. Mine.

"Just as real as you are," he replied, in his usual soft tone.

In the midst of all that was going on around us, it seemed like time was frozen and that I was suspended in disbelief. His clothing was not getting wet. In fact, I saw steam rising off the dry cloth. There was no water dripping from his face. We were in the middle of a hailstorm and he was still dry. I was soaked to the bone, having been pelted with hail the size of baseballs. But nothing was touching this younger version of Surrender.

He looked at what must have been a very puzzled face. Mine.

"I accept that Mother Nature needs to do this for her own reasons, therefore I do not resist. In not resisting I ask myself, what do I need in order to co-exist? In this situation, I asked for warmth, youth, and a dry body, allowing myself to be free of the limitations of the mind. And here I am. Flesh and blood.

"Yeah, but, but, you're so young."

I was too stunned to take in what he was saying.

Staring me in the face was a 20-year-old version of the 70-year-old man who had just been coming down the hill only moments ago.

Memo to self: *I'm so off lattes.*

"Remember how I spoke to you of past, present and future being in the *now*?"

"Uh, yeah. OW!" I got another whack on the head by a hailing baseball.

"I'm simply choosing a time in my youth when I was happy, comfortable, and most importantly, dry."

He continued attempting to install knowledge into my brain. "I'm just co-existing with what the situation calls for in this planetary moment. I'm not harming Nature by being here, and Nature is not harming me by continuing with her natural processes."

Hmmm. There could be money in this.

The pelting began to lessen and I slowly rose out of my crouching position. I started to massage the top of my head where the last ball of hail had landed and left a burning sensation.

"Close your eyes and imagine the hail stopping completely, birds singing, and the sun shining brightly."

With another crack of thunder piercing my ears, I figured I had nothing to lose. The idea of being some Greek God's toy did not appeal to me at all. I did as the young Surrender suggested.

Closing my eyes, I thought of birds in the early morning, tropical sunlight and no more "Hail Mary" baseballs bouncing off my head.

"And don't forget to breathe," I heard Surrender say softly.

I became light-headed as I inhaled and exhaled quickly.

"Allow the breath to travel in and out of your body. It doesn't help to force human nature either."

No sooner had he finished giving his advice than, yep, the hail let up completely and I could hear the birds start to sing. I could feel the warmth of the sun begin to penetrate my wet clothes and shivering body.

I opened my eyes and there, standing before me, was the older version of Surrender.

"Now didn't I say I would carry the water when it was necessary?" he said as he opened up with a huge grin. The laughter that soon followed came from the depths of our bellies.

"You know you're an odd man, right?"

He laughed even harder.

I observed my clothes quickly drying in the sun's heat. Nothing was surprising me anymore.

"Why thank you," he said. "Shall we dance?"

Well, almost nothing.

He opened up his arms and tilted his head as if to say, "Well?"

I had to laugh. This man's idea of fun was refreshing.

"Are you going to stay the same age?"

"But of course," he replied, bowing towards me and sporting his ear-to-ear grin.

I got up off the grass, which was now dry, and stood in front of his five-foot frame, also extending my arms outwards.

"May I lead?" he inquired.

"Don't you always?"

And with that, he laughed, took a step toward me, and stretched out his left hand to meet my right. Clasping our fingers and palms together, he put his right arm around my waist as I put my left around his, and together we danced through the merry daisy fields, laughing and giggling like a couple of ten-year-olds.

If only my mother could see me now. "This came from me?" she would say.

~ 15 ~

I found myself sitting in the common room very much alone.

At least an hour had gone by since Surrender had left me to check on the others.

"I hope you'll continue to enjoy this room while I'm away." What did he mean by that? Was that code for a poltergeist situation about to happen? By this time, I was prepared for anything.

Strangely enough, I found myself not craving food. It had to be at least mid-day. In my other world, I would have been eating lunch and settling into my big comfy chair to watch "the game." That seemed like such a foreign world at this point. Anyway, with only solar power running in this ancient house, watching "the game" was not an option.

I wondered how they squeezed the juices around here. By hand? Ugh. I'm sure that Surrender didn't perform that primitive chore. Just us plebes.

Perhaps dinner would be over some medieval fire pit with big cast iron pots for boiling rice? It all seemed like so much work. My mind drifted into thoughts about the wonders of frozen dinners.

An hour passed by. I had been doing nothing except daydreaming, an occupational habit of mine that has made me a lot of money over the years.

I decided to get up and move my weary body to explore the house. By this time, I had changed into a clean set of regulation white pajamas and was ready for the next adventure. Also, by this time, I had developed a wee bit of curiosity. Not to be confused with courage.

I left the comfort of the common room to begin exploring the unknown. Without the guidance of anyone, I was sure I would get to the bottom of this cult experience. I wanted to be sure that whatever was happening to me wasn't drug-induced or part of an elaborate brainwashing campaign.

For example, where had everyone else gone? What were their special chores? How come it felt like I was the only one left in the house? Weird.

I entered the main hallway but could hear nothing. There was an eeriness in the air. Maybe it was a set-up. I never did see where that axe had ended up. I had difficulty accepting the fact that a group of spacey people would meet in one place without having some satanic ritual take place. Wasn't that what they did in the movies?

Did people really get together around the country to practice mind-control games or demonic rituals? Of course they did. Was this one of those cults? I was going to find out. Again because of curiosity, not courage.

Sure, the experiences I'd been having with Sally and Surrender appeared loving and profound but were they real? Were they drug-induced? Juice-induced? Had I been dreaming? I had nothing with which to compare these experiences. No retreat experiences, no out-of-body experiences, or OBEs, as Sally called them.

This was not a trip I was willing to take if it meant that I was going to re-enter the world a blind fool. Brainwashed to become a false seer, having to ask for donations to help run an organization that fueled some cult leader's Rolls-Royce™. No, a sucker I was not. By exposing fraudulent activities, I'd be doing my own version of service to mankind.

OK, maybe I was misrepresenting the fancy car bit, considering I hadn't seen any cars but mine in the lot. But still, I was determined to uncover the truth.

I continued down the hallway, passing the portraits of what Sally had deemed the great Masters. I had to sneak around in my bare feet because we weren't allowed to wear shoes in the house, out of respect. For whom, I didn't know. Perhaps the guru cleaning lady? Not wearing shoes didn't stop the creaking wooden floors from letting everybody in the house know of my whereabouts. I tiptoed down the hallway, trying to find a piece of floor that didn't scream, "This man is spying!"

I passed a door on my right, put my ear against it, and listened for strange noises. I couldn't hear anything. I gently and quietly tried the handle. Nothing. I bent down and took a peak through the keyhole. Bingo. I saw a partially naked woman lying face-down on a table. She was the one that looked like my co-worker, Janice. Her body was mostly covered with a white sheet of cloth but from what I could see, she was naked underneath.

Coming into view were two large hands. They appeared to be male. A strange white light was surrounding his hands as he hovered above the upper part of the woman's body. A wisp of hair fell over her serene-looking face.

I couldn't see if there was anything sexual going on and I wasn't sure I wanted to. I was there to explore fraud, not spy on people's intimate moments.

The white light from his hands became brighter. I'd never seen anything like it before. Was it a reflection of sunlight or smoke and mirrors? I wasn't sure. All I knew was what I could see – glowing masculine hands suspended above a woman's body.

The woman remained still and seemed very much at peace. Her long, flowing brunette hair fell to the side as she lay there, facing toward me with her eyes closed. I couldn't tell if she was asleep or not. She had the appearance of someone in the land of Oz.

It was at that moment that I saw a blue current of energy flow from the man's palms and penetrate her back, around the heart area. This, my brain could not comprehend. Maybe I was just imagining this, but then it happened again. A blue ray of light flowed from his palms and disappeared into her back.

I took a step away from the door, not believing what I had just witnessed. If it was real, surely the woman would have been jolted right off the table? However, she remained serene.

I moved into my spying position at the keyhole, wanting to witness more. The male hands and bright blue light had gone. However, the woman remained on the table, blissfully unaware of anything that had just occurred.

What made this experience unusual was that I was fully present in mind and body. I was sure of it. It was not an illusion. Or perhaps it was an hallucination, activated by a time-release capsule secretly mixed with my juice that morning?

Memo to self: *No, really! Deal with your paranoia!*

I continued looking through the keyhole, but no male hands appeared. Then, a flash of blue light struck the back of her neck and she didn't budge. Soon there were more rays of light penetrating her frame – yellow, pinkish-red, orange, violet, indigo, and then green. They were shooting in from different directions and going to various parts of her body. The pinkish-red went toward the bottom part of her torso, the orange to the middle of the buttocks, yellow to the lower back, and green to the back of the heart area. The blue still struck the back of her neck while an indigo ray dissolved into her forehead, and the violet ray went into the crown of her head.

I couldn't believe that she was unaffected by all that was going on around her. As beautiful as those colors were, I still found it difficult to accept that she wasn't being harmed in some way.

Just as I completed that thought, a flash of blinding white light sent me backward onto my rump.

What was with the blinding light? Was the sun being reflected by a mirror or was it something from another world? This was yet another experience I would be telling the boys. Um…maybe not.

From my position on the ground and looking through the keyhole, I could see the light becoming dimmer. I got up slowly, and cautiously moved closer to get a better look. I saw a breathtakingly tall, golden-haired hulk of a man. He was stunningly beautiful and, judging by his position standing over the woman on the table, he had to be at least seven feet tall. He was wearing a light-blue two-piece outfit, with a gold and silver shield covering his heart area. To the right and slightly above the shield was a golden insignia of unknown origin and meaning. He looked like something right out of an old sci-fi movie.

Slowly he leaned over the woman on the table and started whispering something into her ear. It didn't sound like English to me but, oddly enough, it did sound familiar.

His blue eyes were even more penetrating than Sally's. His long, flowing blond hair caressed the woman's dark hair as he continued to whisper into her ear. His chiseled features gave him presence.

He stopped whispering, slowly got up from his bent position, and turned his head toward the keyhole through which I was spying. I froze in fear. Perhaps I had just witnessed something that I shouldn't have? I couldn't move away from the door. My eyes were locked into his. It was as if he was putting me in a trance and had control of my thoughts and movements. I felt a flush of warmth enter my body, similar to my experience with Surrender, except this felt even more powerful. I tried to move away. This was too much for me to absorb in one day.

Pictures started to run through my mind. They had an abstract quality not unlike some of my more bizarre recurring dreams. They also had the makings of a sci-fi movie with images of UFOs, planets, stars, and outer space flashing through my brain.

Who was this person or thing? What did he want from me? I asked him to let go of his hold on me. Somehow I had the courage to confront this, whatever it was.

The golden man smiled at me.

"It's so nice to see you again, my friend," and with that, I flew backward onto the hardened floor.

It was as if he had been physically holding my body and then just threw me back, leaving me completely disoriented, both physically and mentally.

Sitting on the floor, I tried to collect my thoughts and check my body parts to see if all were OK. I thought twice about getting up and looking through the keyhole again. Both times the answer was no. I thought about it a third time as I sluggishly got up off the floor. Curiosity always got the better of me. Was what I saw real? Was there really a seven-foot golden man in that room? Did I really see those rays of light enter that woman's body? What did he mean, "So nice to see you again, my friend?"

I remembered what curiosity had done to the cat and thought better of making any irrational decisions. Some things were not meant to be seen, I rationalized, even if it was all an illusion.

I got up off the floor and continued walking down the hallway, congratulating myself for having barely escaped becoming a dead cat.

There were two more doorways along the hallway. I knew that one led to the meditation room but I wasn't sure where the other one led. If I went the other direction, it would lead me to the men's and women's dorms.

I was sure there was something in the attic that would be an inspiration for the next Mary Shelley to write her version of *Frankenstein*. That was an exploration I could do without, thank you very much.

~ 16 ~

I found myself asking more sensible questions like why was I still here? What compelled me to remain with these total strangers? Who was Sally anyway? And what was with that Surrender guy?

I included Sally because it was becoming obvious that she was a major player in all of this.

Was I a glutton for punishment? Did I really need to look through the other doorways only to find more incomprehensible scenarios occurring? What made me stay? The adventure? Maybe it was something bigger than what I could comprehend in that moment. Something was driving me to stay and explore what was really going on.

Up until that moment, I had been living a normal, everyday life with normal, everyday people, existing in a normal, everyday world. Although this was no white-water rafting trip, my recent experiences were awakening a kind of warrior-like competitiveness in me. If there was something suspicious about all of this, then I was going to expose it, if for no other reason than to show Sally what an illusion she had been living.

Anyway, didn't cats have nine lives?

So which door was it going to be? I had explored door number one only to find something that may or may not be real. Would it be door number two or number three that would finally expose this retreat for the fraud that it was? I knew that door number two led to the meditation room. I decided to try that one first.

I crept toward it, arming myself with only thirteen Taekwondo lessons and a lifetime of cowardice. As a precaution, I leaned on the door, listening for any sounds that might accelerate my already rapid heart rate.

Nothing.

The house was unusually quiet. The chirping birds outside were the only sound. I looked through the keyhole and could see nothing other than the occasional pillow and the large crystal in the middle of the carpeted room.

That didn't mean that there wasn't someone or something inside, ready to jump me and force-feed me literature about some god or other, and demand that I donate large sums of money to save their interpretation of the world.

I turned the knob, opened the door a crack, and peeked inside. No sign of human life. I opened it wider. Still nothing. I creaked it wide open. There I stood like a brave soul willing to take on Goliath. Well, maybe not that brave, but close.

My bravado was uncalled for though. The room was as barren as it had been in the morning.

In the middle stood the mighty crystal that had started it all for me in the morning meditation. Fortunately it wasn't doing its humming thing.

The sun's rays entered through the tall clear cathedral window and went directly into the crystal, as if fuelling it for the next session. I could see many lines of formation within the crystal because of the sun's illumination. Fascinating, I thought. Just as long as it didn't start humming again.

The windows were sealed shut. I would have thought that it would get hot in there with that constant sunbeam burning into the space. While entertaining that thought, a cool gust of wind slapped me hard in the face.

"OK, room explored," I declared to whoever or whatever it was, and quickly exited, slamming the door shut behind my panic-stricken body.

Sure, I felt like a chicken but only for a moment. I stood in front of that closed door until the feeling of having been a coward subsided. Three seconds. That was a life skill that I exercised on a regular basis. When there was something I was supposed to do and felt obligated to do, I would wait just long enough for the urge to subside and wouldn't do it. Like buying decaf for example.

Memo to self: *Reflect on whether I'm addicted to lattes.*

Maybe there was a window in there and I just couldn't see it, I rationalized. People could make money off a house like this. I'm sure somebody was but *who*?

There wasn't any literature about any kind of secret society lying about anywhere. Of course it seemed to be a secret society by invitation only. But why had they invited me? It didn't make sense that *I* was having all these experiences, when I'm sure there were people out there who would die to be a part of the "activities" in this place. Hmm. Maybe people did? Die, I mean.

"OK, Mister Imagination, let's continue with this house of horrors," I said to myself out loud, tempting the fate of being discovered and perhaps ending my dangerous explorations.

Deep down, I had always suspected that there was a purpose for everything happening in my life. But it was more along the lines of losing a big account or having a bad meeting. One door closed, another one opened. The red Beamer convertible was out of stock in town and it would take months to get, but I could get the blue hardtop *now*. And so I took it as a sign and did just that.

One door closed, another one opened.

So, door number three. Could this be the door that would blow the lid off the whole organization? I didn't know. Again though, I felt compelled to venture through, if not for myself, then for mankind. Well, it *sounded* heroic.

I used the same procedure as before. Approach, listen, and then peek in. I couldn't hear anything and, looking through the keyhole, I couldn't see anything. Great. A voodoo experiment and I was inviting myself to the party.

It's a fine line between courage and stupidity.

~ 17 ~

I took in a deep breath, a very deep breath, and slowly opened the door. A flash of how few payments were left on my Beamer crossed my mind. Hmm. Yeah. Should have been patient and bought the red convertible with the fancy rims!

I switched the remote for my brain from these distracting thoughts, and proceeded through the doorway.

The air was unusually cool compared to the rest of the house and relative to the time of year. Because of the darkness, I couldn't tell if there were any windows

I could hear a gentle humming in the background, not unlike the crystal in the meditation room. My right hand clung to the doorknob, to shut out spirits and ghouls. Who was I kidding? A spirit could fly through the wall.

My eyes adjusted to the darkness and my gaze immediately went to the back of the barren room, seizing on a large, blue egg-sized capsule. It was sitting on top of a wooden block about three feet above the varnished wooden floor.

Again, a chill traveled up and down my spine. I vaguely recognized what this object was but couldn't place its origin. The word primitive came to mind.

I moved closer, noticing dust and cobwebs attached to the capsule, which was humming steadily. For some reason, I remembered it having a purpose, but for the life of me, I couldn't remember what it was. Was it something I had seen on TV once?

I approached it cautiously. I realized that the humming was coming from inside the capsule. It had to be at least six feet long and four feet high. There was a relatively small door with its hinges facing me, but there was no handle.

Standing in front of the vessel, I could see old copper tubing protruding from behind it, between the wall and vessel. It sprang out in all sorts of twisted contortions, connecting to nothing. The object had the appearance of having been built by a mad professor who never got to finish it because he was chased out of his lab by the irate folks in the village.

I stood about a foot away from the strange yet familiar object, putting my hands on top of the metal. With that, the humming became louder and the cool metal immediately began to heat up. I yanked away my hands and noticed how the sudden heat of the contraption moistened my palms. What could that be? Did it have a mind of its own?

I looked closer at the hatch to see if there was some way to open the door despite the absence of handles. It didn't take me long to discover that there was no way I could open it unless I had the blueprints or instructions.

Why did I feel so compelled to get inside this bizarre contraption? There seemed to be such a sense of urgency. What for?

Every time I moved my hands closer, the humming would increase. When I stood back, it would continue quietly and persistently.

Where had I seen this contraption before? I started speaking to it, a sure sign that I was losing it. "What are you? Where have I seen you before?" Half expecting it to answer me. Of course there was no response.

I turned away to still my thoughts and perhaps give up on this latest discovery when, quite suddenly, I heard the sound of a door opening. I turned back and stood there not knowing what to make of this moment. Was I awake? Was this real? Yes. Should I run? Yes. Could I run? No. I was frozen in fascination.

I *hoped* I was leading a cat's life.

The door hatch was now fully open. I leaned into the capsule to see if that would trigger any recollection as to what it was. Still nothing. There was a small leather bucket seat, a dashboard made of smoked glass, and no instruments whatsoever. Maybe it was a crude version of one of those flying simulators that they train pilots on. Or maybe it was some kind of think-tank.

I looked down at the floor to see if I might have stepped on something that had activated the door. Since I couldn't see anything, I figured it was a heat sensor pad of some sort, like a burglar alarm on a car. Gadgets I get.

I decided to see if I could squeeze through the doorway and into the capsule. I raised my right leg and managed to get it high enough to enter the cockpit. I noticed a handle the size of my hand on the opposite side of the cockpit. I sprang up on my left foot, grabbed the handle with my right hand, and pulled myself through the doorway and into the capsule on a single exhale. There was just barely enough room to slide my legs underneath the dashboard.

I sat there for a moment and glanced at the room. It was strange that it was so empty. The barren wooden floors and boarded up windows were its only decor. It echoed neglect.

I brought my attention back to the inside of the capsule, when suddenly the humming became louder and the capsule became colder. Something was not right.

But when the door slammed shut and I sat there in total blackness I finally knew what I was sitting in. This machine was identical to something I had once seen in a sci-fi movie - *a time machine capsule.*

It was at that moment I cried out, "You Idiot!"

~ 18 ~

I was sitting at a piano, playing a complex concerto that was oddly familiar, and wearing an outfit that might have belonged in the 19th century. My hands were fervently assaulting the keys and my head was spinning just as fast. Then, out of the corner of my eye, I noticed that I was on stage in some Viennese-style auditorium or opera house, and there was a huge audience watching me, all elaborately dressed in outfits of a similar vintage.

Instantly, my hands stopped playing. The regal-looking audience began to clap and I found myself standing and bowing toward them.

"Encore! Encore!" the crowd chanted as I slowly and proudly walked off stage. By the time I got to the wings, they were on their feet and stomping wildly, as if they were at a rock concert.

I was stunned as I stood in the wings of the stage looking out at the sea of well-dressed people. A short, stocky man in a strange black tailcoat and a ruffled shirt, approached me.

"Monsieur, Monsieur! You were absolutely superior tonight! Please, please, go out there one more time and play an encore. You mustn't disappoint them."

I just stared at him. I didn't know what to say to this toad of a man who looked vaguely familiar. I certainly didn't like his vibe!

I was observing everything that was going on and yet I was "in" everything that was going on as well. Could it be that I had gone back in time and taken on the role of someone else? Or was this *me* about to step up to the piano and play another concerto? Back in my usual life, I couldn't play a blade of grass. But in this world I could play the piano, and obviously very well!

I went back for my encore.

Sitting down at the piano, I heard a soft, sweet, melodic sound being coaxed out of the piano by the movement of my fingers. Part of me was engrossed in the music and part of me played the observer.

I could feel the intensity as I attacked and then caressed the keys. What was coming out truly melted the soul - theirs and mine. But how could this be? Why was this happening? These and other thoughts raced through my mind as I played this beautiful fusion of melody, harmony, and spirit.

Was I really a pianist from another time? How did I get here and, more importantly, how would I get back? When I was watching that late-night movie back in the 1970s, I should have been spending more time understanding how and why the time machine worked, instead of being so wrapped up in whether the guy got the girl in the end.

With a slight movement of my head, I glanced at the audience. I was amazed to see young girls swooning and older women enraptured with the music. My music. Meanwhile, the men sat there in their uncomfortable-looking fancy outfits, pretending that this music from Heaven wasn't affecting them.

This wasn't so bad, I thought. I was getting a taste of what it was like to be a rock star, albeit in another era. For some reason I felt very calm, even though the time machine was nowhere in sight. I somehow believed that this really wasn't happening and that I would wake up soon enough. Had I known the seriousness of the situation, I would not have been so nonchalant.

"You must find the time machine!" said Surrender's voice, suddenly popping into my head.

Oh no, was he here too? I couldn't believe the radar this guy had. His travel agent must love him, not to mention the air miles he must be racking up.

"You must find the time machine!" he said again, in a more urgent tone.

"How?" I asked telepathically, realizing that he was not physically present.

"Listen to the voice inside and you will find the way," he responded.

Once again I was out of my league.

"Couldn't you just help a little?" I asked. No response. "A clue?" Still no response. "How about a little hint?"

"Only you will know the will of your way," said the invisible great one.

I would have a better chance understanding the *New York Times* crossword puzzle.

I sat there playing beautiful music, even more the observer than I had been before.

"But I don't know how to do it," I responded, more gently than I would normally feel. This music was having its effect on me.

"Trust your inner voice," I heard his fading voice say.

I was on my own with this one.

I heard myself playing the last of the symphony. The audience was silent. I didn't know how to respond. I didn't even know what I had just played except that it was vaguely familiar. Then I heard a clap. Then another. And another. Soon there was a deafening thunder of applause. People stood up, cheering, stomping on the floor, pounding on their wooden benches and chairs. I was more than a little embarrassed as I stood before them bowing. Surely it wasn't me who had played this music.

People were idolizing me as if I were some sort of god. Flowers were being thrown all over the stage. I picked up a rose, held it to my nose, inhaled its intoxicating fragrance, and then, putting it in my teeth, took a royal bow. The crowd ate it up. I had them where I wanted them.

As I walked off stage, the toad in the frilly shirt was waiting for me. The word "sleazy" came to mind every time I saw him. Actually, come to think of it, he looked like an old client of mine.

"Please, please, Monsieur, take another bow."

Why not, I thought? Why not? I turned around and walked out to center stage to take my final bow of the evening.

As I stretched out my arms to inhale the audience, I took note of a rather plump young woman to my right. She stood there looking at me, like someone who had just seen a ghost. My ego was disappointed that she wasn't clapping, but then, compared to the rest of the audience in all of their regalia, she looked like a commoner.

When I came up from my bow, I looked over and saw that she had disappeared. Strange. However, I didn't give it a second thought because of the adulation I was receiving. I turned, gave a last wave, and slowly exited.

"Monsieur, Monsieur! I'm sorry I called you a drunk. I should have appreciated your struggle to find artistic purity. Please play for me next week."

I didn't know what this joker was talking about, but I was feeling a con job in play. I just smiled.

"I'll think about it," I said, as I walked away, in an absentminded search for the time machine.

He tugged at my sleeve, got down on one knee, and started groveling in earnest.

"Please, please, they want you back. We can do at least three shows and sell them all out."

I stopped and regarded his desperation for money. His greed was similar to mine except it was even more shameless. This game I knew how to play.

"I'll tell you what, I'll play, but only if I can take home 70 percent of what the audience pays at the door, and if I can personally select the people who will be collecting the money."

His sudden pallor told me I had just stabbed him where it mattered most.

"But Monsieur," he began with a nervous laugh, "be reasonable. It is unheard of, the musician making that much money."

"Not where I'm from, bubba," I said, as I walked past him, preoccupied with finding the time machine.

He quickly got up off his feet and grabbed my arm, pulling me toward him.

"OK, OK, Monsieur. Seventy percent of the door. But please don't tell any of the other musicians. I don't want to start a trend here."

"Deal," I said, as we shook hands. He was looking as if he wasn't sure what he had just done. I felt very sure.

As I walked away, I noticed a young boy and his father standing in the wings, both just looking at me, smiling. I think they overheard my conversation with the sleazoid. The little boy looked familiar. He winked at me as I walked past him. I turned back to see the little boy walking onstage and sitting at the piano amidst the cheers of the crowd. Mozart? If only I had paid more attention in history class.

As I walked down the hallway, I couldn't help but wonder if I was the cause of the high-priced tickets for today's musical events. I think some rock stars out there owe me.

"*Peter!* What are you doing here?"

I stopped dead in my tracks, looked over my shoulder, and there was the plump girl who had caught my eye earlier. Her voice was unmistakable.

"Uh, Sally?" I turned at her in disbelief.

"Yes, Peter, it's me. What are you doing here?

"Uh, good question."

"How did you get here? I hope you didn't come here with that time machine capsule."

I looked at her blankly.

"Peter! You didn't."

The little boy inside took over as I reluctantly nodded my head and shrugged my shoulders.

"Sorry. I guess I kinda did."

She let out a stifled shriek of disbelief.

"You know, you look cute as a brunette. And the few extra pounds are working for you."

"This is no time for humor!" she said, momentarily unaware of the well-dressed people rushing toward us, wanting to congratulate me. Even with the little boy playing beautiful music on stage, they appeared intent on tracking *me* down. My ego was loving this. I was beginning to like this time-travel stuff.

"Brilliant! You were absolutely brilliant! We love you!" The accolades were coming toward me fast and furious.

"Teach me how to play," said a voluptuous, dark-haired woman.

Teach her how to play what?

Sally whispered urgently, "Come on! We have to get away from here!"

I looked down at her wide-framed face.

"In a minute. I can't just abandon my public," I said, as I walked toward the oncoming mob.

Sally grabbed me by the arm and pulled me in the opposite direction. "Now I see where your huge ego comes from."

"Aw, come on! Just a couple of minutes. They love me!"

"We don't have a couple of minutes. Now quit your whining and let go of your ego!" she demanded, as she pulled me down the hall and through a doorway.

A scattered few of my supporters were still in pursuit of what must have seemed like a strange sight to them - a fan kidnapping their version of a rock star.

Sally was right about there being no time to further gratify my ego. It would have been disastrous had we not met up with each other at that precise time. I'm talking about altering history and changing the world as we know it. Yeah I know, these New Agers, they're so serious.

We ran down the dark cobblestone alley.

"Where are we?" I asked, panting harder by the minute.

"Vienna. Nineteenth century." She answered quickly, not missing a beat in her step.

"What is my last name?" I asked, wanting to see if there was any truth to the rumor that people are usually famous in past lives.

"Schreiner," she said in her serious tone as we continued jogging.

Schreiner? It sounded so unromantic, so prosaic. "I was kind of hoping it was Liszt."

She slowed down the pace but still gripped the sleeve of my jacket in case I had any crazy notion of going back to the adoring crowd.

"Sorry to deflate your ego. You're Seamus Schreiner. You had an Irish mother who married a piano builder from Vienna. While your father was in Vienna attending to the death of your grandfather, your village in the hills of Ireland was attacked and your mother was killed. Your father brought you back to Vienna to be close to his brothers and sisters. They helped raise you and they introduced you to music. Later you were discovered by a famous composer who taught you everything he knew and then opened up the concert halls for you."

I felt so distant from the story that she was telling me. No connection to it whatsoever.

We had slowed down to a brisk walk. The dark alley, lit only by moonlight, had me a bit worried but I figured that since I was with Sally, I would be safe.

"You're a commoner in fancy clothing. That's why people love you so much. You're just like them. Yet such beautiful music comes from the depths of your soul that people from all social categories come to hear you play. You're a unique attraction in this part of the world."

Even in the 19th century people were brought together by music of the soul.

"How do you know all of this?" I asked, curious as to what history books she had read.

Sally was silent for a moment.

"Let's just say that part of my journey is to know the history of All and its relationship to the Self."

I think she was skirting the issue. I didn't press it because it was probably another story that I wouldn't be able to comprehend with my limited knowledge of metaphysics.

Sally looked over her shoulder and saw that we were no longer being followed. She turned to me, stopped, and looked me straight in the eye.

"Peter, your coming here, in this way, could upset history and the future of mankind."

"What are you talking about? What about you? Aren't you upsetting history?" I felt a tad defensive that I alone could be the ruin of mankind.

"This is only an aspect of me."

"Talk to me, babe. Pretend I know English. What are you saying?"

"I'm saying that you're standing here with my astral body."

"Sally, please. Fill in the blanks. Speak French if you have to."

Sally squeezed my hands.

"I am but a mere observer of this time. My physical body is back at the retreat meditating under a tree."

"What the heck are you talking about? You're right here in front of me, flesh and blood." I squeezed her warm but unfamiliar hands.

"No. You are here in flesh and blood. I am here in spirit. Sure you can feel me and see me, but this is only an ethereal representation of who I really am."

I felt confused as I stood there, looking at this stranger with whom I had such a strong soul connection.

"You see, I'm allowing an apparition of myself to be seen and felt in order to fully experience this moment."

I think a space shuttle just zipped over my head.

"I was not incarnated in this time period. You were. I came here out of curiosity, to experience myself in a different culture and time frame."

"Most people go to Mexico, Sally."

Sally moved closer to me and caressed my shoulders.

"Physically you are really here. Any action that you take that does not reflect what you did when you were here the last time, could result in you not existing or worse, you could accidentally cause a war between nations."

"Come on, Sally. How could anything I do or say cause a war between nations?"

She gripped my shoulders firmly.

"Honey, I'm not saying that you would do anything like that on purpose. But look at what happened between you and that greedy theatre owner back there. Your simple demand caused a ripple effect through time."

I thought about that for a moment and could see what she was getting at.

Memo to self: *Call upon wealthy rock stars for dividends of their huge paychecks when I return to the 21st century.*

"OK, I'll roll with what you're saying, but what do we do now?"

"First of all, *we* have to get you away from here right now. *We* can't let anyone have any contact with you. Understand?"

I wondered if that included the voluptuous woman back there who wanted lessons.

"Would you quit your kidding around?" Dang. I guess she could read my mind in this century too. This lack of privacy was a tad annoying.

"I heard that too!" she said, and yanked me along the cobblestone alley. Sure it was dark and a bit creepy but there was really nothing to be afraid of, I reasoned. After all, I was with a ghost and she wasn't scary at all.

Suddenly I felt a cold chill pass through my entire body. It left as quickly as it arrived. I chalked it up to the dampness in the air.

I looked over at this woman, Sally. She looked like someone on her way to becoming an old spinster like in a Saturday morning cartoon. In a nice kind of way…

"Sally, how come you don't look like yourself? I mean your real self, like at the retreat?"

For some reason Sally didn't respond.

"Why are you here looking like a different person?" Still no response.

As we continued our silent walk down the windswept alley, I could feel Sally's wheels turning.

She finally broke the silence. "When we inhabit our astral bodies, we are made up of molecules that vibrate at a higher frequency. Our molecular structure is operating at such a rate that a simple thought transference can rearrange our astral body to another form. I wanted to experience what people's response to me would be in this form rather than the normal feedback I get."

"Because you're a sexy babe?"

"I see male chauvinism knows no century. Anyway, when I look like this, I get to experience a different energy feedback."

"What's the food like here?"

Sally laughed.

"So you're checking out other places with different bodies?

"Something like that."

"What? Are you checking out other guys too?

Sally caressed my face. "It's not about relationship with others, it's about relationship with Self."

I felt my head drowning in confusion.

"Get right with God and everything will be right with you. Get right with you and everything will be right with God."

"Hang on, I thought you just said this was all about getting right with Self. What's this about getting right with God?"

"You are God, Peter. God is all." she said, in a strikingly serious tone.

"Oh great, great. I suppose now you're going to ask me to stand on some hill and chant, 'I am God, I am God.'" Sally chuckled, remembering the TV movie she coerced me into watching with her when we first started dating.

"If that's what it takes for you to get serious about your Self, then that's what we're going to do," she offered, as she put her arm through mine and gave me a soft kiss on the cheek. At least some things felt the same through time.

It was then I noticed the silhouette of a man coming toward us. Sally followed my gaze and saw the same dark figure. She pulled me quickly toward a doorway but when she tried to open the door, she couldn't. I gave it a try. Nothing. We stood there holding our breath. I wasn't sure if it was Sally's apparition of a heartbeat or my own heartbeat that I felt pulsating through our clasped hands but it was beating hard. Especially when the dark figure stopped directly in front of us.

For some inexplicable reason, I leaned toward him instinctively, as though I was going to jump him. Which was ridiculous since I felt faint with fear.

Sally pulled me back. I thought to myself, if Sally really is a ghost of some kind then why doesn't she just disappear?

"Because if she did, it would leave you vulnerable to an attack by a vampire," said the dark silhouette of a man, in his deep menacing voice.

Oh dear.

~ 19 ~

"You know the laws, sir, you cannot attack unless the victim is willing to participate," Sally said, bravely coming to my shell-shocked defense.

"You're one of those damn New Agers I keep hearing about from the future, aren't you? You have to remember young lady, that in order to fully realize its multidimensional nature, the soul is responsible for the choices it makes. Read your books, sweetheart."

Unfortunately, he sounded like he knew just as much as Sally about all this stuff. That scared me. But then who wouldn't be scared standing in a dark alley, holding the hand of a ghost and talking to a vampire? I wondered if they had scotch in that pub we just passed.

"The name is Richard Galbraith the Third," he said as he extended his hand towards me.

"Don't shake his hand!" Sally said, snapping me out of my daze. "Don't invite him into your being!"

The vampire took another step toward me. The sliver of moonlight offered just enough light for me to see his cold yet penetrating eyes trying to reach into the depths of my soul.

Whoa!

"Jack?" I blurted out.

"Who?" replied the Vampire.

"Peter! Refuse him or he'll steal your soul – *forever!*"

He looked just like my boss, Jack. Funny, his nick-name was "Vampire" too because he was always sucking us dry in the guise of productivity. Regardless, I had an uneasy feeling that Sally was more Casper the Friendly Ghost than a scary spook. This was bad. Real bad.

I could feel the vampire's hold on me getting stronger. I found myself wanting to take a step closer to him. Then I heard Surrender. Never thought I'd be so glad to hear that voice!

"If you let him take your soul, you will become a part of his soul group. You will evolve playing the role of vampire and your history will be erased in all dimensions, altering not only your life but many others' lives as well. Make your choice a wise one."

It was always life and death with these New Agers.

The thought of traipsing through dark alleys looking for easy prey in order to extend my wretched existence for another couple of centuries didn't appeal to me. The thought of not having my life, no matter how perilous it seemed in this moment, did not appeal to me. The thought of not having Sally in my life, especially now that my feelings for her were entering uncharted territory, didn't appeal to me *at all.* And the thought of some vampire stealing my soul for what sounded like an eternity made me scream, "Noooooo!!! NEVER!!!"

There was a long moment of silence.

My body trembled from fear and primordial strength. I looked over at Sally and saw her great relief and joy at my decision. Then I looked at Richard Galbraith the Third and discovered that he had jumped back into the shadows.

It was unusually quiet and tense.

I wasn't sure what was going to happen next but I knew I wasn't going to let him steal my soul - no matter how primal I needed to get.

"We get such a bum rap," Richard the Vampire said, breaking the silence. "All we want to do is live forever, like everyone else. What's wrong with that?"

"Maybe it's in the way you do it?" Sally said, always willing to offer unsolicited advice.

I could sense the vampire's indignation.

"My dear young lady, please don't try any of that New Age analytical crap on me. I've been around far too long to listen to that rehashed Lemurian, Atlantean, Aztec, Mayan, *Spiritual* holier than thou drivel!"

He certainly could stand up for himself.

"I know I am God as you are God. So I choose to experience God in this way. So what? What's the problem, lady? I'm still evolving like you, aren't I? Sure, the picture may not look as sweet but I'm still growing, right?"

Sally mumbled, "Well, um, yeah, I guess."

"Despite what everyone thinks, we vampires don't continue in some eternal Hell of damnation. Well, at least not forever. It's only until we're ready to move on to the next evolutionary stage. We have our choices too; we choose to live the way we do for our own reasons. So please keep your sugary idealism to yourself. Why can't people just accept other entities' ways of growing? I tell you, if that writer Anne Rice ever comes back to visit me again for advice, oh boy, her chum Lestat is going to have to take a number!"

He clicked his heels and tipped his hat.

"And now, if you will excuse me, I'm going to catch myself some fresh meat. Of this century. It's a lot simpler."

I watched with great relief as he gracefully slithered away from us.

Sally and I just looked at each other, expressionless, yet full of emotion.

I loved this woman even more. She had courage in more ways than one. It seemed the closer I got to the truth of all this and myself, the closer I got to Sally. Even in a ghostly skin and a less slender frame, she was as beautiful as ever.

We started to giggle. I leaned in for her kiss but was interrupted by Richard Galbraith the Third's voice echoing down the alley.

"You should have no problem finding the time machine now. Oh, and by the way, give my regards to Surrender!"

And with that, I could hear his bellowing laughter and fading footsteps fade as he moved toward his next prey.

I tenderly held my 19th century Sally, humbled by my love for this woman who was touching my soul.

"Has anything like this ever happened to you?"

"Just once," Sally said as she straightened out her dress, "but not in the same way. I was by myself when it happened. The bottom line was I just had to learn how to say no. It's all about boundaries. It was one of the ways that I've discovered my true power. It was a huge turning point in my life."

Sally snuggled into my chest. "I'm so proud of you, Peter."

I put my arms around her much larger waist and gave a sigh of relief that I had survived another one. Another test. I certainly felt a lot stronger for having said no. However, it still left me with one problem. How was I going to get back to the retreat?

I pulled Sally in tighter as my thoughts tried to recollect any of the clues Surrender might have given. I was drawing a blank. I couldn't remember anything and Sally seemed as lost on this one as I was.

I leaned back against what I thought was the wall. Suddenly, a humming sound kicked in. I quickly turned around and there it was - the time machine capsule!

"Sally, look!" I felt like an excited little boy.

"I thought you would never lean back," she said, pinching my cheek like she was my auntie.

"You mean you knew it was behind us all along?" I asked. My voice sounded like a pubescent boy's.

"Yes," she answered, laughing.

"Well, couldn't you have at least given me some sort of hint so I wouldn't have had to meet Mister 'I vant to sock your blod'?"

"Peter, there are some initiations that you have to undergo entirely on your own. Now get in there and let's go home for some lunch. People are waiting for us."

I turned back around and looked at the capsule. "But there's only room for one!"

I didn't like the thought that one of us was going to have to wait here in this dark alley all by themselves while the other went to the retreat and sent back the machine. I'm not sure I had it in me to deal with another vampire and I didn't want to put Sally through that.

"I am but spirit in motion, remember? I just need to will my way and I'll be home in a thought."

"I often wondered why you never drove."

"Get in there, Seamus Schreiner. We don't want to meet another vampire, do we?"

Now that was a thought that moved me.

I turned to the vessel, remembering to face away slightly. The door opened.

"Hey I'm getting good at this. By the way, why does it only open when I am in this position?"

"Sometimes it's just better to accept 'what is' rather than getting wrapped up in 'how come.' Now get in there!" she said, gently pushing me into the capsule.

I climbed in and observed this woman whom I didn't recognize visually but knew from deep within.

"Just stay focused and concentrate on where you want to go. I'll meet you back at the room," she said, quickly giving me a kiss.

The door automatically closed. I sat in total blackness as the humming reached a fever pitch.

It reopened in what seemed like a nanosecond.

There was Sally back in her familiar form.

"Welcome home, Sweetie! Now hurry and get out of there before I have to fetch you in Lemuria."

Not knowing where that was or what century that would take me to, I quickly hustled out of the contraption.

Upon exiting, I looked up at the inside of the opened door and noticed for the first time a worn out label that read "*RX4Z23 Model: Nuclear Thermal Radiation Connection of Time and Memories*." Yep, a heck of a sports car.

"I've worked up an appetite for lunch. What time is it?" Having just returned from another century, I had definitely lost track of time.

"It's about two o'clock."

Sally took my hand and we walked away from good ol' RX4Z23. I was surprised at how much time had gone by, but given all that I'd experienced since four a.m. that morning, it would add up.

"What's the deal for lunch again?" I asked, trying not to wince.

"Vegetable juice," she answered with a grin, knowing that my stomach would much prefer a hamburger with greasy fries.

We ambled toward the door, leaving the room of distorted time and memories.

"It's so beautiful outside. This has got to be one of the nicest Sundays I have ever experienced here," Sally said, innocently.

Sunday?

~ 20 ~

Sally was laughing and running away from me like a little girl who had a big secret.

I was a little boy in shock, stumbling down the hallway after her. She stopped running when she reached the end of the hall.

"When I didn't see you at lunch or dinner last night, I became concerned and asked Surrender where you were. He just smiled and said that you were on a little journey and not to worry about anything. He suggested I use the time to trust and send my light and love to you. But I never imagined that you had gone for a joy ride in a time machine." She burst out laughing.

"I'm glad you find me amusing."

"Ohhh, what's a matter, Baby?" she said, tickling underneath my chin, "Did my Baby have an unpleasant experience with his little time warp trip?"

I moved her finger away from my chin.

"A little? I missed a whole day and night. I wouldn't call that little."

"Not really," Sally said, her laughter subsiding, "it's only your perception of linear time that makes you think that you missed a day and a night."

This was getting to be like the twilight zone.

"If it makes it easier for you to understand what's going on, then yes, it is like the twilight zone." Sally said, as she turned away and headed towards the back of the house.

"Stop reading my mind!" I followed her through the doorway and out onto the back porch.

Sally stopped. "I'm sorry, but sometimes your thoughts are so loud when you're freaked, it's hard not to pick up on them."

"It's not fair! I can't read yours!"

"In time you will be able to. I'll try not to listen to you when you're freaked."

Which would be difficult at this rate.

Sally took my hand and began to lead me across the back porch to where a group of people were sitting at a picnic table. I stopped her before we entered the polite space of having to accommodate strangers.

"Could you please simplify what just happened to me? To us? And use words from a *modern* English dictionary. *Please!*"

Sally took in a deep breath. I didn't know what was going to be harder, clarifying what we just experienced or listening to her version of modern-day English.

"What I did was a self-induced astral projection. That is when my soul, the essence of who I Am, is able to leave the physical restrictions of my body and go wherever my thought takes me. What you did was put your physical body into a time machine, which actualizes the thought manifestation of where one would *like* to take the physical and spiritual bodies. Subconsciously, you knew you needed to learn something from that lifetime."

"Yeah, right. I was just itching to play the piano in another lifetime. *Subconsciously!*"

Sally laughed.

"Well, what's the difference between what you did and what I did?" I asked, bravely.

"Your de-molecularization of the physical body came from a man-made object. What I did was from spirit. What you did came from man's desperation to duplicate spirit for his own gain."

"Pretend I'm thick."

"Peter, since the beginning of time, the unhealthy aspect of man's ego has wanted to be superior to Nature. That's not possible and never will be. I know I talk a lot about Spirit, Mother Nature, and other things that may bore you or may be difficult to understand. But it's really important to remember that body, mind, and spirit must be working together in unison, in order to harmonize with Mother Nature and the God Self."

I wasn't fully understanding what preacher girl was saying here. However, I did understand the feeling of being lost, hopeless, and not being able to comprehend what was really going on in the world.

I stood there in silence. Did I know that little about what is really going on with this planet? With the Universe?

I looked at the people sitting at the picnic table. Were we all going through these experiences together? Was I the only one behind in class? Why had I come here to this so-called retreat in the first place? Was it predestined? Was it a matter of free will and choice? Why did I need to know about any of this? Other than my career being soulless, I was reasonably happy. OK, I was miserable but that didn't warrant a meeting with a vampire! I had one at work.

There was something to be said for that cliché, ignorance is bliss.

"Bottom line, Peter," Sally said, interrupting my musing, "Science is not viable when it is not connected to Spirit."

For some reason that statement stung like a wasp.

"Then why is that time machine here?" I asked, challenging her logic.

"Surrender brought it here for those who needed to experience science without Spirit because some needed to learn the difference and have physical proof. Most people who come here never use the time machine because it's dangerous."

"What do you mean dangerous?" I asked slowly, already having an inkling of the answer.

"The scientist who built it was taking it to another time frame and, according to his assistant, had done so at least a hundred times. But this last time was different. He shook his assistant's hand and said good-bye as usual, but when the machine reappeared and the door opened, there was no trace of the scientist. When Surrender got wind of the story, he approached the assistant and asked if he would take it out of harm's way. The assistant happily agreed."

I felt sad for the scientist because here he was on the verge of what could have been one of science's greatest inventions and he disappeared. "No one has ever heard anything from this scientist?"

"No, his assistant put the time machine out of commission. He really didn't have the nerve to get in it and find him."

"I don't blame him."

Sally turned and looked out toward the backyard and said softly, "I once asked Surrender what had become of that scientist."

"And what did he say?" If anyone knew, it would be him.

"He told me the scientist met up with a vampire in a dark alley somewhere in Vienna, and allowed himself to be a victim. Now he strolls those very same alleys, looking for unsuspecting victims of the past, present, and future."

"Was that him?"

"No."

"Was it Jack?"

"Good question."

I stood there in bewildered silence. I couldn't speak.

"Let's go eat," she said, as she passed through the doorway.

~ 21 ~

I slowly opened the screen door and wondered what it was that made me survive these precarious incidents and receive this information. Surely there were more qualified people in the metaphysical world who would have loved to be in my position. There must have been some reason that this was happening to me. Was I doing this in accordance with some Master Plan?

OK, maybe there was something bigger than me out there. Maybe there was someone or something that had me on a computer, monitoring my every movement, making sure I didn't get off track and screw up the Master Plan.

Was that the role of this so-called God? Was there a God? Had those priests at my school been talking legit? If they were, then why were there so many different religions? Were there as many gods? If so, was there one that was better than the others?

All of these thoughts were swimming around in my head as I walked toward Sally and the group of friendly New Agers sitting at the picnic table.

"Welcome back," they said in unison.

"Talked to any vampires lately?" one said, laughing. Obviously they were aware of what I had just experienced.

"I heard that you're quite the pianist, Mr. Schreiner," said a burly man, known as Bobby.

"I was just making sure the scientist wasn't building any more time machines in Vienna." They all laughed.

"Here's your lunch," Sally said, handing me an eight-ounce glass of vegetable cocktail.

Yippee, I thought. I haven't eaten in over twenty-four hours and now I'm doing the "Slim Jim Juice Fast." I should have grabbed a burger in Vienna.

I chugged it in one big gulp and handed the empty glass to Sally with a slight burp.

"No more, I'm full. Thanks anyway," I said, with obvious insincerity.

"Oh Hon, it's all in your head," Sally said.

"Well it's certainly not in my stomach," I replied, sitting down with the rest of the disciples or whatever they were.

Sitting near me were three interesting people with diverse backgrounds. Sally introduced me.

Alice, to my immediate right, was at one time a registered nurse at the local hospital. Her husband was a doctor at the same hospital and, when she became interested in energetic healing modalities, he considered it nothing more than voodoo and black magic. That was the end of their once idyllic marriage.

It started for her when a dying elderly patient on her ward said to her, "It's time to share your healing powers with the world. Use your hands." These were the patient's last words, whispered to Alice with her last breath of life.

This inspired Alice to go to her local New Age bookstore and research different methods of healing with the hands. One book led to another, which led her from one teacher to another. Alice is one of the most sought after healing hands practitioners in town, much to the chagrin of her ex-husband.

Beside her sat Bobby, who was the size of a pro football tackle. Despite his long hair and beard, he would have had a tough time convincing anyone that he was Jesus Christ. But I liked him from the get-go. It was very calming to be in his presence. He exuded the feeling that everything was going to be OK, despite having lost his whole family in a severe car accident. When he was in a coma, he saw his wife, son, and daughter walking toward him. His wife said, "It's OK, my love, all is as it should be. The kids will be safe with me. We'll all be OK. You rest." All three smiled at him and then turned, waved good-bye, and walked toward a blinding white light. When he became conscious, he found himself in a hospital bed with a doctor standing over him saying how sorry he was that his wife and two kids couldn't be saved.

I had always felt sorry for anyone who experienced a loss, but it didn't make any sense in this case because Bobby seemed at such peace. Losing his family was the event that had awakened him to embark on his journey into the Unknown.

Sitting opposite of him, was the woman that looked like my co-worker. Again, this was the woman whom I had seen being administered to by the tall, golden-haired man when I looked through the keyhole. She wasn't open or friendly like the rest of the group. I wanted to catch her eye to make some sort of contact but it was impossible.

"Merinda, this is Peter," said Sally. Merinda didn't look at me, just nodded her head. She *looked* normal. However, there was something mysterious about her. Her walls were up and they were made of concrete.

"How are you liking your stay at the retreat so far?" Bobby asked me.

"Oh, well, I have to say it certainly has been very interesting staying here amongst you space cadets."

"Space Cadets?" Sally blurted out in surprise "Is that an insult, Monsieur Schreiner?"

"Not at all. Space cadets are people who live *way* out there. I mean it as a compliment," I chuckled. Sally gave me a playful slap.

"You were right, Sally," said Alice. "He is a wily nut to crack."

I didn't know if she meant that as my reluctance to "join the cult" or if she meant that I had a hard head. I was trusting that it was the latter.

"I just like to make light of situations."

"Good. The more light workers, the better," said Bobby, laughing.

I guess I walked into that one.

I looked over at Merinda, still silent.

"Are you one of these so-called light workers?" I asked, trying to bring her out of her shell.

She looked up into the partially clouded blue sky.

"That's what I'm told. All I know is that I miss my home." I could feel her sadness.

"Well then, why don't you just go home? Or can you?" I wanted to console her on the one hand, and for selfish reasons I also wanted to know if she was being held here against her will. She turned to me and looked straight through my eyes and into my soul. Her penetrating gaze caught me off guard and almost sent me backwards off the bench.

"It's not that easy. *Don't you remember?*" And with that, she got up off the bench and walked toward the forest.

I felt compelled to go after her, feeling that in some way I must have offended her.

"Should I-?"

"No, no, she'll be OK. She's just getting used to being here," said Alice.

"If she's so unhappy here, why doesn't she just go home?" I asked.

Alice gently touched me on the arm. "It's not that easy for her. She lives light years away."

"Well, tell her to take a plane. I mean it can't be that hard to figure out," I said, thinking how easy it was for these New Age people to lose touch with reality.

"A plane couldn't take her where she needs to go," Bobby interjected.

"What do you mean?"

He turned away, noticeably trying to avoid the question. I looked at Alice and she just looked at me for a moment before turning to Sally as if to say, "You'd better handle this one."

I looked across the table at Sally and could see that she was hesitant to respond, which was very unlike her.

"Come on, Sally. What gives? What's going on here?" Sally took in a deep breath, which meant trouble.

"I know we've never talked about this before, and you may find this hard to believe but-" She looked down the pathway where Merinda was walking.

"But what???"

"Merinda is not from this planet," Sally finally blurted out.

"No kidding. None of you are from this planet."

"No, I'm serious. Merinda is from another planet. Not Earth."

Flies were condo shopping in my open mouth.

"Huh?" was all I could manage.

"Merinda is what is called a walk-in," said Bobby.

"Huh?" Once again, I grunted through my open mouth as flies engaged in a bidding war for a two-bedroom bungalow.

Alice picked up the ball. "There are some people who are on this planet and yet were not born on this planet. To put it in simple terms, they have made a deal with another soul to enter his or her physical body and help out with mankind's conscious evolution."

The flies were now looking for beachfront property.

Sally reached over, taking my hands into hers as she took over.

"Merinda entered her physical body last year, after a train wreck. When one enters the physical body of another, they must complete the previous soul's karmic duties before they can continue their mission on Earth. That's part of the agreement. Merinda chose to come into her body without remembering why until she had completed the first part of her newly assumed karmic task."

I looked around the table at these people and could see that they actually believed this story. But I also knew that what they were saying had some connection to my life. I became slightly distracted by the hawk circling above us. Was I now going to find out that I was dinner? I couldn't think of a TV show that was stranger than these people and their philosophies. That includes the Sunday morning one with the preacher who was always asking for money to build another building for the people to come to so they can give more money for the next building to be built and so on. "Many mansions" indeed.

"Let me get this straight. She flies in from another planet, lands in some strange body that is about to kick the bucket, comes to some 'soul agreement,' finishes living out that soul's duty. Now she is this totally different babe ready to help save the world, in the body of somebody else?"

No response.

"Kids, kids, please! Doesn't this sound a teensy weensy farfetched to any of you? Maybe she's a psycho from Gill Street just waiting for a chance to remove any part of us that moves in the night."

Alice laughed. "You do have quite the imagination, Peter. I'll give you that."

"Maybe, but I think I have some stiff competition here."

Alice ignored my comments and continued trying to bring me to some sort of understanding.

"Merinda is just in the mourning stages right now. You see, on a cellular level, there is a release that needs to take place before she can continue with her own journey."

Despite my skepticism, this could explain what I had witnessed when she was lying on the table. But was that real?

"Her space brothers have been working with her to help accelerate the releasing process so that she is available to guide others," Sally continued.

"You know, I did witness some strange happenings when I peeked through the keyhole in one of the rooms this morning. Or was that yesterday morning?"

I stopped. I was getting caught up in their illusions. Also, I was admitting to spying, which may not have been acceptable at this retreat.

Sally squeezed my hand. "It's OK, Peter. For whatever reason you were meant to see what was happening in that room. None of the rest of us have seen the space brothers' acceleration process, only a select few have that opportunity."

I didn't know whether to feel privileged or just plain weird.

Bobby now entered the fray. "The space brothers like to use this facility because of its extreme privacy, sacredness, and high vibration. Hundreds of years ago, these grounds were used by Native American Indians for their special ceremonies with the Sky People," he finished, pointing up at the sky.

I looked at these three people who surrounded me. I knew Sally, obviously not as well as I thought, but nonetheless, I had grown to accept her flakiness. As for Alice and Bobby, they seemed so normal despite what came out of their mouths. I find that when you know what people are about, you can deal with them one way or the other. But when you think you do and you don't, it gets a bit tricky. Who do you believe and what do you believe? Then something that Merinda said stuck out in my mind.

"What did Merinda mean when she said to me, 'It's not that easy. *Don't you remember?*'"

Everyone grew silent. I could tell no one wanted to touch this one.

"Oh come on, you're not going to tell me that I am some 'walk-in' from another planet, are you?"

Still no response.

"Are you?" I repeated, not sure if I wanted to know.

"I wouldn't say you are a walk-in. More like from another planet, but then-" Bobby clammed up.

"But then what?"

They all looked at each other. No response.

I was getting that familiar chill up my backbone. The government would make a good dollar setting up a toll booth, given the amount of chills that had traveled up my spine since my arrival here.

"Oh, come on," I said. "Are you trying to tell me that I'm from another planet and that I've just dropped by to help save the world? Oh please."

Alice piped up. "You know, maybe it *would* be good for you to have a little chat with Merinda.

She said it in such a serious tone that it rattled me. Was the con artist being conned? I looked at Bobby. His usual goofy grin had become a fatherly smile. Sally let go of my hand, nodding in agreement with what Alice had just said.

My heart started beating faster. This couldn't be good for my sanity. I could just hear the rumors. "Hey, did you hear the latest?" "No, what?" "Peter's really a Martian." No, this was not acceptable. I had to deal with this crazy situation – *now*!

I got up, politely excused myself, and proceeded to stride toward the disappearing Merinda. If I was from another planet, I wanted actual *physical* proof. If there was one thing that I was learning this weekend it was to ask questions and take nothing for granted, even if it meant being an outcast. Mind you, if I was from another planet, I was already an outcast.

My heart was racing even faster, and my imagination was chasing me from behind with wild hallucinations. I picked up the pace, running away from my imagination and towards what I hoped was the truth. *My* truth.

~ 22 ~

I quickly jogged along the worn pathway toward Merinda, a pandemonium of thoughts running through my mind. Although I had never disputed the fact that there may be other intelligent life forms out there, I hadn't given it much thought. I wasn't sure if it was something I wanted to resolve in my life, in this moment. I'm not even sure if I had the strength or the courage to do so. If these two worker bees had decided to go on strike while they looked for a saner employer, I wouldn't have blamed them.

I could see Merinda in the distance, just off to the side of the pathway. I slowed down so as not to frighten her with my approach. Who was this woman? What was she *really* doing here? What was my connection with her?

Then something happened that stopped me in my tracks.

I saw Merinda standing amongst the silent whistling of the evergreen trees when she turned to her right, slowly and methodically, raising and extending both of her hands in a cup position above her body. I didn't know if she knew I was there, but it didn't seem to matter as she carried on in her ceremonial manner.

Quite suddenly, a bright golden orange flash appeared in the palms of her hands. This ball of flame slowly rose from her palms and hovered a few inches above them. Her eyes remained closed as she appeared to be communicating with the orange orb of light. Soon, the orb began to flicker and change its colors, as if it was trying to communicate with her, much like the crystal in the meditation room.

I watched as the globe slowly became infused with all the colors of the rainbow. It appeared to be communicating in a kind of colored Morse code, each pulsation seemed to have something to say. As this flickering array of colors continued its glorious display, a stream of tears flowed down Merinda's face. They didn't appear to be tears of distress. She seemed overjoyed, as hearty laughter overwhelmed her. The multicolored orb of fire seemed to be comforting her.

I just stood there and observed this beautiful private moment.

Soon, the orb of fire became smaller and smaller, until it disappeared. Its dying flame visibly affected Merinda and yet I could see that somehow she had gained strength from this experience.

Now that the ball of fire had gone, Merinda brought her hands to her face and began to slowly wipe away the tears. It was then that I felt like an intruder and softly backtracked, not wanting to be seen or heard.

"It's OK, Peter," she said, turning toward me, "I'm glad you saw what you did. It was meant to be."

I stood there like the little kid who had just got caught with his hand in the candy jar.

"I, I, I'm sorry, uh, to interrupt, ahh, whatever it was that I, um, interrupted. I just came to apologize for maybe being out of line back there."

"You weren't out of line," she said, walking toward me. "You were just getting a step closer to knowing *who you really are.*"

I didn't like the direction the conversation was heading, so I slowly kept walking. I was becoming paranoid of this New Age lingo.

She came at me with an intense stare in her eyes.

"Uh, I, uh, should really get back to the house. I'm, ah, sure that Surrender needs more wood chopped."

She quickly caught up to me before I broke into a panicked scurry.

"Peter, it's OK. I know what you're going through. I went through the exact same feelings. It's taken me a while to adjust to what has been happening in my life, but I now have, and so will you."

I wasn't buying it. I'd seen this tactic before: Sympathize with the victim, get his trust, and then go for the kill.

"How do you explain what I just saw?" I asked, bravely.

"It appears that you've adjusted quite well for someone who's new at the game." She suddenly looked down to the ground. I could sense a million thoughts going through her mind. Problem was, I didn't know what they were and I didn't want to stay and pursue any line of questioning whatsoever. Whether this woman had any revelations as to my origin didn't matter. She just felt like too odd a person to hang out with, in a forest, with no one close by. How could I possibly believe that I was from another planet? I turned and began to walk away.

"Wait. Peter," she said, stopping me with unexpected urgency, "Let me tell you a little story about myself that may help explain a few things."

I turned and stood there for a moment, looking into her big dark brown eyes. I could tell that this was important to her. Since I had made up my mind that I wasn't from another planet and since I was taller than her, I figured I could at least help her go through some therapeutic process by listening to her story. Plus, I could run faster than her if it got too weird.

"OK, but please give it to me in simple English. I'm still not proficient with the language that goes on around here."

She took my hand and led me away from the house. If worse came to worse and I had to make a run for it, my athletic prowess would kick in. I hoped.

We walked a bit before anything was said. I could feel a warm, pulsating energy coming from the palm of her hand as we both enjoyed the silence of the trees waving in the wind.

But soon my curiosity got the better of me. "First, explain to me what I just saw." I wanted to find out if what I had just witnessed was reality or illusion.

"Why don't I just tell you the story that leads into that?" She said.

"O-kay," I responded, hesitantly. I couldn't tell what a set-up was anymore. "But give it to me straight, and in English!"

She laughed, let go of my hand, and put her arm through mine. I suddenly felt a rush of energy surge through my body as we were immediately transported to another place and time.

We now stood before a train wreck. I was silenced by this new experience while her story unfolded before me.

"As they may have told you back there, I was in a train wreck about a year ago. When I say *I* was in a train wreck, I'm really talking about my physical body being in the train wreck. It took me awhile to comprehend that the previous occupant of this body had decided before birth that she was going to leave her body at that point of time. Apparently I, meaning my soul, had made an arrangement with her soul to come in and take over: She had learned all the lessons she needed to learn in this lifetime for her soul's evolution. All I had to do was complete her family ties and karma and then I could continue my phase of the journey in her body."

I watched her and this other person hug. They melted into one.

"Wow."

"Wow indeed."

The woman laid back down amongst the wreckage as rescue workers rushed to her side. Merinda squeezed my arm and we were back in the forest. It took me a moment to regain my bearings.

"Shouldn't I be running in fear?"

"Why?"

"I just did that travel thing and, yeah, why? How is it any different than the rest of my weekend."

Merinda smiled.

I took a deep breath, embraced the present moment and took in her calmness. My curiosity knocked on the door again, searching for answers of the great unknown.

"So what do you mean 'family ties'?"

She looked away toward the evergreens as we continued our walk. She was very methodical and deliberate in everything that she did and said.

"When we enter this realm of reality, we have various soul groups that we associate with."

"I think Surrender mentioned something about soul groups. Remind me."

"Soul groups are souls who choose to evolve with each other through various lifetimes and life forms, in order to learn their lessons. Together. We each, through a number of lifetimes, attract our soul group members because we know on a deeper level that we can fully trust them. We are able to surrender to the experience and not hold back on our growth."

"Excuse me. Before we continue this orbiting around my brain, what the heck do you mean by 'evolve with through various lifetimes and life forms?' What do you mean by 'life forms'?"

"Every aspect of the universe has its own consciousness, its own world, its own reality. For instance, those evergreens are learning something at this very moment about themselves and the world around them, thus evolving their own consciousness."

"Wait a minute. Are you trying to say that I was once an evergreen or that in the next lifetime, if there is such a thing, I could very well end up being an evergreen? Come on!"

Merinda laughed, which was an interesting sight. That mode of expression seemed foreign to her.

"I can't answer that fully other than to say that we as souls either evolve to a greater consciousness or we remain stagnant. But we never go back. It's always ascension to the Light. As to whether you were once an evergreen, I'll let you figure that one out on your own. I'm still trying to figure out my own story, which I will shed some light on if you could slow down on the questioning."

"OK, boss. No more questions. Maybe."

Merinda playfully squeezed my arm as we became more relaxed with one another.

"I made sure that her family was taken care of emotionally and that they didn't have to worry about her any more. It was a co-dependent relationship that needed to be addressed before I could begin my journey here. I tell you though, Peter, it wasn't until I came close to completing those co-dependency issues, that I could remember who I was."

I thought about my own issues around co-dependency and remembered that I had just recently observed that my parents and I were getting along much better. It was as if they had finally let go of me as their only son and had begun to treat me like an individual. Somehow I had managed to let go of my identity only coming from them and had begun to recognize and appreciate myself as a strong, independent individual; someone who could handle himself in the world without his parents and yet still love and appreciate them as beautiful beings. Uh oh, my lingo was changing.

Memo to self: *Review English dictionary!*

Merinda's words began to fill my wandering mind, bringing me back to the moment at hand.

"One night, I felt as if there was a presence in my room and yet I couldn't see anything."

"Was something there?" I asked, getting immersed into her story.

"Yes."

"So what did you do?" recalling when that had happened to me and how I had quickly gotten up and turned on the television in the living room.

She squeezed my hand and we suddenly appeared in a room, viewing Merinda's physical body sitting up in bed.

"Could you at least warn me when you're about to do that?" I whispered.

Merinda smiled.

We watched her struggle with her new identity. It seemed like days past before us in seconds.

"At first I was scared and didn't know what to make of the feeling. It kept recurring every night. It was like something or someone was trying to tell me something. Now you have to remember that at this stage, I was totally unaware of what was going on anywhere other than my own little world. So I grinned and bore it for a while until it stopped. Still though, I was curious and tried to find out what had happened to me. Eventually, I came across a book that taught me how to meditate. I found it very difficult to learn in the beginning but slowly got the hang of it."

"Meditate? Ew!"

We were back in the forest.

"Warn me please." I said, looking at the familiar surroundings.

"Sorry. Of course it was difficult for me to sit in one place for any amount of time breathing and trying to clear my thoughts. But it was only a matter of time before my life slowed down and I learned to listen. Soon I began to get answers to all of my questions. That's when the presence appeared again."

"Who was it, or should I say, what was it?"

She stopped me from walking and turned to me.

"Do you believe in angels?"

"Uhh." She totally caught me off guard with that one. "Ahh, well, to tell you the truth, I never gave them much thought." I was at a loss for words.

"Here comes the warning."

We appeared again in her bedroom. I watched her story continue to unfold before me.

"One evening, I felt a spine tingly chill in the room."

I could definitely relate to that feeling!

"I got up to reach for the light and, before I could turn it on, the whole room lit up with a blinding white light."

Oh here it comes. I once saw the perfect comic for this great white light mystery. The doctor was leaning over an unconscious patient on an operating table during surgery, shining a flashlight in the patient's eyes. Naturally, the patient saw God.

Merinda continued her thoughts, which penetrated mine. "It was so bright that I had to shield my eyes with my arms."

We all did.

"Warning."

We were both back in the forest.

"We don't get to see what it was?"

"I already saw it. You will in time."

"Saw what?"

"Within moments, this seven-foot angel appeared at the foot of my bed. It was both stunning and glorious. Not to mention scary. I stopped peeking through my arms and gradually lowered them as the light in the room became bearable. I just sat there in awe of such beauty that was so foreign to me."

"Hmm, what does a seven foot angel look like?" I asked, trying to humor her.

"Peter, I don't know of any words that could describe a seven foot angel and do it justice."

"Try me."

"It was absolutely *stunning!* I know, a boring word to describe something so magnificent. He had long golden hair and wore a long white gown. Behind his back were two enormous wings that extended to the ceiling."

Do I stop her?

"I'd never experienced so much love before. It seemed like a man and yet it could have been a woman. It was full of love."

"Did this, ahh, angel say anything to you?" I asked, wondering what her imagination would come up with next.

"Yes. The angel said, 'You are one of the chosen ones. It's time for you to wake up and carry the message of Truth.'"

Merinda checked out my reaction, sighed, and walked away from me, sensing my obvious disbelief. I decided to follow her. I wasn't sure why.

"How do you expect me to react? It's like you're telling me that you're the female version of Jesus Christ."

Merinda ignored me.

I caught up to her and saw that she was upset. She continued walking with her head down, maintaining her silence. For a woman who had appeared to be cold-hearted, she had turned into quite the mush bucket.

I found myself apologizing to her, yet again.

"Look, Merinda, I'm sorry. I didn't mean to make light of your story - no pun intended. But you've got to understand that it's quite a tale to swallow. I mean seven foot angels telling you that you're one of the chosen ones? They lock people up for statements like that in some countries."

"I don't expect you to believe me. I'm just telling you how it was, how I experienced it." She slowly walked down the pathway.

"Why don't you just show me that angel like everything else you've been doing?"

"You get shown certain things when you're ready, whether you think you're ready or not." she said softly.

I began to feel bad. Who was I to judge another person's experience of reality? I'm sure if I told some people about what had happened to me this weekend they wouldn't believe me. I wouldn't believe me. I'd lock me up. Although I also thought that I just might wake up and realize that this was all a dream.

She finally spoke through the silence.

"Peter, that wasn't the hard part."

"OK, lay it on me. I'll do my best to believe."

Merinda stopped and turned to me. "OK, I'm from Sirius and it is important to reconnect with that source in order to fulfill my mission on Earth."

I took in what she said before laying it on her.

"So you're saying that this seven foot angel came to you in the middle of the night, not only telling you that you were one of the chosen ones but that you were also from the star Sirius?"

"Yes. That's right."

I was about to continue confronting her but thought better of it. My mutable self was inclined to accommodate a woman who needed to get things off her chest.

If she was making this up, she was doing one hell of an acting job. If there was one talent that I'd picked up in the ad game, it was how to spot the con. You don't spot the con, you don't survive.

"Um, did this angel say anything else?" I asked, hoping I wasn't enabling her delusion.

"No, that's been the hardest part. This vision of beauty just came, spoke, and then left me hanging there, trying to figure out what it all meant."

"Bummer," I said. "So what did you do?"

"I didn't do anything for the first while. I was still restless at nights and felt that someone or something was in my bedroom. I kept asking in my meditations, 'Who are you? What do you want?' But no response. Finally, in a last desperate bid for my sanity, I went to a channeler who told me that one of the space brothers was trying to connect with me."

Sally's talked about channelers. Apparently they're passé now.

"Was this channeler a couple of thousand years old or was it just one of those three-hundred-year-old jobbies?" I asked.

"Look, I can understand your skepticism. We had a flood of channelers a few years ago because Earth was ready for new information. We needed to get it as soon as possible, so some of the more sensitive people on the planet opened up to their predestined arrangement to help bring through new information. Unfortunately, what started to happen was that some of these 'sensitives' became greedy, and preyed on people's vulnerability and willingness to grow.

"Soon, the channelers ran into their own problems. Earth kept increasing her vibration and a lot of them stopped doing their work on themselves, causing a great imbalance in their lives and therefore their inevitable downfall. Unfortunately, they discredited the whole process, making it impossible for many new people to learn."

I twirled her words around in my brain for a moment or two.

"That's a nice hypothesis, but the fact remains that there are still charlatans going around taking people's money and promoting lies."

Merinda remained silent for a moment as a cool breeze swept over our faces.

"I could have a long discussion with you as to why channelers do what they do, why charlatans do what they do, and why people still go to them. But the bottom line is, most people don't want to listen to what's going on inside of them. More importantly, when they do listen, they don't have the courage to act on the little voice shouting at them to do something; to change their lives. They don't want to take responsibility. They don't want to "respond to their ability." I mean, anyone can channel, Peter. Even you! All you need to do is tune into the creative Source, the universal energy, the God force, or whatever you want to call it. The information is there for everyone, not just those who know how to twitch their faces or lay a card."

I still wanted my twenty-five bucks back from the channeler who said I was going to be an astronaut.

"It makes me sad to see people give up on their dreams. They're really not as far away as they think they are from living them out. That's part of my mission here, to help people realize how important it is for them to live out their dreams. Because if their dreams are their truth and they're living out their truth, they are assisting in the healing of the planet. They are making the ascension into the Fourth Dimension a lot more graceful than it would be otherwise. We are here to live out our dreams. Really. We are meant to experience Heaven on Earth. It's programmed into each human's genetic coding. Too bad society doesn't support individuality."

"What do you mean?"

"Keeping people ignorant about the fact that they are truly multidimensional beings and can experience Heaven on Earth is the name of the game. Sadly though, if we maintain this negative course, there is great potential for catastrophes on this planet. Earth changes will eliminate those who have never had the chance or courage to wake up and live out their essence. If we could only have the courage to live our dreams *now*!"

I'm sure that's what folks in Ethiopia are thinking every day, 'Hm, what's my dream today? I think I'll live out my poverty. That way I can heal the planet while I'm at it too.' I don't think so. I'm sure they were just dreaming of eating and growing old. This was *way* too doom and gloom for me. I didn't know how much longer I could hang out with these New Agers.

Merinda looked over at me, taking my hand. "It's not so much about doom and gloom as it is about being aware and conscious of the inevitable evolution of this planet."

Why is it that everyone can read minds but me?

"Peter, this time period has been prophesized by many. It can't be ignored. You only need to look deep inside to know that something major is happening with this planet. To put it bluntly, you either get it together or you'll be taken apart. It will be much better to make the choice consciously. Trust me on that one."

I didn't know what to say. Here I was with a complete stranger who was telling me her version of a potential Armageddon or whatever they're calling it these days. How could I believe this any more than I could believe the angel story? Was I to continue walking with this lady of limitless imagination? Was I to invest in a bomb shelter and begin stocking up on dry foods? I really didn't know what was next. All of these people were starting to affect my psyche; I was actually starting to believe some of this. I was actually starting to believe in something, which was definitely a new place for me. But was that a good thing?

"OK, a little step back here. Let's get back to the space brother thing. How does all this tie into floating balls of fire above your palms?"

Merinda held my gaze before looking away.

She did it again. A simple touch and we were now standing in a room with the physical Merinda and a channeler, who actually looked like my grandmother.

"This channeler told me that a space brother by the name of Rinaldo wanted to come through me to speak. The channeler said that I would need to go through a major cleansing of the emotional, physical, and spiritual bodies before that could happen. Rinaldo told her that my vibration was too dense for any transmissions to come through clearly."

"What do you mean by cleansing?"

The channeler looked up at us, smiled and went back to talking to Merinda.

Merinda took in a deep breath. "The way it was explained to me was that the type of fuel that bodies require for the New World is of a very high octane."

"What, we have to start drinking gas?" I inquired, knowing that wasn't the answer.

"No. We are talking about the food we eat. What we put into our bodies is going to become a major issue in the next few years. The old saying, we are what we eat, is certainly applicable now. It affects everything."

Suddenly, both the channelers' and Merinda's physical bodies turned into pure molecular energy. I was wide-eyed. Impressive trick! Ironically, I could see certain blockages in Merinda's energy pattern. Bad food? Maybe. And I knew nothing about this stuff.

"Are you going to tell me that eating red meat is bad for me? Because I'm not going leafy green!" I asked, as I inwardly clung to my fast food lunches.

"What I'm saying and what I've been told is that anything containing man-made chemicals – preservatives - additives, et cetera - will not carry enough nutrition to enter the Fourth Dimension. When you think about it, Peter, our thought processes are partly being controlled by the major manufacturers of food."

"What do you mean?" She had hit a sore spot but I sensed she was right about that one.

We were back in the forest.

"Can't you see, Peter?" She was almost pleading. "There are people who are controlling what goes in our food. It is these same people who dictate to us what is healthy and what is not. What makes them money is that which can be made the cheapest and sold for the most profit. People continue to pay good money for their man-made product, so they continue the cycle. In the last few years, the big food manufacturers have begun to panic. 'What if the people get tired of our product? We won't be able to make any more money.' It was at this point that they started putting in the addictive chemicals that convince man's subconscious that the product is essential. Take our addiction to white sugar or caffeine. These are not substances that have always been part of our diets. It's only recently, when man realized that they were both addictive and profitable, that the manufacturers began to really saturate our market and our collective psyche. We're hooked on man-made chemicals and don't even know it."

All I could say was Amen to that one. I had first-hand experience and knowledge of this dirty deed from the ad business.

This information, as unscientific as it may have been, weighed heavily on me. Many were the times I had watched clients talking only about dollars and cents when they were marketing a product that was being branded as "healthy for your diet." As I said earlier, these were the products I had made a mental note not to buy.

"So what you're basically saying is that there are millions of people walking around addicted to their hamburgers, fries, and breakfast cereal, none of which is good for them to begin with, right?"

"Absolutely. Some people are addicted to the foods they eat, the liquids they drink, and I'm not just talking about alcohol. Some are even addicted to the air they breathe. Especially the polluted air."

"People are addicted to pollution? You're kidding, right?"

The world changed around me. The evergreen trees had now become a huge projection screen for Merinda's tale. I saw every type of pollutant to mankind appear before me, from the steel industry to garbage dumping into the lake by the average person.

"It's human nature to adapt and survive. Unfortunately, we've adapted and survived to the point where we are trying to accommodate our own man-made chemicals, which are lethal. We have effectively created a tapeworm that won't stop until all is gone."

This left me in silence. The images of pollutants were fast, furious and plentiful. The screen flashed to a blinding white light and then disappeared. Merinda looked at me and shrugged.

I took in the silence of nature.

It seemed as though I was on a never-ending path called "knowledge input." This thought brought my attention to where we were walking, which also seemed like a never-ending path. Where the heck were we?

The sun was beginning to go down behind the trees and I felt an evening chill coming upon us.

I looked over at Merinda, only to find her lost in thought too.

Was what she was saying about man's addiction to chemicals true? If so, was I continually perpetuating these lies by helping to come up with ideas to market these products? Um, yes. But I already knew that. I wasn't proud of my actions but I knew exactly what I was doing. If you're not part of the solution, you're part of the problem. I knew that too. But geez, the money was good!

It didn't start off to be about the money. I thought it was fun and creative. I didn't think it was going to turn into something that was so destructive to humanity. Maybe there was another way of doing what I do to serve mankind as opposed to fooling it?

Whether Merinda's angel existed or whether the channeler was telling the truth about the space brother wanting to connect with her, didn't matter. This conversation was making me take a look at the lies that I had been living for years; trying to tell myself that I was contributing something to the community when deep down inside, I knew that there was a big lie going on and that I was playing a major role in perpetuating it.

Something else was nagging me about this conversation.

"I think you're avoiding telling me something," I said, stopping Merinda's continual long strides.

She looked at me, folding her arms and giving a slight smile. "Guilty."

"What haven't you told me?" I asked, wanting to finally get to the bottom of this.

She took hold of my hands. "In a nutshell, I'm a star person and so are you."

Pop! I felt my world shatter. I momentarily lost consciousness and literally went to the stars and back. She was speaking the truth and I knew it.

My knees began to shake involuntarily. I knew I had been hit with something deep. Part of me didn't want to know any more but my gut said otherwise.

Merinda put her arms around me. I could barely hold myself up. I knew I was about to hear something that could mean a major personal change. Did I have the courage to ask what she meant? Could I take the answer? No doubt this was hitting me at a soul level and was going to be hard on me but I knew I had to ask for the next piece of the puzzle.

"What, ahh, what do you mean when you say that I am a star person too?" I asked, slowly pulling away from the embrace.

"Are you sure you want to hear about this now?" she asked, softly caressing the cheek of a very frightened man. That would be me.

I could no longer see this woman as a cold-shoulder type. She was obviously a caring and loving soul who was genuinely concerned for mankind. And like Sally, she was beginning to touch my soul - territory rarely explored by anyone!

"It's getting dark out," she said, leading me toward the retreat center. "Let's talk about it as we walk back."

She put her hand in mine and I allowed myself to feel a great love for this woman as she led me down the path toward home. Once again.

~ 23 ~

Merinda and I walked hand in hand, down Mother Nature's smooth pathway. She was one of many who were leading me to the questions that I had been asking myself for years without realizing it. Who was I? What was my purpose here? And what was I going to do about it?

But I had lived my life in such a way as to silence these thoughts. I worked hard and played hard, never taking time to reflect. There were moments when I would get a glimpse of who I really was and I would know that I was living a big lie. But so was everyone else so why should it matter? Why did I have to take it any further? Who else knew my lie? Who else cared? I lived in denial of my truth, and therefore in denial of my existence. I knew the glimpse of who I really was wouldn't last forever. If I waited long enough, it would subside and I could continue my denial.

I became very adept at denial.

There would be times when I would be watching my boss making a pitch to a prospective client, knowing full well that his promises were empty, and yet I still supported him when he went in for the kill. I conveniently chalked it all up to the system.

I would hear the lies going on around me and I would feel a burning sensation in my stomach. I knew something was wrong but I didn't have the courage to admit it. I would quickly suppress my feelings with a ceremonious drink after the deal was made. What a liar I had become. Not only to others but also to myself. Sally was able to call me on my lies and this was one of the reasons I resisted going out with her in the beginning. That and because I thought she was too straight, and, uh, honest for my liking.

I met her at a housewarming party. The theme of that party was "things that go bump in the night." I should have known.

I knew in my gut that she was good for me and not only as a girlfriend. I must have known intuitively that she could help me get out of the lies that I was drowning in. I knew I needed help, I just didn't know how to ask. She was there for me right from the beginning. I was always grateful.

"Shall I begin?" interrupted Merinda.

"Yeah, sure. No turning back now."

"Good. You know how people talk about time traveling to other places in the past, present, and future?"

"Know it, done it," I said.

"One of the reasons you experienced that 'adventure' was so that you would understand time as man sees it, as opposed to time as it really exists."

"Which is how exactly?" I asked, wanting to get to the bottom of this "time" issue once and for all.

"Time is nonexistent. Time does not exist anywhere but in man's head. It's just man's way of trying to have control over the Universe. Well it doesn't work any longer - *in any way!* That's why we have this continuing collapse of the third dimension: It's being forced out of man's hands."

"You do like to dwell on the abstract, don't you?" I said, interrupting her before she went on a completely different tangent.

"Sorry, sometimes I get carried away."

Now there's an understatement.

"I think I'm still trying to understand it myself. Anyway, if you can assume for a moment that time really doesn't exist, can you see how entities from other planets relate to us?"

"Um, nope."

"In the absence of time in human terms, they can travel through space to any destination, in a wink of an eye. There are other intelligent life forms out there that can appear to us even if they are light years away from our point of view. They don't see us in a time reference. It's all a vibration of energy to them."

"What the heck are you talking about?"

"In a roundabout way I'm saying that we have visitors from other galaxies here on Earth, and those who can raise their vibration and operate as multidimensional beings are able to communicate with them."

I still didn't know where this was leading. The idea of other entities visiting us from other planets and galaxies did seem a tad far-fetched, even taking into account what had been going on in my life the last few days.

"OK, Merinda, even if what you're saying is true, and I'm not saying that I'm buying it, what does all of this have to do with me?" I asked, wanting to finally get a straight answer.

"Let me put it to you this way. As you know, man has been on this planet for thousands of years."

"OK, I can buy that."

"Did you ever stop to think about where our evolution began?" I thought back to my history classes in school.

"Uhh, didn't we just evolve from monkeys or something like that? Or, wait a minute, I think it was apes. Um, well, I haven't really given it much thought, to be honest."

"Darwin's theory of evolution is man's attempt to put a label on something without involving Spirit."

"What are you saying?"

"The seed of humanity is from another planet," she replied, almost knocking me over with those words.

"In saying that, I'm also saying that you are from another planet. As am I."

Once again her words fell heavily upon me. I couldn't remember much history from school or Bible studies but I'm sure there wasn't any mention of us coming from another planet.

"I would like to lay it on you thick and you can just take it or leave it. However, I feel that I need to ask your permission to continue."

My head stopped spinning long enough for me to answer, "Sure, why not? It's only an illusion anyway, right?"

She laughed. "Of course, Peter. Of course. Now this is where it gets a bit heavy, so just bear with me for a moment. I'm just coming to grips with it myself."

"OK. I'll hang onto your hand in case we start flying off to other planets."

Which we immediately did! Well, at least a part of us left planet earth because I couldn't see our bodies as we shot through space. Ironically, I wasn't freaking out over it.

"Sorry. Forgot to warn you."

"I'm getting use to it," I said, fascinated by the planets whizzing by.

"I'll try and make it simple for both of our sakes. There are many universes and galaxies out there. There is even a parallel universe that is doing exactly the opposite of what we are doing here on this planet, in order for us to maintain balance within our own solar system."

"You mean there is someone on another planet Earth who is like me except he's having a good time watching the football game?"

"Simply put, yes."

Wish I could get in touch with him and find out what the score is.

"If you can accept that there are other intelligent beings in the other solar systems, galaxies and universes…"

"I'll roll with it."

"Then try and accept that within our own universe there are other forms of intelligent beings besides humans."

We shot through the rings of Saturn.

"I'm still rolling."

"Some of these beings are looking for places to conquer, some are looking for places that conform with their own natural habitat, and some just want to observe. There are also those who are watching over us until we decide to become a planet with a higher vibration. They will assist us in achieving this higher understanding, thereby increasing their own vibration and bringing us all closer to the God source."

Did she really think I was getting all this? For the sake of my ego, I tried asking her an intelligent question as we whizzed past Mars.

"Are you saying that these Martians or whatever have the same alleged God as we do?" I asked.

"Does that seem far-fetched to you?"

"How can I answer that? I don't even know if we have a God."

"Never mind that for now. Let's imagine there is an evolved planet that needs assistance for its next evolutionary process toward the God source."

We glided over a futuristic looking city for but a moment and then shot back into space.

"And this planetary community has the technology to travel through other universes, looking for fellow planets to help with this process. This evolved planet chooses a barren planet called Earth because it has a relatively safe position in the Universe and because its own inhabitants are capable of evolving in this environment."

Odd, a UFO just zipped by us.

"Now let's say, hypothetically of course, that as a genetic experiment, these beings then plant a seed whose purpose is to bring mankind to a higher frequency of consciousness. Once again, their ultimate purpose is to understand themselves, thereby bringing them closer to God."

"Assuming there is one."

"Warning."

We were now back on the path through the forest. For some reason, all that bopping around had a familiarity to it.

"Of course. There are even some who have been taking samples of this planet, vegetation and humans, in case there are major changes on Earth. This will help with the replanting of the new Earth as we enter the Fourth Dimension."

"OK sister, hold it right there. Just hold it, OK? You mean to tell me that we are some sort of genetic experiment from another type of alien race and that they are really just watching over us like, like, babysitters?"

She took her hand in mine.

"We, meaning you and me, no. We, meaning the majority of mankind, I would have to say yes. I would use the word guides as opposed to babysitters when referring to entities like us."

"And why aren't you and I genetic experiments?"

She took one of those ominous deep breaths.

"In a way, we all are. But more specifically, you and I asked to be assigned to this planet in order to help raise the consciousness of mankind; to help mankind acclimatize to the fact that our space brothers, along with the angels and others, will be returning in the near future to assist with the planetary shift."

"Okaaaay. So what you're saying is that I didn't come from my mother's womb but instead, dropped into this body at some point in my life when I bumped my head?"

"No, unlike me, you chose to enter at birth to get the full benefit and understanding of man's greed before going out to teach."

"Teach? Teach what? What are you talking about? Wait! Before you answer that, are you saying that I was hovering in some spaceship above Earth just waiting for my parents to do it, and then popped out like Baby Alien?"

"No, I meant-"

"Because I think my parents are going to be a little shocked when they find out that they raised an alien."

"Peter, you have to understand that everything is being done as part of the Divine plan to help save this planet and others; to help raise the consciousness of the beings on this planet and others by bringing them into the Oneness of it all. The God force. The Source. Give it any word you want."

"Which brings me to a point I made with Sally. If there is such a thing as this God, why did this God thingamabobber kick us out of the Source in the first place?"

"First of all, no one was kicked out. We have always had free will within the Divine plan."

"But within the Divine plan, I only have so much freedom, right?"

"Hm. Don't know about that one yet. Fate, destiny, and free will are all a bit of an enigma at this point. All I know is that some of us chose to enter another realm of understanding and live in dense circumstances to grow and to help others. Unfortunately, understanding the multidimensional life-force was forgotten when man started to push free will and choice to its maximum, trying to reshape the Divine plan. Thus disconnecting us from the Source.

"While man is by nature an enlightened being, he can be greedy when he doesn't work within the universal laws. Some beings began to abuse the privilege of choice and went against the Source of their very own Being. They felt that they 'should' have full control of their own destiny and play outside of the Divine plan whenever they wanted to. Some people call them fallen angels. There are fallen angels who are trying to earn their wings back so that they can go home and there are others who choose to rule the material world because they can't rule the spirit world.

"Ultimately, we are all being guided homeward and are protected by the Oneness - the Source, God, Spirit, whatever human term you would like to call it. Even the fallen angels are being guided. Albeit, sometimes against their will."

I felt a cool breeze caressing my face as I stared into the distance, trying to see my reality.

"I think the most important issue is that we reconnect with Spirit in our own unique way because that is how we will find our true home. We do that by going inside our own heart, not someone else's. How fast we go home is directly proportionate to how much we call upon Spirit for guidance."

I just stood there, looking up into the indigo sky, trying to take it all in. I was with her on the free will and choice part, and then I drifted. The richness of the unusual sky fascinated me. Some people have ADD, I have NADD - New Age Distraction Disorder. Sally starts riffing on this stuff and I get easily distracted with shiny things. But out of respect for Merinda, I tried to refocus and get back into the conversation.

"So, are you saying that there are extra-terrestrials and angels floating around this planet, even as we speak?"

"Yes. What happened at some point in the journey is that man was exercising free will and became so wrapped up in greed, desire, and other dense states, that he excluded spirit and negated his own multidimensional nature. Most extra-terrestrials, star beings, and angels are here to help remind mankind that it is very capable of experiencing matter and spirit simultaneously. Most of them. There are some exceptions but you don't need to know about that now."

Yep. This was becoming, once again, waaaay too much to absorb. But I had taken in so much information and had experienced so much in the past few days that I really didn't know what to scoff at anymore. Some of this strange new information was feeling familiar to me. I took in a deep breath.

"Sooo. Exactly what am I supposed to be teaching again?"

"All of this and more. When you're ready. You still have some remembering to do and some choices to make."

"Great."

Memo to self: *Start taking Gingko Biloba!*

"What's with that ball of fire that I saw you with earlier?" I had some vague idea that she used it for communication, but with who or what?

"It's one of the ways I talk with my people. The ball of energy allows me to see and communicate with them directly. I only use it when I'm really confused and need a more direct form of communication. Over a period of time, they have come to me in my dreams, slowly assisting me with certain understandings. Sometimes, in the middle of the night, they take me to their spaceship to continue my lessons."

"You mean they abduct you and do weird experiments on your body?" I asked, thinking of the stories I had seen on the front pages of those supermarket tabloids.

"No, not like that at all. Those people who have apparently been abducted have been taken according to a voluntary, prearranged agreement."

"Tell that to them. Any movie I've seen, they're squeezing their butt-cheeks and screaming their heads off."

"Warning."

We were standing in what seemed like a room in a castle. A castle made of crystal. A wooden table stretched out before us. A tall, odd looking man with the skin color of a reptile and dressed in Royal garb, entered the room. He looked at us, smiled and bowed. I heard a buzzing sound and we were back in the forest.

"What was that?"

"It's important to understand that we are all here serving God in our own unique manner. There is not just one planet that's communicating with ours, there are many. We are all here to learn from each other."

There was one question that had kept popping into my mind, back when I was drifting in my own little world. "Is Sally from the same place as you and I?"

Merinda paused for a moment.

"Sally is an angel."

"Well, I know that but is she from the same place as you and I?"

"No, listen. Sally *is* an angel."

I was silenced. I didn't have it in me to go there.

~ 24 ~

Merinda and I sat beneath the starry sky. The chill coursing through my body wasn't just from the cold.

"Am I *really* one of those star people that you talk about?" I could barely choke out the words.

Merinda turned to me, and put her hand on my shoulder. Feeling the heat come from her hand and surge through my body, I quickly became lightheaded.

"As God is my witness, you are."

Energy more potent than I can describe shot through the top of my head. I felt my body tremble. I had no thoughts.

If this were even remotely true, how could I continue to exist as I had for so many years? They say everything happens for a reason, but this, this was heavy. Was this my new reality or was it a dream? Was there any separation between the dream state and the waking state? If so, which state was I in? I felt unfamiliar emotions welling up from deep within.

"What does it mean to be one of these star people?"

"As with all beings, it means service to God. It means fulfilling your true purpose for being on this planet. It means understanding your*self* so well that you can understand others and be of service to them. We are just another form of the same Spirit working toward the evolution of this planet. Bottom line? It means getting real with yours*elf* first, and then with others."

Merinda put her arm around me. "Your time has come to remember *what you already kn*ow. Some may not be as fortunate as you. Others will have more revealed to them than you, but the journey is the same. You are who you are and there is no turning back."

She pulled me in closer and whispered softly into my ear. "You are a child of God who came here with a mission to awaken the souls of others. Soon you will meet your old friends from the planet that is your real home. You'll work with them a lot, as I now do. They will help guide you. They will come to you when you are able to meet them halfway. It is very important that you begin to discipline your body, mind, and spirit, starting now."

She caressed my hair as I felt my emotional response to her words. As with Surrender, I was able to feel what it was like to express from my well of emotion without holding back for fear of being judged.

"Peter, I won't be seeing you for awhile, at least not on this planet. I must go and fulfill *my* purpose. My adjustment period is over. It is my time to go to the people. You have only just started your period of adjustment. Try not to be as hard on yourself as I was. You're a beautiful man with a lot to say. So please, for the sake of mankind and for the other people who carry this knowledge and need your help, don't give up now. Always explore and ask questions of the Unknown, for in that you'll find the true answers of the Self and its connection to the Source.

Please remember not to forget.

This information is being passed on to you as it was to me. One day it will be your turn to pass it on to many others who need to remember. Whether on a cellular level or on an intuitive level, it will strike a chord in them. They too will begin to remember. So don't hold back. Don't fear. Your truth is very near. It is deep inside you."

I could feel her crying as she was playing the protector of my newly awakened soul. I felt sad that she wasn't going to be around to talk to. It seemed that we had so much to share.

Was I feeling love for this woman? Or was it simply that there were no boundaries to love and no time restriction on love. For the first time in my life I was able to feel love for more than one woman without feeling guilty.

Was it possible to love many people and still be the lover of one? I didn't know.

But I knew that there was genuine love and camaraderie between Merinda and me, and it far surpassed any restrictions that I had ever put on love. I was beginning to grasp the reality that love does indeed transcend all, and that we have a responsibility to love one another in the purest, most altruistic way. There was no room for games or abuse. Love just *is*.

We sat there under the winking stars. The stars knew something and were letting us know that everything was going to be OK. But how? I knew I wasn't going to be able to hang out with the boys in the way that I had before. What was I going to do with my life now? How could I walk around with all this information and not have anyone to share it with? I was appreciating having Sally in my life more than ever. The work that she must have done on herself to become the person that she had become gave "self-respect" new meaning.

I could see Merinda's point about attracting like-minded people in order to build a stronger energy field of awareness. This was not something that all people were going to be open to. Would I really attract those like-minded people she had talked about? Or would I be branded as some sort of freak? Would I care?

My mind was moving beyond mere optimism. Something was happening to me, something greater than I could explain. My only hope was that one day it would all make sense.

"Peter, what you need to do now is allow time to de-program. This is going to be difficult at first, but the more aware you become, the more you will see how essential it is to be concerned about your lifestyle. The people you surround yourself with, they've got to share your beliefs; otherwise it will be too hard on you. Build a strong support system. Be aware of where you live. Listen to the inner whispers of the wind. Know where it is that you need to be at any given moment and trust that it will be OK.

"Be prepared to move at a moment's notice because that's how fast the winds can change. And be aware of what you eat. It's the fuel that will help you become stronger and have the courage of the spiritual warrior. Everything in your life will be altered dramatically. Please be prepared to listen to Spirit and your higher Self."

It struck home. I knew that what she was saying was true for me. I didn't know if I had the courage or strength to do what I was beginning to know intuitively had to be done. I didn't know if I could let go of my habits and attachments and fully trust in Spirit. I could feel the tears warming my cheeks as they streamed down my face.

"Remember that there are and will be people all over this planet going through what you're going through. You are not alone and will not be alone. When you start to meditate, you will know what I mean. Your new friends will come to you in your dreams, your meditations, and your waking state. There will be so much love in your life." She pulled me in for a big hug.

"When you feel alone, look up at the stars and talk to them. They will hear everything. They will always be sending their love."

Merinda gently wiped the tears from my face, and then tilted my head toward the sky.

"See that star? It's called Sirius. Somewhere around there lies your true planet." Then she pointed toward my heart. "And somewhere in there lies your true home."

I lost it completely. Crying uncontrollably in Merinda's protective arms. I knew that those stars held a truth that had been buried deep within me. But, even more importantly, this was the first time I realized that deep within me was my home. Not some house, condo, or planet, but the essence of my soul.

Merinda and I slowly made our way back to the house. My mind was swimming with thoughts of the Unknown.

How could I have been on this planet for so long and not remember my true origin? My soul? And if there was such a thing as reincarnation, how could we incarnate from one planet to another? Who was really in charge of this world? Who were our *real* world leaders? Were they from this planet? Was there a more developed race than ours on another planet that had come here to plant seeds and monitor our growth, taking a few samples along the way? Was there an Armageddon, biblical or otherwise? Were we going to experience planetary catastrophes of major proportions? Could anything be done to stop the prophesized demise of this planet? Was it going to be a demise or a rebirth into the next dimensional reality as Merinda had been saying? Or both? Were they going to take the children first? Would I be able to raise people's awareness of Truth? Could I go back to my day job and pretend none of this existed? How could I relate to my family in the same way, knowing what I know? Was I really a star person? If so, then what was I to do about it? My mind raced from thought to thought.

Finally, I couldn't take it any longer. My mind had completed its last lap.

"Merinda, I really need to lie down and relax. I think - no - I know. I'm on information overload."

Merinda held me up as I stumbled toward the stairs leading to the back porch. I couldn't conceive of walking up those stairs by myself.

"Perhaps we should take you straight to your room and lie you down on your cot for a little nap? Unless of course you're hungry?" Merinda let out a chuckle.

"No, no, I'm really not in the mood for food or polite conversation. Let's take me to my room."

We entered through the back door. Sally was there to greet us.

"Peter, are you all right?" she asked, as she rushed to my side, obviously noticing my mush bucket state.

"He just experienced a little de-programming. He'll be better with a some sleep," Merinda said to Sally. "Why don't you get him a cold wash cloth for his head? I think his crown chakra is about ready to fry some eggs. I'll bring him up to his room."

Sally went rushing off to the bathroom for my rescue cloth. I could vaguely hear her mumble something about a little remedy to help me out. If that meant a good stiff belt of scotch, bring it on!

~ 25 ~

"I'm going to need you to help me get you up these stairs, Peter," Merinda said, as we looked up the staircase leading to the sleeping quarters.

Slowly we made our ascent. Never in my life had I found it so difficult to coordinate my legs.

"Does absorbing this information get any easier?" I asked, wondering if I would always turn into a jellyfish.

"As you become a lighter being in body, mind and spirit, you will have less difficulty accepting information because it just *is*. The lighter you become, the more you will remember who you are. You won't feel any necessity to retain it because it just *is*."

I needed a break from all the lingo. I needed to just lie down with my own thoughts and go to sleep. It was getting close to bedtime, which was ten o'clock according to the clock we had just passed. I was emotionally and physically exhausted. I had missed a night of sleep somewhere in all this "de-programming," or was it brainwashing?

Merinda brought me through the doorway and laid me to rest on the cot. Just as I hit the old cot, Sally arrived and stood there watching Merinda put me to bed.

Merinda kneeled beside me and said in a whisper, "It won't be long before you meet your space brothers and reconnect with your home planet and true purpose. I'll see you on that planet before I see you again on this one. Take care, my friend."

"Funny, you look just like a co-worker of mine." I whispered back.

"When it comes to life lessons, people look like whoever you need them to look like." Merinda said softly.

She leaned over and gave me a kiss on the cheek as her forefinger hovered over my heart. I felt an electric current pass from her forefinger into my body. The sudden warmth relaxed any muscle that was fighting to stay in charge. From my semi-comatose state, I saw her give me a warm smile, get up, and leave.

Sally followed her out into the hallway. I saw the two give each other a loving hug and I heard Merinda say, "So long for now."

Smiling, Sally began a slow, sensual walk toward me. I wasn't in the mood. I couldn't believe I was thinking that but it was true. My body was drained of energy; I couldn't even comprehend a "quickie."

"You look so beautiful lying there, all vulnerable and silent," Sally said, in a soft sexy whisper.

"I'm sure I bring new meaning to the term sexy beast," I offered, truly unable to protect myself from any woman with lustful desires and marathon capabilities.

Sally knelt down beside me and put the cold cloth on my forehead. I'm sure I must have had steam coming from my head. I felt as though there was a drill burrowing itself through my skull. I can't say that it was painful as much as uncomfortable.

"Sally, something's going on with my head. My whole body for that matter." I tried to muster up some final commentary before I went lullaby.

Sally pulled out a little bottle and motioned me to open up my mouth as she put a few drops of some kind of Homeopathic remedy into my mouth. This was something she used frequently after teaching one of her yoga classes. I didn't know what to make of the taste but it seemed like there was a smattering of alcohol in it. I motioned for more.

"That's enough for now. You're experiencing a physical reaction to all the information that you've been receiving. You're remembering your interconnectedness with All. It's quite common that, on a cellular level, you will have these physical and emotional reactions as part of remembrance and letting go. It's as if there are miniature time capsules that go off at certain times in order for you to receive the information. It never happens unless you're ready."

"I don't recall saying that I was ready for this. In fact, I recall wanting to spend the weekend watching football. *That* I recall!"

"That's ego talking, Sweetie. It's all unfolding as it's meant to. I didn't see it coming either. But I knew that one day you were meant to be here at this retreat."

"A little heads up would have been nice."

Sally chuckled.

"What's exciting is that your chakra centers are opening up to a new frequency, helping you see the worlds in and around you in a whole new light."

"Yippee."

"Now, now."

"Uh, these chakras, is there any way of turning them off so that I can go to sleep?"

Sally laughed.

"These chakras are high vibrational energy centers comprising the many layers of both your physical and spiritual bodies. You don't ever want to turn them off, especially since they've been reactivated. They are beginning to find their harmony and balance within you. All of you."

"Sally, you're scaring me."

"Why?" she said softly, as if I had just hurt her feelings.

"Because you're starting to sound like Merinda, that's why. Do me a favor, don't say anything else and be the angel that you are. I just need you to be by my side in silence."

She nodded in understanding, took my hand in hers, and gave it a soft kiss.

I took in Sally's loving presence. I had been noticing lately that whenever I felt lost, the thought of Sally helped me feel good. This was one of those times. What was I lost about specifically? I didn't know. But what I did know was that her warm glow always brought peace and serenity to my heart. It had taken me several months to finally admit to myself that Sally was different from the previous women I'd dated.

Sally placed her hand on my heart, slowly bringing the focus from my burning head to my warming heart. I just stared into her glowing blue eyes as the lights began to dim. The last thing I saw was the serene angelic smile of my loving mate.

~ 26 ~

"It's your time. It's your time," was like a mantra in my mind as I rolled over onto my side into the fetal position.

"Come on! Wake up! We'll go for a ride." The squeaky voice echoing in my mind sounded oddly familiar.

Was I asleep? Was I dreaming? I opened my eyes to total blackness. What was going on? Seeing nothing, I turned on my back and tried to resume my sleep.

"Come on! Let's go have some fun and help you remember home," I heard again.

Now the voice was coming from somewhere in the room. I opened my eyes. As they adjusted to the darkness, I could see an odd figure standing at the foot of my bed. At first, all I could make out was a little boy with a pear-shaped head. But then a small beam of white light with a humming sound started to enter the room from the window, casting a shine on something incomprehensible. I was more curious than shocked.

I quickly looked around the room to see if there were others who could witness this extraordinary sight.

"Don't be a dweeb, nobody sleeps in this dimension. Come on, let's rock and roll. We'll pick up a couple of babes from Sirius and go cruise the universe."

As the room filled up with more white light coming from the window, I began to see this figure more fully. His origin was not human.

"Hey Pete! That's what you call yourself here, right?"

I just lay there, my jaw resting on my chest, staring.

"Loosen up, bud! We're going to do some cruising. Maybe by the end of the night, you'll remember me."

I was speechless. This four-foot, whatever he was, looked like a fetus that could walk and talk. He had huge insect eyes and a small mouth that didn't move at all while he jabbered fifties jargon stolen from *American Graffiti.*

The humming became louder and the room brighter. This midget ant thingy was extraterrestrial green and looked exactly like a figure from an exhibit I had seen with my dad when I was seven years old. It had scared me so much that I ran out of the building screaming, "They are real! They are real!"

It had taken my dad hours to calm me down again. If this creature was one of those things from outer space, I was surprisingly calm.

"Hey bud, I know you guys are still stuck in this linear time thing on this planet, but the little binko flying the saucer wants to get a move on. So why don't you hop out of bed and we'll get beamed up together?"

I slowly began to raise myself up with my elbow. This Martian munchkin was yapping at me telepathically, not unlike Surrender and Sally. Why wasn't I afraid? Why didn't I scream? Why did I get up out of my bed and stand beside him? For some reason, I was game for this new experience.

"Allllright! This is gonna be a piece of cake. The screaming that goes on sometimes, I have to hit them with a needle just to shut them up. Man oh man, I tell you, it's a good thing I don't have human ears. A little patience and understanding go a long way, right Bucko?"

Bucko? Where did they get this guy? I was thinking about all the times I had read about people being taken away and how terrible it was. Now it was my turn and I ended up being abducted by a regular comic from planet Mars' improv club.

"You're lucky you got me, bubba. Some of the space bros are sooo anal! Oops, poor choice of words. Sorry. No worries here, bro. No probing gonna be done. Yo! You OK? You with me?"

I probably looked like a shell-shocked mannequin as I continued staring down at him.

"You're not going to freak out on me now, are you?

I managed what I hoped was a nod of encouragement.

"Good. Yeah, them bros take their jobs sooo seriously. They scare the crap out of you humans because they think it has to be done all serious like. Not me. If I've abducted one human, I've abducted ten million. Why not enjoy the process? That's what I say. Show the human a good time. That way when they get up in the morning and we allow them to remember, they'll be left with a good impression of us light workers. Right?"

"Uh yeah, right," I heard myself say.

"Relax. Save your vocal cords. We'll communicate telepathically. Oh, and by the way, swallow the pill. It makes for a better ride. I'll explain later."

He then pointed to my right hand that was clenched into a fist. I guess I wasn't all that relaxed, or maybe I was getting ready for a fistfight with a Martian.

I opened up my fist and in the palm of my hand sat a pill. I'm not sure how he put it there but I noticed that it was very similar to the one that Merinda had given me earlier to get me through our little journey. I hesitated. Was I going to have another breakdown? Was I really communicating with a four-foot, loudmouth Martian who was about to take me on his spaceship? Was this yet another elaborate dream?

"Yeah, I know. It looks very similar to the one Merinda gave you, but it's not. This pill is gonna help your molecular structure adjust to the way we travel in our spaceship. Oh yeah, that Merinda, what a knockout! Such a brain on her! Aye karumba!"

I think I would have preferred the shock abduction scenario.

"Oh, one thing about the pilot. He really gets antsy if you go near the control panels. If it were up to me, I'd fly the damn thing myself but I can't. OK, I can, but, well, there was a time when I was allowed, but I, I kinda got grounded. Ever since Roswell! Bum rap, man. Me and Buddy were playing chicken. I went right, Buddy went left and he crashes! And they blamed me! Hello? We were just having some fun. I mean, if I had to dissect one more cow. And you know, it's not like Buddy's soul stuck around and gave away trade secrets. His astral was out of there so fast, especially when your government boys started probing his body. *Ew.* Saw the new him recently. He's great. Wife. Kids. Doing the Venus-Jupiter postal run these days.

"Excuse me-"

"In the end, we did have to throw your government a few flying saucers to shut them up."

"Who – Are - You?"

"Cripes, now we gotta listen to your binko scientific fly boys tell us how to fix one of our own saucers. Talk about your dense matter. Captain Buckwing is flying some pre-historic tin can that practically needs duct tape to hold it together, and he's trying to expound on his theory of quantum physics. To us? Hello?!"

"What - Are - You?"

"The arrogance! We practically handed them the blueprints and those pencil rockets are the best they can come up with? They scare the slime out of us every time they put human beings in one of those firecrackers! Can't believe it. Just can't believe it. So then the big guys upstairs decide that they need help down here and send your government a few of the brothers to train your guys how to maneuver those flying saucers that we gave them. Yeaoh! Now there's something to watch, human beings at the controls of one of our babies. Ha! I mean, there's not a lot you can do in the big leagues if you don't know yourself. Take control of your*self* first and the rest will follow. Bunch of knuckleheads can't hear that!"

He gave off a strange noise that might be his version of laughter.

All of a sudden, the humming became louder and there seemed to be static in the air. I had the sense it was time to go but my loudmouth stranger continued to blab on. Just then my new green friend looked out the window, toward the source of the white light.

"Yeah, yeah, OK. Relax! Take another Dweeb pill, will ya? I tell you, these new space cadets they've got coming out of the academy, no sense of humor. OK partner, now remember, stay away from the control panels and, oh yeah, pay no attention to the third eye in the middle of his forehead. Exchange student and all. He gets kind of sensitive if you stare at it."

I didn't know what to make of this little munchkin, but I thought I might as well be entertained if I had to learn yet another lesson on this journey through time and space. I was getting a lot better at these surprises. I could feel my sense of adventure arising from deep within. This was *my* journey. I felt it. I was on it and I was going for it. Sometimes courage shows up in the strangest places.

The light was blinding and the humming had become a sizzle. I felt myself being raised up into the air and through the closed window. Was I now a ghost? I didn't know. I felt my body and it seemed…different. Ethereal-like.

The munchkin was floating beside me. He held my hand. I embraced the new sensation of being on a beam of light and going to another place of unknown origin.

I could hardly wait to see the thing with the third eye.

~ 27 ~

I'd seen them on sci-fi shows and this spaceship wasn't much different, except maybe a smaller version than most. Nothing surprised me anymore.

My new little green friend was sitting beside me in a bucket seat similar to my own. I felt as if I was fastened to my seat but I couldn't see any seat belts. I had the feeling that it was some type of force field strapping me in. My bug-eyed friend sat silently, staring straight ahead. His appearance was a tad repulsive back at the house but it didn't seem so bad in this shadowy light.

Directly in front of me, at about ten feet, was another high-backed chair in front of what appeared to be a small, dimly lit control panel. Because of the height of the chair, I couldn't see anyone or anything but I had the sense that something was sitting in it. Perhaps it was the tiny three-eyed monster?

"Have you ever been to sea, Petey?" I heard the munchkin say, interrupting my observations.

"Sure glad you humans are trying to clean up your act about accidentally catching our dolphin buddies. Boy, talk about a tough gig. My hats off to the dolphies from space. I mean, the great sacrifice they're making just so a few humans can get their act together. I tell you, if your people only knew what the dolphins were trying to tell ya. I'd probably be out of a job! Ha! Oh!"

I noticed his body starting to squirm in his seat.

"Having a little problem with my digestive tract. I just had lunch before I came to pick you up. I tell you, I never learn. That dematerializing and rematerializing gets me every time I do it right after nutrition break. I'm not as young as I used to be."

I couldn't tell if he was young or old. He appeared ageless.

I checked in with my nerves and was quite impressed that I wasn't in shock.

"I talked to the space cadet flying the ship. Told him I have orders from up above to take you down to Lemuria and Atlantis for some rambling ceremonies."

I could have sworn he said, "Secured ya at Atlantic City for some gambling ceremonies."

"You know about those old lost continents that sit at the bottom of the Pacific and Atlantic, that the humans annihilated a long linear time ago?"

I just shrugged.

"Never mind, we'll be there soon enough. I'm telling ya man, these underwater trips get me every time. I dig it, man. I just dig it."

I just dig it? This oughta be good.

"By the by, you can call me Lenahtal. As for the hot shot flying this craft, you can call him Space Cadet."

I could hear his high-pitched laughter echo in my head. This was good. Perhaps he didn't take his outdated version of the English language too seriously.

"Oh, do you mind if I call you by your real name or do we gotta go through some dramatic process for you to figure it out?"

"Ahhh, I guess, ahhh, it's OK to call me by my real name." I didn't have a clue what he was talking about.

"Great, 'cause I like Bleakus."

"Bleakus? Yuck!"

"It's a cool name where I come from."

"Where are you from?"

His tone became quite serious. "Don't worry, I'll take you there when everything is in alignment, dude. But right now you get yourself ready for one crackerjack of a ride into the ocean." He then lifted up his long, gangly arm, tilted his hand forward, and said, "Hit it, Bubba!"

A sudden force hit me so strong I thought I was going to bust through the back of the seat. But the acceleration was only intense for a moment and was over in the next. I could feel the craft had stopped, but where or how I didn't know.

There was complete silence. I couldn't hear anything coming from Lenahtal or Space Cadet.

I took this opportunity to catch a glimpse of the interior of this small craft and its various chambers. Its rooms were not unlike those inside a rectangular craft, and were partitioned off by walls that didn't quite reach five feet in height.

I wasn't sure what type of metal this craft was made of. It looked like pliable aluminum. But as I reached over to see if the partition to my right would budge, it moved away from me. When I moved my hand back, it went back to its original position. Maybe this wasn't made for people to touch?

There was a humming sound coming from the center of the craft, directly behind us. A partition made of the same pliable metal shielded the humming sound unit. My guess was that this was the power source.

"Kids! Give 'em a space age toy and they break it," Lenahtal said, interrupting my thoughts.

"Excuse me?" I said, waking up from observation mode.

"Well, young Buckwheat up there was trying to show off to you how much power this baby has. Got here quicker than what was right. Not cool. Just can't allow that stuff to go on. The big guy doesn't like it. All your body parts in the right place?"

I did a quick body check.

"Uh, yeah. I think."

"That's the nose you had before?"

I felt it.

"Um, yeah. Feels like it."

"Huh. Weird. Anyhooooo, lucky we didn't have to leave the galaxy. I might have had to take over the controls. I'll deal with him later."

"When you say 'big guy', do you mean God?"

"No. My commander. He's about seven feet tall. Gangly sucker."

What is it with these seven-foot creatures, I thought, remembering the golden boy who had administered to Merinda.

"Basically what I do is train young Roger Ramjets and send them off to other parts of the universe to continue their training."

He looked toward the front of the ship where Space Cadet was sitting, still with his back to us.

"The jury is still out on this one."

"Where do you get the English lingo from?" I asked.

"Hey listen, when you've been doing this as long as I have, you better occupy yourself with a hobby or put in for a section eight. I specialize in languages. I know most of the languages in this Universe."

"I'll take your word for it."

"Now, let's get up and stand over there," he said, pointing at a porthole that I had just noticed for the first time. Had it always been there?

"Take a look out there, Bleakus."

Bleakus. Yuck.

I got up, bumping my head on the ceiling. Lenahtal laughed until I gave him a look.

"I told 'em to give me the bigger model. They never listen."

I looked out the small window and, true to his prediction and much to my amazement, we were now underwater. There was a light beaming from somewhere on the outside of the spaceship that allowed me to see schools of colorful fish swimming by.

Suddenly, a dolphin swam up to the porthole. I swear it said "Hello" in my head and proceeded to tell me that they were the protectors of the sunken one's treasures. It then welcomed me back once again, saying that it was a great honor to be in my presence. It then thanked me for the "messages of another time" and swam off to meet another dolphin.

No wonder I got the feeling that everybody and everything around me knew everything and I know nothing.

Memo to self: *Every can of fish I buy better have a "No Dolphins" label on it!*

I wouldn't want to find myself eating a brother or sister from a past life and listen to them screaming at me from inside my head at the injustice of it all. Uh oh. Now I'm starting to think like Sally.

"Hey Buckwheat! You a good swimmer? Because this is where I let you off," I heard him say in my head.

I started sweating.

"No, no, I'm not, please!

"Got to. Part of the Divine Plan."

"Oh no, you can't! I'm afraid of deep water. Please!

"Gotta follow orders, bubba."

"I'll do whatever you want. Don't force me to swim! Please!!!"

I only felt safe swimming in man-made pools. Lakes and oceans scared me for some reason. When my head went underwater at the beach, I panicked.

"Bleakus! Bleakus, relax. Take a downer. I was just kidding, dude."

It took me a moment before I could breathe normally again. I wiped the sweat from my forehead.

"I tell you, I've seen more humans screwed up because of what happened when Lemuria and Atlantis sank. Relax, bro. You're not going swimming here and you didn't drown in Lemuria or Atlantis, OK?"

What a relief.

He easily disarmed my fear with his humor. I was surprised at how my body went into terror with the thought of going in the dark ocean for a swim. I had never stopped to question my uneasiness at swimming in oceans and lakes. I just never did it because I didn't like it and left it at that.

"Let me sum up what this trip is about for you, Bleakus."

What a strange thing to call someone. How had I ended up with such a weird name?

"You are at the beginning of remembering your purpose on Earth. This is essential for all star beings who are preparing to assist with Earth's ascension process. The first stop for you is Lemuria. Since in my books time is irrelevant, let's forget about the whens and focus on the whys, shall we? Space Cadet here has us in a holding pattern around the lost city. When all is aligned appropriately, we will enter the dimension of Lemuria's current reality. Not a pretty picture, compared to what it was in its heyday."

I was taken aback, as though I was being let in on a big secret. Sunken continents? Lemuria? Atlantis?

"How could this have happened?" I asked my little friend.

"The nuts and bolts of it all is that people got greedy. Kinda like the way they are on your planet right now. This was a very advanced civilization, ancient within the framework of your linear time. It was recognized intergalactically."

"Which means what?"

"Which means that this civilization, Lemuria, like Atlantis, worked openly with the Space Brothers Federation and the Ascended Masters. Lemurians were a universal civilization in every sense of the word. The great teachings were shared throughout the population. All were willing to learn, up to a point. That point began and ended with greed.

"It's like your story about Adam and Eve. A great story! I use it as an example for beings in other galaxies. Sometimes it gets lost in translation; they don't have fruit on most planets. But for the most part, it works. This guy Adam gets beamed down to Earth. He's having a good time, enjoying the nature, taking some peaceful walks, meditating, and so on. Then they beam down this babe they call Eve to give Buddy a little company. It gets hot and passionate, a few kids pop out, and life is hunky-dory. Then some snake of a character comes down and says, 'I can show you a good time if you come my way. Forget about your God. Forget about your old space buddies. I'm going to show you what *real* power is all about. I'm going to show you how to control your own destiny and planet without God.'

"Enter lust, greed, murder, abuse of power, et cetera Of course, Adam and company thoroughly enjoyed these newfound 'pleasures,' for a time. Then they began to realize that something was missing, something was not the same as it was before. And that something was their good ol' fashioned connection to the Source. The God force. You forget about that, you forget about living, Bucko.

"Adam and Eve soon forgot about God and instead, lived out their little fantasy life with opposing forces - light and dark. Duality. That's when their Garden of Eden became their Garden of Hell. Of course, it's never too late and Hell is only Heaven with the lights turned off. Eventually, they were brought back through Heaven's gate. But not before they learned the lesson of never forgetting about God! Met him once."

"Who?"

"Adam. Nice guy. Bit whacky for my taste. I think you earthlings call those types hippies. Can't fly a spaceship worth beans. Lost his license."

I couldn't stop my mouth from hanging open as he continued.

"Now *she* was right out there! Sweeeet! Anyway, the same thing happened with the dudes in Atlantis and Lemuria. I'm just amazed at how many people on your planet don't know their own history. Mind you, all your history books would have to be rewritten if the true stories were to be told. In simple terms, God and company allowed some sinister forces to play out their hand, which meant a little shake, rattle, and roll with the Earth. As expected, these dark forces overplayed their hand, and ended up shuffling Lemuria and Atlantis underwater. At least until it's time for them to resurface again. Meaning, when people are ready to appreciate and be of service to the Godmiester once again.

"It's so simple. It constantly amazes the Federation how come you humans don't see it. And you know, it's gonna be happening again. Soon. Big shift. That's why the major debriefing with some of the people of your planet and others. A few of your nations are going to go under and a few more of these lost lands, like Atlantis and Lemuria, are going to reappear, after a little zap from the big guys in the head office. Gotta change the structure of the planet so that it can breathe again. Now these new nations are going to include dudes like us, so that we won't have to fly around pretending we don't exist when we visit this planet. I used to take that stuff personally until I began to see where it was coming from. Now I just laugh it off. Always look at the source."

I stood at the porthole looking out as he continued his ramblings. The stories seemed unusually familiar, but I couldn't place them. Perhaps they were my grandmother's bedtime stories from long ago? I didn't know. They were coming from a much different-looking storyteller than

Grandma. I was in a daze and lost in thought as I looked at the dark water, occasionally getting the odd doubletake from fish swimming by.

"Why am I here? What's all this about?"

"Ah, Bleakus." Ugh. I didn't know if I could ever get used to the name Bleakus. It reminded me of science class, "Pass the bleakus, I mean bleaker, please.'

"You are here to get reacquainted with some of the Elders who have remained close by, in preparation for the rising of Atlantis and part of Lemuria."

"What do you mean the Elders? People actually live down here?"

"You are here, my friend, to become reacquainted with the process related to the reactivation of Lemuria and Atlantis. There are certain beings from your planet and others that are responsible to help reactivate both Atlantis and Lemuria. Ya think you're up for it, Buckwheat?" He echoed in my head like a high-pitched chirp.

Looking into my four-foot friend's bug eyes, I was perplexed and fascinated with everything that was being said and with everything that was going on. It felt as though a very important task was at hand and I was supposed to be a part of it. It gave me a strong sense of purpose.

Lenahtal's eyes revealed no physical indication of any outward emotion. His pear-shaped head and four foot green leathery beer belly body had no facial features except for a small slit for lips and two holes where the nose would be located on most heads. This would get attention at a bar, albeit not the kind I would want to hang out in.

I could feel him looking deep into me. I could feel strange movements around my intestines, as if a doctor was examining me. What was going on?

"Got to stay away from that milk chocolate - it will be the death of you, my friend. Try pure cacao or at least organic dark chocolate. White sugar kills!" I heard his childlike laughter bubbling up inside my head.

I thought these things weren't supposed to have emotions and were bald and ugly. OK, Lenahtal was definitely bald and ugly, but he had a sense of humor that compensated for his looks.

I felt sudden warmth entering my body; somehow I knew it was coming from Lenahtal. Soon, I could see a circular yellow glow at the centre of his large, protruding forehead. Then it turned to indigo. I looked over at Space Cadet to see if there was any reaction from him, if this was at all "normal."

Space Cadet was still hiding in his high-backed bucket seat. I could just catch a glimpse of silver boots just barely sticking out from the base of the seat. The boots looked like they would fit a ten-year-old. I tried to move closer to get a better look and maybe communicate with him like I could with Lenahtal, but my body was frozen. I couldn't move from my spot.

"Everything's OK, dude. He's still in training. He's not allowed to communicate with beings from other planets yet. That is a privilege that has to be earned. There are a few Dweeb initiations that have to take place before he is allowed to open up with the communication skills."

I heard all this from my little friend as he floated in front of my face, so that we were eye to eye. A ray of indigo light shot from the middle of his forehead to the middle of mine. The tingly, surging, burning energy in my body kept increasing in intensity.

"Everything is OK, Buck-germ. We're just going for a little ride without the saucer," said Lenahtal, in a sleep-inducing voice that was making me feel drowsy.

Soon there was a sizzling sound as I felt us lifting in the air. All I could see was white. My physical body had no definition, nor did his for that matter. All I knew was that we were in motion.

I wondered if I would ever get used to this sort of thing. I wondered if I was still alive. Then I heard Lenahtal whisper softly, "It's time to meet the Ascended Masters."

I wondered if it was still possible to get nervous.

~ 28 ~

I felt us floating to a stop in total blackness. My friend's attention was elsewhere. I think he was trying to communicate something to someone else. Judging by the moistness and the smell of the cool ocean air, we seemed to be in a darkened cavern. I could see absolutely nothing.

"OK, I just spoke to him. We'll have to wait in the waiting room until he's finished meeting with the Federation dudes," I heard Lenahtal say to me, as we both floated in complete darkness.

Before I could have another thought, we were in a room filled with blinding, brightly colored light. We floated to the ground. It took a moment for my eyes to adjust. I quickly scanned my new surroundings and found myself in a cave of unusual richness. It was filled with boxes of priceless jewels.

At the opposite end, there was only one opening and that led to total blackness.

The light coming from the crystal wands sticking out of the walls fascinated me. What was their power source? I looked down at my feet and noticed that I was standing on a white marble floor covered in markings and drawings from another era.

I turned to see where Lenahtal was and found him sitting on a huge pile of gold coins and bars. Beside him was another huge pile of diamonds, rubies, and other precious jewels. There were also some stones that I had never seen before. It was an incredible high to stand in the midst of such splendor

– jewels, artifacts, statues, ornaments, all glistening for attention.

However, I was surprised the room felt as though no one had ever taken care of it or put anything in order.

"I was going to take you to the games room but I thought this would be more impressive for someone from your type of society. Pretty nifty sight, eh?"

"Uh, yeah, I think you could use the word 'nifty' in this case."

"Greed is such a big thing with Earth right now. Not that I'm calling you greedy. You did stop doing the car campaigns. That bought you some brownie points!"

"How did you-"

"No secrets from me, Bucko! Right now you're pretty much a byproduct of your society."

My eyes were spinning around the room, looking at all the priceless objects. Absolutely stunning.

"What is all this?"

He got up and started to float around the room.

"See this one? This is to help heal the immune system. He pointed to another mixed colored rock, "And this one is to help the alchemist in each of us produce enough energy for our personal needs and purposes for a lifetime. No more paying for electricity for you guys."

He stopped floating.

"About this one, well, well, ahh, actually I'm not really allowed to go into much detail because the last time you guys understood this one, you blew yourselves up. The greed thing. Nothing personal."

"I can assure you, Lenahtal, I have no desire to blow myself up or anyone else for that matter. I like life too much."

"Yo! Dude! I know you're hip. Otherwise, I wouldn't have been allowed to bring you into this room in a temple of the lost continent of Lemuria. Naw, you're one of alchemists for the future rising of Atlantis. Actually, you already exist there as an alchemist."

"What?"

"Never mind. We'll have to get into that time thing again and I know the kind of problems you're having trying to understand that one. Perhaps another linear time," he chuckled.

He was right. I didn't want to get into the time thing again, even if I was already living in the future.

"See this?" he said, holding up between his long green fingers what appeared to be a small shiny clear red ruby.

"Just one of these babies could fly one of your tin cans into space, just one. But would your four-eyed scientific fly boys listen to us? They think they've got all the answers. I can't believe some of your folks who think that they need to struggle for years for the Truth to be realized. And now it's too late. Your linear time's up."

"What do you mean too late?"

"Basically, they've gone past the point of no return with their greed. This room of jewels is waiting for star beings like you to remember and reactivate your original purposes for being on Earth. Then and only then will these mysteries be released."

I stood there looking at perhaps all of the answers for mankind's disease, lying before me.

"Excuse me for being naive, but this seems so unfair. Why don't these Masters release these healing jewels and mystery remedies to those dying on Earth now?"

For some reason this made me angry. It always had. If there is a God, then why are so many people allowed to suffer, especially when the remedies lay below in a sunken continent.

"Yo Bucko! Back off. I'm not the one in charge. The old man up there calls the shots."

"The old man, as in God?"

"No, Dweeb. I mean old man, as in the old man in the cavern upstairs with the long white beard. Now just cool your jets, bro. I can assure you that no great injustice is being done here. The old man will be here in a bit, so just relax. Oh and, uh, he may appear a tad, uh, dramatic to you. Just go with it. That's the way he likes to be seen."

Here I was, in one of many rooms filled with what could be remedies for many of the mysterious ailments on our planet, and there was nothing I could do about it.

"Yo! Buck-germ! I said don't take it personally. It's just the way it is. For now. Things are going to change, you'll see. Your people are beginning to believe in themselves again, starting to trust one another, finding God within and all that. In a matter of space and time you'll be living on one hunky-dory planet. Honest! Trust me."

"And when will all this happen, Lenahtal?"

Thinking of Merinda, Sally, and whoever else I'd asked. None of them ever seemed to have an exact time for when things would happen. Or should I say an exact *linear* time.

"On one level, it has already occurred and aspects of Self are now living in that ideal reality. On another level, the mass consciousness hasn't made a decision, hasn't chosen its own path. It's inevitable that Mother Earth will stretch and expand in order to get rid of the toxic elements that don't serve her well-being. As for what's going to happen to your people, that's another story. The jury's still out on that one and you people are your own jurors."

I was grasping hard at the reality of what he was telling me.

"Let me get this straight. The planet is going to experience some major catastrophes, or major physical shiftings, with or without our help?"

"To a point, Buckeye. The planet is going to experience some major shifts, all right, but if you people work at it together, you can all help ease the pain."

"How?" I asked, with a growing concern for the planet I lived on. Maybe after this retreat I could bring back some message to the world to help solve this one.

"It's your planet, you figure it out," he answered, sounding almost humorous. Almost.

"What did you mean when you said we are the jurors of our own fate?"

"Let's say, as of this moment, in your linear time, that you decide that you can make a difference. Then you go out and try to connect with someone else who thinks that they can make a difference and so on. Soon, you will be working with a lot of people who think that they can make a difference. Collectively, you will make the difference. This is what you need to pass on to your people. The light workers need to all come together *now* and work with each other in the ascension process into the Fourth Dimension. It's gonna happen, dude. Believe me, it's gonna happen. So you can either go for the smooth, aware transition version or you can go for the rough, unaware version. If I were you, Bucko, I'd go for the smooth one. Because that rough one will knock your teeth into the middle of next week. Linear style, of course!"

"You're saying that if enough people get together they can make the difference with the healing of this planet?"

"You got it, Pontiac! A widespread shift in consciousness for the healing of self and planet is what's needed to make a conscious entrance into the Fourth Dimension. You need to be with as many like-minded people as possible in order to spread the awareness of what is really going on with your planet. Just don't get fanatical about it, that's *soooo uncool.* Maintain a silent confidence about your*self* as you gather up the light workers. Feel good about who you are and what you're about. Again, be *cool* about it. Don't start preaching, don't become some whacky guru. G-U-R-U. Gee! You are you! It's about self-realization, bubba, not following some clown who thinks he has all the answers. Ya gotta run from those ones!

"Don't worry, when you put the vibe out there, you'll find your peeps and hook into the right groove. Oh, and one other thing, you've got a bunch of light workers coming from different angles, working for the same cause. Don't pass judgment on how someone sees God. God is looking through the eyes of everyone."

I couldn't stop myself from blurting out that one question that had been with me all weekend,

"Lenahtal, what the heck is God?"

"Ouch! Whoa doggy!!" Lenahtal did a sudden full somersault in mid-air.

He looked at me with bewilderment. Well, as much as an alien with insect eyes could look bewildered, and floated upside down. "Dude, you didn't hear that ring?"

"No. I didn't hear anything." Was he just avoiding the big question?

"Dagnabbit, the big guy gets me every time. His call signal brings new meaning to 'ring my chimes.'"

"What are you talking about?" I was getting dizzy watching him bouncing off the cavern walls.

"I'm talking about the big guy. He's ready to see you now."

So much for the big question. At least for now.

"OK then, this should be interesting."

"Oh yeah, this will be. And you'll be on your own for this one. We'll meet back at the ship. Just think of me and you'll be able to get yourself back on the ship. Piece of cake. Ciao, babe."

"Wait! Wait! How come you're not coming with me?!" No way I wanted to be alone.

He came to a floating stop. "Um, I think I might owe the big guy from a poker game we played eons ago."

"Poker?" Martians played poker?

"Naw, I'm just pulling your leg. Light workers like me don't usually meet with the Masters. Only when it's necessary, like for a briefing when someone of your vibration comes to meet them. They just give me the info: Tell me what to do, what to say, and where to take you. Dude, did you forget that you're an important leader of the new world to come?"

I just looked at him.

"Ohhh maaan, Bucko! When they erased your memory they did a thorough job, huh?"

I was speechless.

"Hello? Hello? Earth to Bleakus!"

I managed to blink to let him know I was still there.

"OK, forget the leader thing for now. Here's the scoop, poop. Before you travel, imagine bringing in the violet light to fill your body. Then imagine surrounding yourself with white light and ask the Almighty Creative Force for protection."

"Uh, why?" I asked. It seemed redundant after the amount of traveling I'd gone through.

"It will protect you from the subtler dark forces who try to control virginal light forces like yourself. Ultimately, they can't, well, if you don't let them. Anyway, who needs indigestion and a bad trip, know what I'm saying?"

I was beginning to like this guy, Lenahtal. I wondered if he might be androgynous? I wondered if he had sex?

Lenahtal floated in front of me. "OK, OK. Enough mind chatter. In answer to your rude questions, none of your beeswax! Do I ask you about your sex life?"

"Uh, no. I'm guessing you don't need to. I was just curious if-"

"Never mind! Let's get you up there before the big guy rings my bell again. By the way, that Sally of yours? A *babe!*

How did he know about Sally?

"Quiet! Quick! He's about to ring the bell again. Close your eyes."

I closed them.

"Now inhale the violet light."

I did.

"Now surround yourself with white light and ask the Almighty Creative Force for protection."

I did and within moments I felt very lightheaded.

"Now touch your nose with your right forefinger and try to walk a straight line."

I tried and tripped over a bar of gold.

"Ha! Caught ya! Simon didn't say," he chuckled.

I opened my eyes and stared at this four-foot prankster.

"Hey, I'd have a boring job if I didn't have a little fun now and again," he said, laughing inside of my head.

Then his voice took on a serious tone.

"Now hurry, he's waiting. Same procedure as before but this time, as you begin to feel lightheaded, say 'Master Amos' three times."

I repeated the procedure. The lightheaded feeling returned.

"Repeat the name three times!"

I did as I was told and repeated 'Master Amos' three times.

I didn't know what was up for me next but with each stage of this journey, I felt more and more confident. Sally would be proud of me now!

"Smell ya later, dude face!" was the last thing I heard Lenahtal say as I felt myself move into the darkness of time, merge into formless matter, and experience a peaceful lightness of being.

Yeah, my lingo was changing.

~ 29 ~

I felt so much love when I opened my eyes. If home was indeed in the heart, I finally knew what it was like to be at home. I felt like I was in a chamber of peace. When everything came into focus, I was facing a wall of solid rock. I may have felt good on the inside but the outside didn't look anything like the last place. I thought I was supposed to end up in front of this Master Amos guy?

"That was only because you didn't trust our humorous light worker fully. The direction is more precise when there is *full* trust, my son."

I listened intently as this deep, rich voice resounded in my mind. My body wasn't able to turn around. I was frozen in the very spot I stood, but a warm energy was embracing me.

"Now you may turn around, my son," I heard the voice say, as I felt the loving embrace release me.

I turned around and there was Master Amos. He was seven feet tall, with long white hair and a beard to match. Yup. Just like in the movies. I stood there in awe. In no way did I feel threatened. If anything, I felt the opposite. There was no word to describe the love that came from a being like Master Amos. Standing before me in his white flowing robe with attached violet hood, he appeared ageless. He radiated youthfulness.

"Our little friend Lenahtal has quite the sense of humor. He is also a Master in disguise. One day, he too will learn to trust who he really is and express it accordingly. In the meantime, we let him share his humor and tell his jokes.

There is perfection in everything. Do you know that you too are a Master, my son?"

I was barely listening. His powerful presence was mesmerizing.

"Ahh, me? Ahh, no, no. What's that?"

"Masters are entities who are in complete alignment with their multidimensional nature. They must be if they are to impart their wisdom to others. The great Masters, including your future Self, have chosen you, my son, to remember your being, your essence, your entire nature. Now. In its entirety. Do you remember any of this?" As if he didn't already know the answer.

"N-n-not evvvv-en the sligh-test," I answered, with all sincerity.

"This is why you are here. For your journey of remembrance is upon you. Come, follow me."

He turned and we left the barren cave room, and entered a hallway of treasures.

"Who does your dusting?" I asked, in my feeble attempt to bring some light to the situation. No reply. Nothing was said as we continued down this dimly lit hallway. I was astonished to see so many valuable jewels lying around in the unattended hallway. Must be serious camera security in these caverns.

"Where are we going?" This seemed like a reasonable question.

Not a word. He maintained his graceful stride ahead of me. It wouldn't come as any great surprise if he were really floating along that corridor.

"Are these healing jewels as well?"

Still no answer. My guess was that my little conversational tidbits were of low priority.

"Your stay in Lemuria will be a brief one. However, we felt it was important that you meet your fellow light workers who will assist in the raising of our sister continent, Atlantis.

From now on, you will be in complete contact with me and the other Masters in everything that you do," he said, without even turning back to see if I was still there.

I'm sure he was floating. It's no wonder these folks hardly eat; they don't have to move a muscle to get anywhere.

He pointed to his right. "This is the chamber where all the Masters who have chosen to help in the raising of Atlantis and Lemuria will meet. You will be a part of special meetings about both here and Atlantis."

I had the feeling that this was going to be a pressure cooker type of job.

"Ah, excuse me, are you saying that I chose to be here and help out with the raising of these two civilizations that I've never heard of? Why? What's the connection?" Why would I want to be having meetings in damp caves? My idea of roughing it was bad room service at a five-star hotel.

Master Amos stopped in front of the doorway and looked down at me. "You are one of the reasons that both Atlantis and Lemuria sank."

If a disembodied human could gulp, I just did.

"Simply put, you were in charge of the crystal division that later became infiltrated by the dark forces. You gave into them. They told you they wanted to bring the continents to a higher vibration, but their real motive was to use the crystals to overpower the light force. Which they almost did, until the Light Brotherhood Federation ruled that it was best to put this phase of the experiment to rest. At least until mankind could handle power in unison with the Source."

I was part of the demise of these underwater continents called Atlantis and Lemuria? That was ridiculous. How could plain ol' "I feel like a brewskie" me, with only a slight ego problem, be responsible for a disaster of such massive proportions?

"My dear son, it's not that you were a willing participant. You soon realized what they were really up to. It's when you tried to stop them that they annihilated your molecular structure for what they thought would be an eternity. What they didn't realize, because of their obsession with darkness, was that God does oversee all. Your molecular structure was reorganized and returned to your home planet for a long rest period before you were sent back to Earth to prepare and assist in recovering these lost continents.

"Now, my son, I'm very pleased to be able to say that the alignment of the stars and Spirit is such that both you and the lost continent of Atlantis are ready for a major shift. Your focus will be on Atlantis, others will focus on Lemuria, and together all shall rise to be One."

He was beginning to scare me, although I was still fascinated by his story. Why would he lie to me? What would he gain? If he were a dark force, then my intuition was mud. This person, or whatever he was, exuded love and wisdom. Surely he was on the up and up. I couldn't retain much of what he was saying and yet there was that familiar ring of truth. It said, 'Hello, remember me?' in a deep part of my soul.

"We must proceed," he gently bellowed.

We walked through the wooden doorway into yet another room filled with bright, sparkling artifacts of this lost culture. I was blinded as I walked through the doorway, but as my eyes adjusted, I saw none other than my sweetheart Sally, standing there in a golden robe laced with white. She looked like an angel. Wait a minute, *She was an angel*! She was hovering above the marble and gold patterned floor. Her hair was a pure light blonde and her piercing blue eyes penetrated me like no others could.

Sally gracefully floated over to me and telepathically said, "I love you."

My heart melted, as I knew it was coming from the depths of her soul, touching the depths of mine.

"I love you too," I heard myself say to her for the first *soulful* time.

She just hovered in front of me, as we transmitted nothing but love energy back and forth. Had I not been standing beside a seven foot Master, having been brought here by spaceship - underwater no less - with a four-foot Martian munchkin as a tour guide, I would probably be having a difficult time accepting Sally as a beautiful angel, floating in front of me. But I wasn't. I was in love and that's all that mattered.

"Sally was part of the collective soul from which you both emerged at the beginning of Creation, in order to serve mankind. You are both very blessed children of God. The God force has rewarded your commitment to Truth by allowing you to share your sense of purpose with one another. Are you now ready to serve, Peter?"

I didn't want to take my eyes off of my heavenly angel.

I finally turned to Master Amos and responded with love in my heart, "Yes, Master Amos, I'm ready to serve." I said it wholeheartedly. I either was being severely manipulated or I felt a greater sense of commitment than I had ever known in this lifetime.

Master Amos bowed toward me as I instinctively did toward him. I then turned back to my angel, Sally, feeling all the love between us become even more boundless, if that was possible. It was then that I became aware of other presences in this treasure-filled cavern.

Over Sally's shoulder floated two dancing angels. One was Bobby and the other was Alice. I couldn't help laughing at the sight of these two dancing together in their angelic joyfulness. I was happy to see them but their huge white wings took me aback. Had I not experienced all that I had experienced, I'm sure I would be in *fear* mode as opposed to *love* mode. If this was a test, I must have been passing with flying colors because everything was beginning to *feel* OK. I was more fascinated than anything else.

I had always thought angels were a myth, something for artists to paint. I guess I was wrong. But if Sally was an angel, why didn't she have any wings? Sally could see my confusion, obviously knowing my every thought. After all, as I was now beginning to realize, we were part of the same soul group.

"Some of us choose to wear wings and some of us choose not to. I chose to meet you in this way. I thought it would be a lot easier for you to handle."

"Ya think?" We both laughed.

Of course she was right. Seeing your mate flying around the room wearing huge white wings on her back would throw anybody off, I'm sure.

"Welcome to the memory chamber," said Bobby and Alice in unison. It was a strange sight to see these two together – one tall and wide and the other short and petite. Yet, in their flowing white robes and huge expansive wings, they looked perfect together. Actually, it was more of a feeling than a visual impression.

The guys would never believe this even after *20* beers.

I turned to Sally as she gave me her warm and loving smile. She then turned and floated over to where Bobby and Alice were hovering. I wanted to join them but I felt myself being pulled backwards out of the room.

"It's time to continue your remembrance journey," Master Amos said.

I didn't want to leave Sally.

"It's OK, Peter. We are together forever in the Light of God. Just think of me and I'll be there."

With that, she sent me a warm surge of energy that relaxed my body. How these people did this was beyond me.

I began to calm down. Although I still didn't feel comfortable being apart from what I had spent so long to find, my soul mate. I can't believe that word came from me.

The girls at work always talked about soul mates. I used to think it was just an excuse to dump one guy and take up with another.

"I have to leave you. I've found my soul mate." "Yeah right, lady, you just got bored." Maybe they hadn't gotten bored. Maybe they had found someone special in their lives. Maybe there was someone out there who was willing to work side by side with another for the purpose of fulfilling their journeys and serving this thing called God.

"What Sally said applies to me. Think of me and I will be there. Call on me for purpose and strength and I will help you remember," Master Amos said in a half-whisper, as he escorted me out of the room, leaving me to catch a glimpse of Sally and the others.

What a sight. Three Angels - two with wings, one without - floating around a room full of lost treasures, ancient remedies, and secret scrolls. Another Elder, similar to Master Amos but wearing a long blue robe, appeared. The angels hovered before him as he held up a precious jewel of some sort and began to explain its purpose to them.

I could see how greed and lust might kick in here for the average man who wasn't a Master of his Self.

"When do we get access to these lost jewels and secret remedies?" I asked, as we continued down the long hallway, lit only by the glowing crystal wands protruding from the walls. I was curious as to what purpose they were going to serve in the new world.

"You will know. You will be told when it is right." With these words, he stopped gliding down the hallway and turned toward me. For a seven-foot ghost, he was beautiful in his radiance and grace, although I got a sore neck looking up to him.

"I am honored that you have chosen to awaken at this time. For you see, my son, some do not choose to awaken, but remain asleep in the darkness of all time. It pleases everyone when one of the chosen decide to play out their destiny.

I was getting a lot of credit for *choosing* to do this – whatever it was. I don't know when I made this decision but I decided to accept it; it was making me feel good.

"Now my son, it is time for you to transfer back to the ship. You will find it the same way you found me – by closing your eyes, bringing in the violet light, and surrounding yourself with the white, asking for protection. Focus on Lenahtal and say his name three times. More of our purpose together will be revealed as you continue down your path. I am most grateful it was time for us to meet again. But for now, the reason I wanted to see you face to face was to apologize to you.

"Why!?"

"You see, my son, I was the dark force that led you astray. I'm very sorry, my friend. Very sorry." His voice tapered off as he bowed his head.

Hearing that shocking bit of news, a little explosion of remembrance went off in my head. This was the man who had always come to me in one of my many recurring dreams, pleading, "Please forgive me. Please forgive me. I am truly sorry for what I have done."

I recognized his eyes. I would always wake up and try to think of who I knew that had done something wrong to me? In the Ad game, one has a lot of enemies and you tend to remember them. So this one was always a mystery. But this was the man. These were his eyes. Finally, a missing piece to another lifelong puzzle.

I found myself saying, "And now the time of forgiveness is upon us all. I thank you, my friend, for having the courage to apologize and be here also."

My vocabulary was changing, which made me a bit nervous. The thought of sounding like Sally scared me.

Although maybe it wasn't so bad. My confidence was reaching an all time high, hanging with these ghosts, angels, and alien types. Maybe there was something to all of this.

We gave each other a warm, loving embrace and felt our energies meld together. I pulled away, looking into his deep, penetrating blue eyes.

"You have been down here all this time?" I asked. This had to be a very lonely job.

"Yes. In the beginning, they weren't too happy with what I had done and I was shattered into many particles across the galaxies, until every molecule of my soul understood what I had done and had asked for forgiveness. Slowly, my soul connection to the Source was fully reawakened. The Council asked me what I thought would be a fair compensation to the God force for my previous deeds. I said I would like to assist in the ascension of Atlantis and Lemuria. That is why I spend my time between here and Atlantis, meeting with other Masters like you. Atlantis is especially critical since it will be the first of the two continents that will rise as a result of the planetary shifting. I've waited so long for this momentous occasion. This moment of perfect alignment. I am truly happy." His voice then tapered off, perhaps overcome with emotion, if that was possible.

A Master who was humble? Maybe.

For some reason, I felt like I was his equal; no greater, no less, but the same.

"I understand that look, my son. It is true, we are all equal in the eyes of God. God looks through us all. We are all God. My friend, we'll have other moments to share. Right now, it is imperative that you get aboard Lenahtal's ship to continue your journey of remembrance. God bless you, my son. Remember what Lenahtal told you to do to protect yourself," he said, as he rubbed his thumb on the middle of my forehead, mumbling something in a foreign language.

"Ahh, thank you, and God bless you too, my friend," I said, awkwardly, not used to the New Age language that I was now muttering on a regular basis.

I closed my eyes and began the process of inhaling violet light, surrounding myself with white light and asking the Almighty Creative Force for protection. Then, I focused on my space Buddy, Lenahtal, and repeated his name three times. Just before the third Lenahtal, as I began my disappearing act, I could hear Master Amos' parting words, "And tell that Lenahtal that he owes me from the poker game."

I had to laugh at the thought of these spirit guys being high rollers.

After the third mention of Lenahtal's name, into the darkness I went.

~ 30 ~

"What's shakin' bacon? Glad to have you back, Jack. How's your meter, Peter?" Yes, of course I made it back to the spaceship. No one on Earth talks like that.

"Ready for another blast of the past?" said Lenahtal.

I looked around the ship and everything was the same. Nothing had changed. For some reason, I was expecting something different. I still couldn't see the three-eyed wonder.

"Where to now, chief?" I said, becoming more enthusiastic about my journey. Who cared if this was real? I was enjoying myself.

"We're going to take you to a place called Atlantis. Ever hear of it?"

"Of course," I said, having recently become hip to my underwater continents.

"It's no wonder. You blew that place up too."

What kind of person was I in the past, I wondered?

"I'm kidding. Just having a bit of fun with ya." He began flying around the room, not unlike a little kid.

"I'm surprised you've lasted this long on the job," I said, a little annoyed at his idea of fun.

"Chill, bud. Sit in your chair, bear, and Space Cadet will take us there with care," he said, floating in front of the Space Cadet, who still remained in that high-backed chair with his back to me. I was just itching to peek.

As soon as I sat down, that same force field locked me in. Lenahtal floated back into his seat and said to the three-eyed monster, "OK Roger Ramjet, don't play hero. Just get us there safely."

Then he turned to me. "Nothing worse than crashing underwater. You think changing a flat in a thunderstorm is bad news."

It only took a nanosecond to get us to our next point of destination.

We maintained a holding pattern underwater, somewhere around Atlantis, I presumed. As I looked down at my physical body, I noticed that there was something different about it. Was it ethereal? I didn't know. There was a physical form and shape, but when I went to touch my hand or any other part of my body, it felt insubstantial. Maybe I was an apparition.

I looked over at Lenahtal and, being able to read my mind, he said, "For the kind of tripping you're doing, we couldn't take your physical body. Well, we could, but then there is all that preparation and going in and out of chambers. Blue pills, pink pills, yellow pills. One time I got it mixed up and the guy's eyeball was hanging off his butt. Traveling through space is tricky. A real pain in the posterior. So I got the big guy to give me the OK to take your astral body and leave your physical body at the retreat. I'm getting too old for that other stuff. Anyhoo, it's all a formality. It kind of feels like your physical body but it's not. Cool, huh?"

"Is this your astral body as well?" I asked.

"Yes and no. Yes, in the sense that I have an astral body and I'm here with it. No, in the sense that what I left back there at the retreat is merely an illusion, a hologram of who I am. Its purpose is to serve as a warning if anyone or anything tries to penetrate the space in and around your physical body. Two things – you don't mess with the dark forces and you don't mess with God. Anything in between is up for grabs. We have to make our choices accordingly. In your case, you're kinda thick-headed about remembering what's going on, so we gotta protect you from those who think they can enter your body and take over. Strictly a precaution. Nothing to freak out about. That aspect of me that's serving as your protector is kinda my protector too. Anything happens to you and the big guy kicks my butt! Big time!"

"You really fear this big guy, don't you?"

"Naw, not really. It's just that he wants to promote me but I'm not ready yet."

"How come?" I asked. This was the first time I could feel him letting his guard down.

"Yo, yo, back off, Buckwheat. Just cuz you're rubbin' shoulders with the big wigs doesn't mean you got the right to analyze the alien."

I figured I'd better quit while I was ahead.

He sat up straight in his chair.

"OK now, back to business. There was a time when Atlantis and Lemuria were the strongest nations on this planet. Lemuria was older and more traditional, whereas Atlantis was more 'New Age,' you might say. More adventurous. More progressive. Though no greater or less than Lemuria. They both connected with one another and with other planets. The dudes from outer space would quite often visit these places until greed did its dirty work and Atlantis and Lemuria became history. A blanket of forgetfulness covered the Earth, except for a few wise ones, who escaped total annihilation and went to form new nations in other parts of the planet, including deep down below Earth's surface.

"The how's and why's vary with every old guy you talk to, but when you start tapping into the Akashic records, you'll be able to figure it out for yourself."

"The Akashic records? What are they?" I took pride in my knowledge of music but had never heard of these albums.

Lenahtal gave me a look of disbelief, as much as is possible from a bug-eyed Martian.

"I really wish you could remember things faster. All this explaining makes my job harder. OK, OK. Sorry, I know you've been asleep for a while. Akashic records are the recordings of moments in time since the beginning of Creation. Everyone has the ability to tap into the Akashic records, it just takes time and patience. Which it appears mankind doesn't have a whole lot of. You want to learn about events of the past, present, and future, this is the energy field you tap into."

"How do you 'tap into' the Akashic records?"

"It's different for everyone. I sit still and get quiet. In my mind's eye, I travel down a long dark hallway. When I get to the end of it, I meet up with an old grey-haired dude. I give him the magic password and I'm in. The password is different for everyone. Some have numbers, some have sound vibrations and some use colors. You work that out with the grey-haired dude if that's how you want to do it. When you get inside, it's like one of your libraries on Earth. Grab the book of time that you're looking for and presto! You're a psychic and you got yourself a one nine hundred line. That's the way I do it. You gotta figure out what works for you. Like I said before, it takes time, patience, and a dash of belief."

I just looked at him, wondering if I would ever reach the stage where I would know what could happen in the future or could have happened in the past.

"Just remember, Buck-germ, it all comes down to choice. A present choice could affect a past or future choice. That's why it's crucial to tap into your multidimensional being. The more you know about Self, the better choices you'll make all around."

"Whoa, you're losing me." This idea of choice made my head spin.

"Never mind. 'Cause for now, ya got me to trip you to the light fantastic. Not a bad deal, considering you coulda gotten a boring dude who likes to shove long pointy needles in your orifices to take samples and get you to do tricks for them. I say give human beings some credit. They'll respond if you ask them nicely. OK, I see your eyes glazing over with my yakking. Stay focused!"

He took a long look at me, without speaking.

"You know, you're doing pretty good for someone who's been hanging around Earth all this time. Most people are so scared they just sit there and I end up playing my portable video game. I usually don't get to talk this much."

Hard to believe. Oops, I guess he heard that.

"Yeah, yeah, think what you want but it's true. Now where was I?"

I just looked at this chatterbox and started to laugh. My only wish was that everyone would get to ride with this guy. Because if you didn't believe what he was saying, at least you're being entertained.

"You were talking about Atlantis and Lemuria."

"Oh, yeah, Atlantis and Lemuria. What about them?"

"You were giving me a little history lesson about them," I responded, laughing at his absent-mindedness.

"Oh yeah, right. I get a bit spacey sometimes when I travel a lot. OK, so Lemuria was the first to go, and this is where it gets interesting for you and makes me feel honored. You were the first one who signaled Atlantis about what was about to happen in Lemuria. You were able to tell Atlantis who was working with the dark forces and why.

"Unfortunately, that was also your demise. The dark forces in Lemuria heard about this and connected with the dark forces in Atlantis to set you up. They somehow managed to talk you into coming to Atlantis by pretending they were Atlantean High Priests who needed to meet with you to dispel the dark forces and their infiltration of Atlantis.

"Ya see, Bucko, in those days a lot of the transportation was done through a process called teleportation. Meaning, they had this contraption in Lemuria and Atlantis that would disassemble your molecular structure as someone punched in your destination and then reassemble it upon arrival at that destination. In your case, they punched in your destination and in mid-flight to Atlantis, the dark forces cancelled it. Not the nicest way to wake up in the morning, but hey, the dark forces ain't nice. It wasn't long afterwards that the dark forces were allowed to blow up most of Lemuria, using some crystal contraption, collapsing some of the underground volcanic chambers, and burying it below the ocean floor. In time, a similar thing was allowed to happen to Atlantis."

"Why would they be *allowed* to destroy these continents?"

"Good question. I think the board of directors upstairs weren't too happy with all the greed and obsession with duality that was happening on these continents before all of this went down, and decided to let the dark forces go ahead with it. I guess they were hoping that it would teach mankind a big lesson, thereby furthering mankind's evolution. From what I can see, it didn't work.

"Now the select few survivors that remained, thanks to your warnings and a few from the Council of Twelve above, were sent to other parts of the planet to continue the evolution of mankind. Some were even sent down below to protect the sunken treasures until it was time for them to rise again."

"Master Amos said that Atlantis and Lemuria were going to rise again."

"Yep, could be. That's the theory."

"Master Amos said I was going to help with the rising of Atlantis. Any idea when this is all supposed to happen?"

"Don't know any timeline. Time's not my thing. And nothing's ever for sure anyway. It's a free will and choice thing too. The great ones upstairs are still waiting to see what happens with the mass consciousness and the collective choices humans make about their future. Think of yourself as on standby. Mind you, if Master Amos said it was a sure thing-"

"That's what it sounded like."

"Cool."

"Interesting parallel to what happened then and what is going on now," I said.

"I tell you, partner, if your history books had a sliver of truth in them as to what has really been happening on Earth, you folks wouldn't be putting yourself in the same situation as you are now. I guarantee it!"

My curiosity wouldn't let go of the story. "So what happened to those people who survived? How could they possibly live if the destruction was so bad?"

I could tell Lenahtal was enjoying playing teacher. I have to admit that he was good at whatever he was supposed to be doing with me. His casual manner made me feel that no question was too trivial or too stupid.

"Oh, they survived all right. Some began new civilizations around various parts of the planet. A place called Egypt being one of them. The people of Atlantis had more warning than the Lemurians. Some went into underwater caverns around the planet to form subterranean cultures that were far enough away from the collapsing of Atlantis and Lemuria that they weren't affected. Some started civilizations in mountains, that still exist today."

"Really? Where?"

"Sorry, Bucko, that's on a need to know basis, to cop a phrase of yours. But if you're ever in Northern California, check out a B&B at the bottom of Mount Shasta. It's really a doorway to what I call The Tall Ones' world. They're leftovers from Lemuria. Oh, and check out the greasy spoon down the street - *awesome coffee!*"

"So why am I here with you, hovering around this so called Atlantis?"

"Oh man, you're gonna dig this. Your name went down as a legend in these people's minds because you helped save so many lives just by your warnings. As soon as some of the people picked up on what you were communicating telepathically, they left for the other lands, always remembering the name Bleakus. The hero that tried to save Lemuria and Atlantis. Now, as part of your awakening initiation, the people who are looking after Atlantis and Lemuria underwater would like to have a commemorative service to honour you and welcome you back. Part of your remembrance package, you might say. Up for it?"

I was confused. Not only had I helped destroy continents, I tried to save them? And now they wanted to honor me?

"Of course, I guess. Why not?"

"That's the spirit. Ooooh, this is going to be so exciting. You see, for some reason, they want me to go to the ceremonies with you."

In saying that, he flew off his chair and started doing loops in mid-air. I'm sure this sort of thing is not the norm for these space guys.

"This is big time hoity-toity. I've never seen one of these ceremonies before. They are so rare."

"I'm glad I can make your day."

"Don't say 'day.' You don't want to think in terms of days anymore," he said, coming to a halt in mid-air, by the tiny window.

"I'll work on it."

I gracefully and effortlessly glided over to him. I was beginning to realize that I didn't need to walk. By a mere thought, I could be at my destination. I looked out the window. There was nothing but water out there. I didn't notice any fish or dolphins this time. It was pitch black. Perhaps they were getting ready for the big ceremony.

Lenahtal yelled out in the direction of our three-eyed pilot. "Hey bobo, take care of the ship. And no snacking until

I get back." He leaned over and spoke to me, as though sharing a confidence, "Every time I go for a jaunt, he's into the bucket of Earth treats, which I wouldn't mind if he left some for me."

"Earthlings are like that too, Lenahtal."

"Yeah, well, the buck stops here! If there's one thing he's going to learn from me, it's moderation when it comes to snacking. Not to mention sharing. A little advice you could heed yourself, my boy, with your latte and chocolate addiction."

They must have a zillion TV screens in space, watching everyone.

"Yup. And you should see the satellite dishes we use," he said, with his high-pitched laugh. "Enough already, we've got an appointment with destiny. We're meeting the big boys and you're the guest of honor."

I was beginning to feel proud, despite myself. I just didn't know what about.

Lenahtal's mood unexpectedly changed. He turned to me, looking nervous, assuming nervousness is part of an alien's emotional repertoire.

"How do I look? Think I should grow some hair?" he asked, caressing his large bald, green, pear-shaped head. "Maybe wear a cowboy hat? That'll impress them. Let them know I'm down with the Earth dudes."

"I think you better go as you are. It's a lot more dashing."

"Do you really think so? I'm kinda nervous and all. Master Amos said it was a great honor even being part of the ceremony. Maybe I should put in a false mouth with some of those dentures. Those subterranean babes like that sort of thing."

"Lenahtal, relax! You look fine." I couldn't believe I was saying that to a four-foot, green, insect-looking, beer-bellied Martian.

"OK, OK, OK. I trust your judgment. Well, except for that Atlantis screw up…"

"Hey!"

"But, I, I mean, you certainly wouldn't be getting this kind of honor if you were a Nutbag, would you?"

"Thanks for the vote of confidence."

"OK, Buck-brain, here we go. Ready?"

"Yes, but would you at least call me by my real name, even if it is Bleakus? The other names are ridiculous."

"OK, sponge breath."

I knew kids who were more mature.

"You know the procedure; close your eyes, inhale the violet light, surround yourself with the white light, ask for protection from the Almighty Creative Force, and then just focus on me and I'll take you there."

I did as he said.

I heard Lenahtal voice echoing as we traveled through time and space, "Hey, dude brain! Master Amos didn't mention anything about a poker game, did he?"

~ 31 ~

We arrived at yet another empty, damp cavern.

I reflected on my experiences as a time traveler the last few days. Obviously, other people were making similar journeys. Was this something that had always been going on? Or was this a recent phenomenon on Earth? It couldn't have been reserved for those who followed a specific religion because I wouldn't have been a candidate.

How was I to benefit from this knowledge? What was I to do with it? What was all this about being honored? Was it true what they were saying, that I was a hero in these lost continents, Atlantis and Lemuria? And, just to confuse the issue, that I was one of the reasons they became lost in the first place?

I could only hope that my insurance would cover me for therapy, in case all of this was some elaborate cult scheme.

"Ready for your Atlantean Flame of the Light Brotherhood initiations?" my little friend asked.

"I guess, if this is what's up. Let's check it out," I said, as we hovered in the chamber with the crystal wand lights protruding from the walls.

We left the cavern, entered a hallway, and were immediately greeted by another mysterious, white-robed figure with an oversized hood covering his face. Like many of the others I'd met in these strange travels, he was around seven feet tall. They should get together and form a basketball team.

He had obviously been expecting our arrival and stood - no, floated, outside of the chamber in the hallway. Nothing was communicated either verbally or telepathically. From what I could tell, Lenahtal was just as curious as I was about the identity of this hooded figure.

He turned and began to float down the hallway, motioning us to follow.

"Not much of a conversationalist, is he?" I said to Lenahtal, breaking the silence.

"They're not allowed to communicate before these ceremonies. That's what Master Amos told me."

"Why not?" It seemed strange not to communicate with the guest of honor.

"Apparently, they don't want to be tainted by the new energy until it has been initiated. The new beings have to be initiated before our hosts are allowed to interact with them.

"Sounds like a cult."

"Don't get paranoid, Buck-germ. Cults had a purpose. It's just now that most of them are full of phony baloney control freaks who try to take away your power and dominate your mind, leaving nothing of the true Self. They're all ego-driven and no path to enlightenment, that's for sure. Ya see, everything operates on vibration. You dip into the lower, negative vibration of cults and it's hard to pull yourself back up. That's why it's so important to hang with your peeps, hang onto your power, talk to God, and follow your heart. You can't go wrong that way."

"Still sounds like a cult."

"Chill, bro."

As we continued floating down the hallway, I noticed a certain tranquility about this place that I hadn't noticed in Lemuria. Each adjacent hallway was lit with specific colors that beamed from the crystal wands. I'm sure there was some corresponding meaning. There always was with these New

Ager types. I didn't get the feeling that our leader in white was going to let me in on it.

As for my little munchkin friend, he was just as preoccupied in this exploration of new territory. He kept looking down each hallway, expecting to find some new and fascinating toy. It was more interesting to watch him experience something new than to ask questions that inevitably lead to another esoteric history lesson. I was definitely a people watcher, or in this case, an extra-terrestrial watcher.

"You're enjoying this, aren't you?"

"Are you kidding? If I've been to one type of initiation, I've been to ten thousand," he said, looking over to me with an alien version of a smile and a wink. He was like a kid in a candy store.

"All right, maybe this one's a bit different."

The white-robed figure stopped at a pure crystal translucent door in front of us. Its surface was smooth and yet the inlaid markings gave it the look of a crystal rock that had developed over thousands of years.

The white-robed figure turned and motioned to us to stop. When we did, we were amazed to see the figure go right through the crystal door and disappear to the other side.

"Uh, OK, that was different. What's going on, Lenahtal?" I was getting proficient at thought transfer.

"I'm not sure, dude brain. I think we have to wait here until we get our marching orders. No use in getting them mad at us. These dudes look like heavy weights. The real deal."

Lenahtal was right. There was something about this place. You knew they meant business. We stood there for what seemed like an eternity.

Maybe they were watching us on some monitor, seeing if we were really bad guys? But I'm guessing if we were suspected of being bad guys, we wouldn't have gotten this far. Unless, of course, I was about to participate in a huge cult initiation. Fear always showed up when my mind was idle. I would then try to intellectualize what was really going on. Then the Hell would begin.

Memo to self: *Learn to get a grip when in underground, lost continents, floating beside aliens.*

The huge crystal door slowly began to open. The air was charged with excitement. It was oddly comforting to have Lenahtal by my side and not be the only one having this new experience.

As we stepped through the crystal doorway, Lenahtal offered me his long-fingered hand, which was attached to his extremely long arm. I'm not sure if he was doing it for me or for himself.

As we passed through the doorway, a blinding white light engulfed us.

"Lenahtal? Can you see anything?"

"Of course not, Buck-germ. We just gotta keep walking. No probs. Just trust."

And so we did, until the blinding white light subsided and we found ourselves standing at the foot of a long, descending marble pathway that ran through the largest underground cave I'd ever seen. The exquisite marble pathway ended at the foot of an enormous crystal palace, lit with a soft purplish color that seemed to emanate from within the crystal itself.

Never in my TV and movie-watching life had I seen anything as breathtakingly beautiful as what lay before us.

"Bleakus, this is most excellent!" I heard my little friend exclaim in his dude talk.

"I have never seen anything so amazing, Lenahtal. Is this what Heaven looks like?"

"If it is, I'm bucking for early retirement."

The marble walkway was encased by clear crystal inscribed with many different insignia. Symbols of what had once been a prominent culture, I figured.

I noticed Lenahtal checking out the insignia.

"What do they mean?"

"I'm not sure. Some of them look like markings representing some of the planets within this solar system. And others? Maybe this is where visitors left the markings of their civilizations, in order to be remembered. I don't know, Bleak. I don't know." He continued to study them further.

I gazed up at the ominous-looking crystal walls that seemed to be the protectors of this palace. They extended at least twenty stories high, and were made of jagged crystal from top to bottom, including the ceiling. One false move and maybe they would collapse on top of a perpetrator. OK, so I still see negative amongst beauty.

Memo to self: *Step up work on negativity!*

"Are we still underwater?" I asked Lenahtal, still marveling at the idea that we were walking through a crystal palace deep in the Atlantic Ocean.

"Yup. This is definitely the place to take the babes to impress them."

Sounds as though he's from a patriarchal society too.

There were no windows in this palace, only the markings of where windows might go. There was a large, crystal drawbridge-type doorway. Again, everything was made of crystal. Crystal wands, protruding from the crystal walls, were lighting the vast cave dwelling. An exquisite sight. I could only imagine what was behind the drawbridge.

Little fireballs, much like the one I had seen hovering above Merinda's palms, started appearing out of nowhere. They were hovering in flight patterns quite similar to those of fireflies. As they flew around in an excited fury, I wondered what their purpose was. Was this for both Lenahtal and me? Was it an honor of sorts?

Our hooded friend in the long, white robe only gave us a moment to inhale the atmosphere before motioning us to follow him. Lenahtal and I just looked at each other, shrugged our shoulders and thought, "Here we go."

As we began our descent along the sloping crystal walkway toward the crystal palace, we began to hear musical tones echoing throughout the cave. The sound was similar to that of a synthesizer or vibraphone.

Soon, various colors began to appear on the crystal walls, synchronizing with the musical tones. Violet tones coordinated with the high-pitched tones; red came through on the low-pitched tones.

Then, as everything reached a crescendo, more colors of the rainbow appeared on the crystal walls, ceiling, and pathway. We were being greeted by a symphony of beauty. I could tell that this was affecting Lenahtal as much as me.

I began to feel that this space guy beside me was an equal who also had things to learn. This seemed to be a healing experience for both of us.

We continued holding hands, truly in awe of what was happening around us and inside of us.

Our hooded friend was waiting for his spellbound stragglers at the doorway to the crystal palace. This part of the journey was so soothing to my soul, I almost didn't want it to end. I felt a tad strange sharing a new experience with an extraterrestrial, but was beginning to realize that such is the mystery of the Universe. No one was excluded from these kinds of experiences if he, she or *it* was open to it.

We both stood motionless and dumbfounded as we stared up at the large, crystal drawbridge doorway. My little friend must have been going through his own stuff because this was the quietest he had ever been in our entire adventure together.

Lenahtal and I stood there with our hooded guide for a few moments. Were we waiting for approval from someone higher up? The lights, music, and fireballs behind us were all now coming to the end of their "symphony," synchronizing with the opening of the crystal doorway.

I turned around to take one last look behind me, smiled and turned back. The drawbridge was now gone.

The robed one motioned to us to enter the passageway of light. Lenahtal and I looked at each other and then walked into the light. I squeezed his leathery hand for reassurance. We immediately found ourselves hovering in an enormous, cavernous structure made entirely of crystal rock. There were at least fifty white-hooded figures lined up on both sides of an aisle that led to a raised altar. Were we in a church? A monastery?

These white-robed characters faced both Lenahtal and me, as though expecting us to resume our journey down the crystal pathway. I could feel that this was a sacred space. Seeing the inside of this temple, I considered it to be less attractive than the outside.

I soon found out how wrong I was.

~ 32 ~

Our hooded tour guide motioned us to proceed past him. I tried to sneak a glance at his face but he kept his head in a bowed position. We slowly and hesitantly began our journey down the pathway together.

"Does this happen all the time around here?" I asked Lenahtal, who was squeezing my hand as hard as I was his.

"Not according to Master Amos. He said this was only the second time that an outsider has been initiated into the brotherhood since the sinking of Atlantis. The first was some dude named Nostradamus. Trust me, bro, this is serious sacred stuff going down here."

Huh. But Nostradamus was ostracized by society for his troubles. Uh-oh. Maybe being initiated into the brotherhood wasn't such a good thing.

Despite my usual doubt track, I felt a rare serenity that I hadn't felt since I was little and went to the neighborhood church. Some people didn't like the church because they thought it was too old. But I thought it was serene and beautiful. I felt very much at home there. I think if it weren't for the men who always stood up and asked for money, even though they drove expensive cars and lived in fancy houses, I would still be going there today.

I tried to sneak a peek at the hooded figures to see if there was anyone I recognized. Basically, I wanted to know if they were human. But I saw nothing but blackness, and the dimly lit temple didn't help. It was funny catching Lenahtal doing the same thing. At least I wasn't alone in my curiosity.

Were there items in that room that we weren't allowed to see? All I could make out were the usual crystal "candles." The walls and floor were also made of crystal.

I began to hear a low, droning murmur in the background. It seemed to be coming from the hooded figures. As it became louder, it sounded like they were all saying "hum," in unison.

"Are they asking us to hum?" I asked my little friend.

He laughed inside my head. "No! They're saying "Om." It's kinda the universal sound for oneness."

"Oh. Are we supposed to say that too?" I asked, in my full-on pleaser form.

"Well, *you* can, Buck-germ. I don't have full use of my vocal cords anymore - an evolutionary thing. So I'll just, if it's all the same to them…" His voice trailed off. He sounded disappointed.

"Why don't you at least try it? Things may be different for you down here."

"Naw, cowboy, there are some limitations I just have to accept."

Then he looked up at me.

"Actually, you know, why not?" He began to move his mouth.

I heard a little squeak come out. It wasn't quite an "Om" but I could tell that Lenahtal was both shocked and joyful that there was any sound at all.

Maybe this was some kind of magical kingdom where people were able to be expressive without obstruction.

There was no stifling of expression in this temple as I soon found myself chanting, "Om."

We continued walking down the pathway and I began to hear another chorus of chanting on top of the "Om." I wasn't familiar with the language but I was positive it originated in this lost continent.

"Lenahtal, what language is that?"

"I don't know. I've never been here before so it all sounds like monkey talk to me," he said, making an attempt at humor, as we neared the end of our crystal walkway.

Soon there was yet another chorus of chanting in yet another foreign language. Lenahtal kept turning his head with curiosity in the direction of each new chorus, while still maintaining a constant squeaky "Om."

"What do you make of all this?"

"Don't know. It's gotta be some sort of ritual, dude brain. You and me are the main focus here, that's for sure."

We were now steps away from the raised altar and I couldn't keep my panic at bay. "Hey, if this gets ugly, do you think you can get us out of here fast?"

"I'm not sure if I have the know-how, wheatgerm. These dudes are major heavyweights. But hey, no one is better than me when it comes to running from fear. They say it's all an illusion, so heck, if I'm scared, I'm disappearing!"

"Just take me with you." It was unnerving that my personal guide was out of his league. But even in a tough spot, he still found the humor in it all. I had to appreciate that.

"No problem, Buck-germ." he answered, with a slight quiver in his telepathic transference.

I too was out of my league. Waaay out of my league. No way was I letting go of Lenahtal's leathery hand.

We approached the end of the pathway. I noticed a couple of hooded figures in long, flowing robes, coming out of a doorway and approaching the altar. One wore a violet robe and the other a red one. Did they have more power than the others?

I took a closer look at the altar. It was made of solid crystal rock, with crystal stairs leading up to it. It was about four feet high and seven feet long. Nothing on it or around it. No pictures, symbols, or crosses surrounded it. If these people worshipped God or the devil, they didn't have any objects or images to support one or the other. But I was sure this was some sort of secret order.

We finally stopped at the end of the walkway. The hooded people were behind us, chanting at a fever pitch. I could feel myself getting caught up in it all. I felt my so-called astral body experiencing a tingling sensation. I guess even ghosts could feel things.

"This place is rockin', man," said my little green friend.

"If we were at a real rock concert, those hooded things behind us would have lighters in their hands and be holding them up in the air."

The two main figures were now opposite us, standing behind the altar. They motioned for me to come toward them.

"Cover me, will ya pal?" I said to my only friend in this temple of mystery.

"Hey, if they lay you out on that altar like some sacrificial lamb, I'm not sure I'll have the guts to stick around and help ya out, bro. Sorry," he said, as he let go of my hand.

"I didn't even think of that. Thanks for putting that horrible thought in my head. *Thanks a lot!*"

"Sorry, bud. I just finished reading one of those trashy horror books that I picked up in the Midwest. Uh, good luck!"

I left his side and cautiously ascended the stairway to my doom.

I now stood opposite the two hooded figures. By now, all other sounds had subsided and that familiar buzzing sound had returned. I found myself floating straight up into the air. There was nothing I could do to prevent it. I had no control over what was happening to me.

My feet began to lift up from beneath me until my body floated parallel to the altar. I was now floating parallel to the altar. Like a cloud, I softly floated down onto the crystal slab. Was this it? Was my life over now? Was there a God overseeing all? If so, would he, she, it, whatever save me now because I was really scared and I wanted God or my mommy to be there to protect me.

There goes the Beamer, I thought, in what seemed like my last moment before eternity.

Memo to self: *Next time, pay cash for the BMW. And get the red convertible!!*

The hooded figures stood at each end of the altar, invoking something in their strange language. I still couldn't see who or what they were. I was sad at the thought that my life might be over now. I had so much new information to give to people. I had seen the worlds as they really were and it seemed that I was now leaving, never to impart what I now knew.

I could see the red-robed, hooded figure moving his hands around the bottom of my feet, chanting something in his language. I glanced above my head to see the figure with the violet hood gesturing and speaking something equally incomprehensible. I looked over at Lenahtal. He looked just as scared as me.

I lay on the altar looking up at the flat crystal ceiling and saw a blurry reflection of myself.

ZAP!

I saw a current of violet lightning shoot through me from head to toe.

ZAP!

Another current of violet lightning shot through me in the opposite direction. I was paralyzed with fear. I couldn't even scream. I only had my suspicious mind to "comfort" me. Who were these evil men and why were they doing this to me? Was all this an elaborate set-up so that they could steal my soul? Was Lenahtal really an extraterrestrial or was he an operative in a complicated scheme to steal human souls?

ZAP!

The violet fire ripped through my ethereal body once again, leaving me with an even blurrier reflection of myself on the ceiling as I witnessed what appeared to be my destruction. I felt as though something was slowly being taken away from me. If it was my soul, then so be it. I had no power to fight whatever was happening, so let it be done quickly.

ZAP!

Again, the violet light bolted through me from head to toe, but this time I saw a young man wearing a short, white tunic with high-laced leather sandals. Somehow I knew this young man was me, although he looked nothing like me. I was kneeling in front of an older man whose eyes conveyed great wisdom. He might have been my father but had the aura of being a father to many.

"You have been chosen to decipher the ancient design for the molecular structure of the crystallization process. You have been given this assignment because you have proven your worthiness to the Masters. You will always have free will, but if you take away others' free will, then so shall yours be taken. Go now, my son, and serve your people kindly."

It was obvious I had been assigned a very important job within the communities of Lemuria and Atlantis. Could this have been the moment that Master Amos had talked about, when I was assigned as keeper of the crystal?

ZAP!

Another flash of violet went through me, bringing with it another reflective memory.

"You didn't say you were going to destroy everything!!! You said you wanted to help *heal!"* This young self was overcome with rage and grief.

"I lied," said the other young man, who was obviously a younger version of Master Amos.

"You do-gooders make me sick, thinking that there is some God that oversees all. Now hand over the molecular structure blueprints or I'll *destroy* you. Or is that what you want?" he said, in a low, menacing tone.

"No, that's not what I want. Nor do I want you to rule. I thought you were my friend."

"Not even close. Now if you don't want to meet your maker, I would suggest you hand over the blueprints, you miserable excuse for a living organism."

I stood there in defiance.

"If you choose not to hand them over, I will annihilate you with one of your specially designed crystal laser guns. And then I'll do the same to your family," he said, pulling out a long L-shaped crystal.

It was obvious from my demeanor that I understood the danger I faced at his hands.

"You, you…how could you steal from the people of Lemuria and Atlantis? How could you?"

He let out a menacing laugh. "Bleakus, you have no conception of what is really going on in the battle between the light and dark forces. Hand them over. Now!"

I could see the younger version of myself trembling with fear, struggling with the decision to hand over the blueprints that consisted of numerous plates of crystal and were in book-sized form. I could barely make out the formulaic writings inscribed on them.

I watched the younger version of me, falling to the ground, holding out the crystal plates, crying from the depths of his soul.

The younger Master Amos snatched the crystal plates away from me. "You are a pathetic little boy. Why they ever put you in charge of such an undertaking is only an indication of their stupidity and self-destructiveness. My *real* friends and I will be able to work magic with these plans. We'll even design our own species that will work for us and take over not only this planet, but any others that we so choose."

In saying that, the dark figure of the younger Master Amos quickly left the room.

The innocent young man remained crying on the ground. I then began to cry on the altar, knowing that the young man lying on the ground was me.

ZAP!

Another surge of violet light coursed through me. I was beginning to understand what was happening. This was a form of cleansing on a cellular level. This was making me feel different. Lighter. I didn't feel as weighed down by what had occurred in my life to this point. I felt very much in the moment. No longer held captive by my past or future, I felt that I was getting my power back.

"Do you not know what has occurred, young man?" said a booming voice above me as the young me lay there weeping.

"Yes, sir. I'm sorry. I'll try to repair my error, sir."

"It is too late, my child. You have already set in motion that which was predestined to happen."

Having said that, the older man kneeled down beside the young me and began speaking in a much softer tone, sounding almost defeated.

"It was inevitable that man's greed would catch up to our civilization. I was just praying that perhaps our demise could be delayed. We had hoped that, because you are such an honest, pure, and strong young man, you would not be tainted by the dark forces."

"But he lied to me! He was my best friend. I only told him about the blueprints because he said he could help me decipher the codes and help heal the planet and its inhabitants. He said it would bring us closer to God."

"I think he was right, more than he realizes. Do not blame yourself, young one, for it was your purity that led you here and it is that same purity that will always keep you in alignment with the Almighty God force and the Master Plan."

The old man cradled my beleaguered younger self in his arms and caressed my forehead.

"We will all be of light soon enough," he said, bowing and kissing me softly on the top of my head. Then he got up to leave.

Watching him leave, I saw a sudden look of determination come over the face of my younger self.

ZAP!

Yet another violet light pierced through my body as my mind swam in memories. I saw myself in a golden room, arranging crystals - all sizes, shapes, colors, and forms. Then I sat in the middle, amongst the new arrangement of crystals, closing my eyes and mumbling something. Above my head was a pyramid about one foot high. It was made of gold rods and contained various colorful shapes and forms of crystal rock. It was spinning in a counterclockwise motion above my head.

I sat there quietly and motionlessly. Clearly, I was meditating, and it looked like I was doing a lot better job than at the retreat.

Soon, there was a loud humming in the room that was directly related to the crystals. From what I could understand about the process, I was trying to communicate to someone or something. It was urgent. I saw myself sweating profusely.

Then, unnoticed by the younger me, the dark, younger version of Master Amos came into the room. I could tell by his expression on his face that he was not happy with what was going on. He then left the room as quietly as he had come in.

"They are trying to take over. You'll be next, my good friends. Believe me!" I could hear myself pleading my case. This was obviously the moment when I was trying to communicate to someone about what was going on in Lemuria.

ZAP!

Another ray of violet streaked through me. I, as the young man, was now in conversation with another young man. That man was Lenahtal, whose essence was embodied in human form. He had golden hair, a well-proportioned body, pure white skin, and aqua green eyes.

"I'm telling ya, seaweed breath, they want to meet with you tonight. I'll operate the teleportation machine and nobody will know."

"I don't know, Lenahtal, it sounds a bit risky to me."

"Don't be a Nutbar," Lenahtal said in his familiar pseudo-hipster tone, "it's the perfect plan. Besides, we've got to do something. We can't let them take over."

I stood there for a moment, staring at the ground, thinking of my options.

"OK, OK. I'll meet you at the teleportation room tonight, after the eighth star moves into the fourth quadrant."

We then went our separate ways with Lenahtal smiling and the younger me looking very pensive.

ZAP!

A violet ray pierced my astral body as reflected in the slab of crystal above. My image was becoming more luminous as the story unfolded.

"OK, are you ready?" Lenahtal asked me, as I stood on a raised crystal platform, in what was obviously the teleportation room. Golden walls and crystal formations of rocks extended downward from the ceiling. The floor was also made of pure clear crystal, thus adding to the room's solid yet ethereal presence.

"Don't stay any longer than you have to," Lenahtal said. "The dark forces might tune into what's going down."

"OK, partner. In case I don't make it back, take care of those remaining crystal plates with the encoding of our planet's history on them. Give them to the Masters. They'll know what to do with them. We'll need them in the future if the dark forces get their way. And, uh, stash the crystals, jewels, and any other documents in the vault in my lab so that they'll be safe and we can recover them another time. Perhaps when man is more prepared."

"Yes, Sir."

"I'm really worried about those new crystal laser healing protractors and extractors that we created. I don't want anybody using them as lethal weapons against unsuspecting nations."

"Understood."

"Nobody uses them unless they're for healing, got it? Otherwise, destroy the plans. It's not worth the risk."

"Got it, chief. Anything else?"

"Pray."

"Don't worry. Relax, bro. You'll be back soon enough. Prepare for one kick-ass time." Lenahtal proceeded with the formalities of teleportation.

I observed myself standing in the middle of the platform reciting something that sounded like a prayer, likely asking for protection.

"Ready?" he asked.

"Ready," my younger self replied, with a nervous smile.

I watched the younger version of myself dissolve into millions of tiny particles until finally disappearing. I could see Lenahtal smiling. Was he the one who had annihilated me? We seemed like such good friends.

"You little twerp!" The dark figure of Master Amos entered from the shadows.

Lenahtal didn't turn around but I could see fear quickly remove his smile.

"I told you to destroy him last night, did I not?" said the scornful Master Amos.

"It's too late, Snailhead. He's already on his way to meet and alert someone in the Unified Intergalactic Council meeting of the Elders at Atlantis. You, knucklebrain, are going down!"

"Stupidity is an unfortunate quality. You had better hope the Elders are merciful. Your young friend is on a journey to doom. Now get away from the panel!" he said, pulling out a crystal object that was similar to, or at least was wielded with the same intention as a gun.

"No, I can't. He hasn't arrived in Atlantis yet."

"Whether your friend arrives there or I abort his travel escapade here, therefore aborting his life, doesn't really matter. That Elder whom he was going to contact is an ally. Either way, your naive young friend has met his certain end. This way it looks cleaner. Now get out of the way or you will meet your alleged maker for breakfast."

"You just want to rule and destroy, not save and heal. I won't let you do this to Bleakus!" Lenahtal tried forfeiting his life for mine by protecting the panel with his body.

"The world is full of innocents like you and your friend. Time to change that - one by one if I have to. First, we'll start with you."

And with that, a golden ray shot out of the crystal object, striking Lenahtal in the back and dissolving him into nothingness.

Lying on the slab of crystal, I cried for my extraterrestrial friend who truly cared. Not only about me but about humanity.

ZAP.

I felt another surge of energy blaze through my body as I felt the pain of my friend's effort to save my life. Then I saw the evil version of Master Amos approach the panel and quickly press the red crystal button.

"Aaaahhhh! Ahhhh!" I screamed as the pain quickly ran through my etheric body lying on the altar.

"Aaaahhhh! Ahhhh!"

I couldn't stop it. The two hooded figures at the polarities of my pain began to run the violet light continuously through my body, from head to toe, toe to head.

"Aahhh! Stop it! Stop it!" I screamed in tormented silence.

"Aaaaaahhhhh!"

The pain was excruciating and unrelenting, and there was nothing I could do about it.

Then everything became blank. Everything stopped. I saw nothing but white as I felt the pain quickly subside. I was no longer on the altar but I could still feel the two robed figures protecting and healing my soul.

I was surrounded by white. I was in white. I was white and yet, I knew I was moving toward something even greater. The vibration was quickening. I tried to communicate with the two figures beside me. Nothing. Even though they were guiding me, I felt very much on my own.

Soon, I could feel their guiding presence leave as I moved closer to something greater than I had ever experienced. Something that dissolved my thoughts of what was truth and replaced them with Love. I lost all sense of identity. I was moving towards a greater Love. I was moving towards the source of the Creator of All. This was a direct experience of God. It could not have been anything else.

There wasn't a man standing on "the other side" calling all the shots. I was part of something that was greater than me. I was moving toward the Source. The Source of my wholeness. The source of All That Is.

I was losing my separateness and gaining my wholeness. I was becoming a light being. A particle of greatness. A particle of Oneness. I was in God and God was in me. There was no difference. No barriers. No separation. I lost my limited consciousness of boundaries and issues and melted into the power of, for the lack of a better word, God.

I awakened into the realization that I Am God. As are we all. Whether we see ourselves as a child of God, an aspect of

God, connected to God, it all pointed to a common denominator. In this moment, I had finally found my peace.

Yikes! If the guys could see me now, expounding realizations of Self, One, Oneness, God, et cetera I'd be so kicked out of the breakfast club!

~ 33 ~

Gradually, I could hear the chanting. I could see the ceiling. I could see my reflection. However, the two robed figures were nowhere to be seen.

In my grogginess, I turned my head to the right and saw Lenahtal bow toward me. I then realized everyone was bowing toward me. What did it mean?

I was sluggish in my attempts to get off the altar. It felt good to connect my etheric feet to the ground and not have bolts of lightening striking through me.

Facing the bowed figures, I began my descent down the crystal stairway. I felt lighter, softer. For the first time in a long time, I felt my*self*. As Sally would say, I felt my essence, my Being. I felt the "God Mojo" in my Self. I felt connected. I had met the Maker and it rocked my world!

All of those times I had felt superior or inferior toward others when it really was beside the point. I was coming to the realization that indeed, we are all One. We are each an extension of the other. The adage, 'in helping one another, we help ourselves' made perfect sense. All of these people who had been helping me in the last few days had also been helping themselves; therefore, helping the God Self.

There truly is a whole universe inside of one's Self, if only we take the time to go in and explore it. If only we remembered how to listen to the Self. If only we remembered our connection to the Source. If only we remembered the Source. I felt so honored to have had this kick-start in my reawakening process.

Why me? Why now? Why are we all so different and yet the same? These questions and more raced through my mind. This road of questioning never seemed to end.

I was now standing in front of Lenahtal as I watched him come up from his bow in unison with the others. There was so much love being exchanged in that moment. Time doesn't have a monopoly on love.

"Now *that's* the big guy!" he said, as he stepped forward to give me a hug.

I returned the hug. What a sight it must have been, a six foot one ghostly spirit being hugged by a four foot extraterrestrial spirit, surrounded by white-hooded figures softly chanting inside a crystal palace.

He unwrapped his gangly arms from around my etheric body. I felt a strong presence behind me. The hooded figures in front of me began to bow their heads in response to this presence, as did Lenahtal. I turned around and saw the two hooded figures who had been my guides throughout this whole experience, standing at the altar.

Looking at the red-robed figure, I could finally see the face that had been concealed by his hood. It was Surrender. I felt his love penetrate me. I looked toward the violet-robed figure and saw the Elder who had cradled me as I cried at the end of my time in Atlantis. I felt so much love coming from them both that it eclipsed any words that I could express in that moment.

They motioned me to stand beside Lenahtal. I turned and did so, without hesitation.

They each opened up a pouch and pulled out a crystal object. As they stepped toward us, I could hear the hooded figures behind us begin a prayer that was vaguely familiar. On closer observation, I could see that these objects were small crystal pyramids. Each crystal was made of two double pyramids, base to base, with their edges outlined in solid gold.

Lenahtal and I just stood there, transfixed.

They motioned us to bow before them. Then they opened the leather straps attached to the top of the double pyramid crystals and put one around Lenahtal's neck. They moved their hands around the top of his head and began mumbling something from another language and time.

Then they repeated the same procedure with me.

We were each being honored and respected for our respective journeys. I was as happy for my little friend as I was for myself. I could see that he was surprised and deeply touched.

"Thank you for your integrity and courage, but most of all thank you for choosing to remember."

Choosing to remember? This? I missed that meeting. But I didn't care anymore. Sally's right, sometimes you just have to accept what is.

We each rose from our bows and looked at each other. I could see a tear running down Lenahtal's greenish cheek. His bug eyes were filled with love and joy. I hadn't been aware that extraterrestrials were capable of having such deep feelings.

We both turned toward these great beings and all four of us bowed.

"Now go and help the other children of God to remember. It is important to remember *now*. We need them all," said the wise Elder in the violet hood.

Surrender looked deep into my eyes.

"Thank you for being so trusting, coming so far and for getting through all of that traffic. I guess I can put away the nerf bat now, huh?" he ended with a wink.

I laughed. Life. What a world. What a miraculous world we lived in.

They both turned away, walking up the crystal stairs toward the altar. They then turned toward the crowd and raised their arms. Everyone in the crystal palace did likewise.

Surrender and the Elder turned their palms toward Lenahtal and me. The others did the same. The chanting was approaching a crescendo. The dimly lit room was filled with white light as the chanting reached its peak.

"Come this way," we heard from behind us.

We turned to see the same individual who had led us here. We both reluctantly left the two Masters and followed the unknown white-hooded figure.

Taking a step closer to the white-hooded figure, we could see that it was a smiling Master Amos.

"It's time to go back," he said.

I looked at Lenahtal.

"Shall we??" I extended my hand toward his.

"Don't see why not, Buckwheat. I mean, Bleakus." He grabbed my hand.

Master Amos turned and we followed him up the pathway of crystal. The light became brighter and the voices became a magnificent chorus as we passed the white-hooded figures, their palms raised toward us.

Before we passed through the doorway, I turned around and took in one last moment of "remembrance." I could feel their love. If we had more people with the same commitment to God and growth as these folks, would we be in the same mess on Earth? Not likely.

I gave a bow of respect to these people and to their assistance in my journey. Then, hand and hand with Lenahtal, I passed through the doorway and into the white light.

"Remember, you are all Masters. Make your choices accordingly." We heard Master Amos's words echo through the blinding white light where there were no definitions of self.

"Use those crystal pendulums when in doubt and they will connect you with The One. Remember, you are not alone in your journey," were the last whispers we heard from Master Amos as we merged into the light.

~ 34 ~

In less than an instant, Lenahtal and I were back at the spaceship, standing in exactly the same place as when we left. I looked at Lenahtal and he looked at me, each of us trying to digest what we had just experienced. I looked to see if Space Cadet was still in position. He was.

I looked at Lenahtal's crystal pyramid hanging around his neck as he did mine. It was strange that they were exactly the same.

Lenahtal read my mind. "That's because we were brothers then and we are brothers now. We are brothers in time."

He floated up and started his little air dance.

"It's not the skin that keeps it together, it's the soul, brother. Gimme four!" he giggled, holding out his four-fingered hand.

I did. I gave him my first four fingers and slapped his hard.

"All right, Bro! Now all we have to do is make a quick pit stop at the planet where you'll be working in conjunction with Earth to fulfill your mission. After that, you're back to good ol' Earth. Ready, Dude-face?" he asked, as he floated back to his chair, motioning me to do the same.

"Ready," I said, in my newfound confidence.

"OK, Space Cadet, *hit it!*"

In another moment we were hovering above our next destination.

"Hey, Space Cadet! Are those candy wrappers I see on the floor? I'll deal with you later. Dang rookies! OK, now

Zoltron is the name of the planet you'll be working with for now. Remember everything is temporary."

"Temporary. Got it."

"Yo! Space cadet! Take us down."

And the unseen creature in the driver's seat did as he was instructed.

"Basically, I'm going to give you the two cent tour of the planet you already know so well. You've got so much swimming in your head right now, that's about all you can take in."

As we began our descent, I looked over at Lenahtal, and caught him admiring the crystal pyramid around his elongated neck.

"We did good, didn't we?" I was touched by his innocence.

He looked over to me. "Yeah, we kicked some butt, dude! OK, they kicked ours first."

"But at least we tried to do the right thing. Besides, it all worked out in the end, right?"

He started to float out of his seat again. This was turning out to be a favorite habit of his.

"There's even more butt to kick, Bro! The Universe is full of dark forces. But the Force is with us," he said, lowering his squeaky voice the best he could.

"Yeah, yeah, saw the movie."

"*Saw* the movie? I practically wrote it for the guy!"

He floated over to the doorway as it creaked open. "Oops. Needs lubricant. See that?" He pointed upwards as I approached the doorway and looked out.

"This too was once called the Garden of Eden. Unfortunately, like the one on Earth, it became tainted. That's what I'm saying. The dark forces are everywhere. They don't want you to succeed in knowing your truth. That way it's easier for them to control ya. They're always trying to keep entities like you and me ignorant. Can't allow that anymore. You know, Buck-germ, part of the message that has to get out is that the surrounding planets, including Earth, need to understand that we all need to help one another. It's time for major growth - *Big time* - everywhere and with everyone."

I tried to take in what he was saying but I was distracted by the view. I was in awe of the absolute beauty, of the breathless vision before me. Its tropical appearance reflected an abundance of rain and sun. The plush gardens sang in tune with brilliantly colored birds.

"Is this my home?" I wondered if this was what Merinda had been talking about.

"No. You just left your true home, remember?" He said, slipping his hand into mine. "Zoltron is just a place you can go when you need assistance with what is happening on Earth. You've had many incarnations on this planet and it is one of the most developed in all the solar systems."

"I thought you said the dark forces were here too?"

"There is only one place where we don't experience that duality and you were just there."

"Atlantis?"

"No, Buckwheat, the Source! Geez, I think we're gonna have to give you some special herbs for that memory of yours."

I didn't think that was a compliment, but hey, what are brothers for if they can't keep you straight?

"The dark forces here are a lot more subtle than your dark forces on Earth. As hard as it may be to understand, French fry, the dark forces respect God. There's just a few more little tweaks they gotta work out before they see the light. Understand, rubber band?"

I looked at him, trying to comprehend his butchering of the English language. Exactly where did he learn all that slang?

I looked out as we continued to hover above the ground. I thought about jumping the several feet down onto the fresh green grass but something rang inside my head and said, "Not yet."

"Am I going to get the two cent tour or the ten dollar tour of Zoltron?"

Lenahtal squeezed my hand.

"Why repeat what you already know so well? We're just here for a quick memory trigger so that the next time you come back here you won't feel so lost. You'll know exactly who and where you are. The only reason I was told to bring you here now was so that you would have a sensory experience of this planet when we work with you in your dreamstate. Helps reduce the steepness of your learning curve. Don't worry about nothing, bro. We'll have you operating in full multidimensional mode in no time."

I stood there looking into my brother's bug eyes. How I could love a being that looked like this was beyond me, but I did. Unconditionally. This was a love far greater than could be written in a book or expressed in a song. This was a love that just *was.* A love for my fellow space brother. A deep love of truth, understanding, and camaraderie. I was so out of the boys' breakfast club.

Lenahtal interrupted my thoughts with his own. Of course, being able to read my thoughts, he took off from where I left off.

"Once you've experienced The God-Force, there is no part of the experience that is greater than the whole. It doesn't matter what you look like. It doesn't matter what planet you're from. It's all God. It's all One. Remember, it's not a word that you're after, it's the feeling. There isn't a word, thought or concept out there that replaces the feeling of love."

"You know, Lenahtal, you've turned into a pretty good teacher for a squeaky loudmouth."

"I forgot! I can speak!"

He tried again. A little noise peeped out. Not much by human standards but he was quite chuffed by this new experience. He floated up and darted around the spaceship, filled with joy and squeaky noises. Finally, he floated back down by my side and let out one last squeak.

"That's soooo awesome. Wait until they hear me back home."

"Where is your home?"

"Ah, maybe one day they'll let me bring you there. Meet the wife."

"You're married?"

"What? You think that's only an earthly thing?"

"No, I just - well, yeah! I guess."

"You have so much to learn, Buckeye, but I've got to say, you've turned into a pretty good student for a guy who's been asleep for 87 lifetimes."

We both laughed.

"Shall we take you back for now?"

I took in a deep breath.

"Yeah, I guess it's time, huh?"

"Yepper."

"So when will I be coming back here?" I asked, nervous about my future.

"Schmooka, you haven't even left yet. Don't be leaving the present for the future. Live in the present. The future will take care of itself. You'll be back here soon enough. No worries."

I felt a wave of relief come over me.

"It feels peaceful here."

"Whoa, dude-brain! Grass is always greener. It's what's inside that counts."

"Gotcha!"

"We've got lots of work to do together, and apart. This will be our outpost for the majority of the work that we do together. Yessiree Bob, we'll both be coming back here to further our studies as Master communicators."

He paused for a moment and suddenly became serious. "You know, Bleakus, I think I'm finally ready to take Master Amos up on his offer. It's time I gave myself a promotion."

"If it means anything, I think you're ready too, Lenahtal," I said, squeezing his leathery hand.

"It means a lot. It's been so good for me to see you again. I think I almost forgot what I was supposed to be doing with my life too, Buck-brain."

I could feel his energy soften. He let go of my hand and floated back to the chair.

"Come on, let's get out of here before we turn into a couple of mush buckets. This emotional stuff is new territory for me too, ya know."

Just before I turned away from the doorway, I saw another compact silver saucer-like spaceship about to land. I had never seen the outside of the one I was in but assumed that they were similar. As a matter of fact, it looked very similar to a lot of those photographs on the front page of those trashy tabloids in the supermarket. Who knew?

Memo to self: *Buy trashy rag if it has a UFO on the front cover!*

There was a gentle hum emanating from the saucer as I watched it hover about ten feet above the ground. It then stopped its circular rotation and began to smoothly descend onto the soft green grass. I noticed the grass started flowing in the opposite circular motion.

The silver disc then gently landed beside ours. It had to be between two and three hundred feet in length. A perfectly symmetrical flying machine.

Everything was quiet as they went into shutting down mode. I turned toward Lenahtal, only to see that he was preoccupied with his pyramid pendant. Now it was time to play observer to that unknown planet, Zoltron.

If there was a door, I couldn't see it. That is, until an opening on the side appeared. It was miraculous how seamless the door was.

Merinda appeared through the doorway. Yup. There she was, smiling and waving as if this were an everyday occurrence and she was just coming home from a morning at the spa and I was picking up the newspaper off the lawn.

"How did you like home? It's a lot different than Earth, isn't it?"

"It sure is."

"You'll like Zoltron, Bleakus. There's lots of unconditional love here. Fair warning though, various shapes, colors, and sizes of God's children come here. It'll throw you off at first but you'll get used to it. If you can handle Lenahtal, you can handle anything!"

The tall, blond, godlike figure who had done the fancy "light show" work on Merinda's body at the retreat appeared in the doorway. He put his arm around her and gave me a gentle smile.

"Hey, Potatohead, get over here or you'll get your face fried," squeaked Lenahtal.

"I think you better go now." said Merinda, as she snuggled with the blond one.

Merinda and her partner felt like a beautiful couple, very much in love. Maaan, what a learning curve this is going to be.

"Until the next time."

They both put their hands in prayer position and bowed towards me. I did the same. I was still awkward with all this bowing stuff, but they say grace takes time.

Suddenly, I could feel a wave of love flush through my body and I knew it was coming from them. I tried to reciprocate but I wasn't sure if anything happened for them. At least I tried.

"Will you please remind Lenahtal that he owes me from poker," Merinda said with a hearty laugh.

Lenahtal certainly gets around, and he doesn't sound like a very good poker player either.

As my door slowly closed, I watched both of them float down to the grass while waving to me in their blissful state. I was in the middle of wishing them well when our spaceship door slammed in my face.

I stood there facing the closed door for a moment, trying to figure out if I had it in me to float around on this planet Zoltron like them. Perhaps that was for another time, another lesson, and another story. Did the lessons ever end? And if they did end, where would I end up? My guess would be a place called Home.

I made my way back to the seat and felt the force field lock me in.

"That was Merinda out there," I said, noticing Lenahtal shift uncomfortably in his seat. "You're obviously not very good at poker, are you?"

"Uh, well, it's not really poker as you know it. It's kind of like will they or won't they poker."

"What do you mean?"

"'Will they or won't they wake up' poker," he said, emphasizing the 'wake up' part. "Look, partner, I, uh, might as well level with you. I was betting against you waking up," he said, wincing as much as an extraterrestrial could.

"What? How could you bet against your own brother?"

"Yeah, I know," he began sheepishly, "but the thing is, if you woke up, that meant I had to grow up and be a Master too, because of our deep connection. And that was a scary prospect. So, I bet against you. Deep down though, I was rooting for you to win, honest."

I thought about it for a moment. "But you never tried to stop me from trying to remember. In fact, you were encouraging me to remember."

"You're right, buckwheat. That is my service and responsibility to the God-force. This is where Divine free will crosses with 'Do not interfere with anyone's process unless asked' part. Ya see, brother, a very long time ago, you and I made a pact to enter into each other's lives to help each other remember. I didn't remember that until recently.

"When Master Amos told me to try again this lifetime, I was reluctant for two reasons. First, I had almost given up on you because of all the other lifetimes I'd tried. Every time we got close, you would go right back to sleep or you wouldn't even wake up. You wouldn't even get to first base. I became very sad about the whole thing. Ask my wife when you meet her. The second reason was that I knew if you really did wake up to the Divine Self, it would force me to be aware of *my* Divine Self in a much bigger way. It was freaking me out. I would have to become a Master of my own destiny within God's plan. It's a lotta work, dude. And I knew you would remind me to wake up if you remembered yourself."

"We kind of woke up together, didn't we?"

"Yepper! Mind you, I didn't go to home base like you, but you're a bit thicker when it comes to the bigger concepts stuff, so I guess they had to go the extra step with you. Me? I already believed."

"Smartypants."

"Hey, it's a lot of responsibility for a four-foot munchkin to be fully realized."

"You can handle it."

"We'll see. I've taken people on many journeys and most of them, well, they just never want to wake up and take responsibility for their own lives. It's always a great disappointment for me and my buds. We try, but in the end it's out of our hands. Folks got to do the last part themselves. We can probe 'em and jolt 'em, but if they don't want to wake up, it ain't happening!"

I sat there quietly, listening to the process that my own brother from another planet had to go through in order to get to this point in his alien life. At least I wasn't alone.

"With you being asleep for so long, the odds were against you. I have to say though, bro, I knew I'd lost the bet almost from the beginning."

"How come?"

"This time, there was something different. This time, you were willing to ask questions. This time, you were willing to take chances. You can only grow that way. Yup, this time you were ready. Thank God!"

"Yeah, I probably should thank somebody." I took in what he was saying and realized the truth of it all. I did notice that in this lifetime I was always asking questions. Very early on, I knew there were no right or wrong questions when it came to learning. Despite having an insatiable hunger for knowledge, I still didn't understand how it led me to this place, this spaceship, this new planet, this experience, even this greenish-looking brother. But I guess it was all part of the learning curve of life.

"Curious, what did you lose in the bet with Master Amos and Merinda?"

He was quiet for a moment. "I used to think it would be a loss, but as we traveled the light fantastic together, I became more excited about the prospect of becoming a Master. What I lost was my right to continually allow myself not to grow. Which means growing up and being responsible to Self. Responsibility. Respond-to-my-ability. Sound familiar?

"Oh yeah!"

"Might even have to lose some of the corny English lingo. Naw, maybe not."

I laughed.

"To sum it up, bro, I lost my status as light worker and claimed my status as *Light Master.*"

"Gee, sounds like a raw deal, munchkin," I said, smiling at my fellow Master.

I knew he was happy with the loss and, being new at the game of emotions myself, I didn't take it any farther than that. Neither did he. But I noticed a change in his emotions. Looked like I was picking up a few tricks of the trade. I should be floating on Zoltron in no time.

"But why me?" I said, in a calm confusion.

"Why not?"

"But what did I do to earn being a master?"

"You allowed your *Self* to remember."

"Huh. That's it?"

Lenahtal chuckled.

"This is only the beginning, bro."

"I was afraid of that."

I took in a deep breath and let out a long exhale.

"Enough chatter. Time to scat, bat! Ready for blast-off, brother Bleakus?"

"Ready, brother Lenahtal."

The force field locked me into my seat. Lenahtal was about to raise his long right arm.

"OK, Space Cadet, take us back to that planet called Earth."

"Wait a minute," I said, in a telepathic whisper, "what are the chances of getting a peek at three-eyed Space Cadet?"

"Sure. No problem, brother Bleakus." He raised his right arm and I watched the little silver-suited Space Cadet rise from his chair with his back to us. It appeared as though Lenahtal could control Space Cadet with his right arm.

With his back still facing us, he began to slowly float across the spaceship. At about the halfway point, he turned quickly and then swooped toward me, slamming into my face.

I screamed and panicked. The three-eyed little monster was attacking me.

"Lenahtal! Lenahtal! Get him off!!! Get this thing off of me!"

He was wrapped around my head, moving side to side and sliming me with some unknown sticky substance. He squeezed my ears and then dropped into my lap, lifeless.

I was out of breath from sheer panic.

Lenahtal was out of his seat laughing and bouncing around the inside of the spaceship, shouting telepathically. "Yippee! Yippee! I gotcha!"

"What the heck's going on?" I screamed.

"That's my stuffed alien, Wilbur. Some kid on Earth gave him to me. I take him with me wherever I go. Yee-ha! Gotcha good, didn't I bro?"

I was dumbfounded by my little brother munchkin and his elaborate practical joke.

He motioned to unlock the force field. I leaned over to pick up the little silver-suited creature. Sure enough, it was an alien in a silver space suit with chocolate smeared all over its face. Funny, it looked just like the stuffed alien Sally gave me that sat on my desk in my office. What are the odds? I was going to let it slide though. Enough coincidences for now.

I began to laugh at my own fear. Then I realized there was chocolate all over my face. Lenahtal threw me a white woven cloth with a unique black emblem on it, to wipe it off. The emblem had a star in the middle of a pyramid. I had seen this emblem before but couldn't place it.

"That's a symbol of timelessness and multidimensionality, my friend. A symbol of truth and commitment to the One. As for the stuffed alien, folks are always asking me if they can fly this dang thing, which drives me nuts! I tell you there is nothing worse than having people asking all sorts of questions about how to control a spaceship when they can't even control themselves. That's why I came up with the idea of telling people it's a scary three-eyed monster that can't communicate with them because he's in training. Works every time," he said, with his child-like giggle.

"You, my friend, have a very warped sense of humor."

"Hey Bucko, you've got a very warped sense of time. Look who's calling who warped." Lenahtal floated back to his chair and quickly shifted to a more serious mood – for him. "We've got to get you back before you turn into a pumpkin. Ready to go bye-bye?"

I was going to miss my little green brother. I laid the chocolate-covered stuffed alien back on the floor. Yup, looked just like the one Sally gave me.

No sooner did I sit back in my chair when I was locked in again by the invisible force field.

"Ready, my fearless captain."

The constant drone of a hum became louder and then a thought came to me.

"Wait a minute, who is flying this ship now?"

"I am."

"But I thought-"

He giggled.

"How then?"

"Look at the size of my head. How do you think? It's all done with thought patterns connecting to the electromagnetic wave lengths of the meridians encompassing the Universe. Everything created is manifested by thought."

"Yeah. Right. I'll just take your word for it." Would I ever get this concept clear in my head?

"Oh, one last thing to hammer into your brain matter, Bleakus - Law of Attraction is action! Don't *wait* for it to happen, *do* something about it. Thinking about it is one thing, but *doing* something about it is another. And while you're at it, throw in a little *seeing* and *feeling*. You have the power to manifest anything that is in alignment with self and your journey. But I repeat – you have to know your *Self* first!

Otherwise, you'll create illusion and confusion. Know thy self and enjoy the ride while you're at it, one step at a time. Be patient. When you get back, apply these principles. Trust your instincts. Trust the multidimensional being that you are. Make a difference in your life and others!"

"Huh. Okay, I'll try."

"No try. Do! There are no limitations if you're in touch with who you are and what your purpose is. It's all in your head."

"Looking at you, clearly."

"Ouch! Leave my head out of this."

We laughed.

"I can see we have a ways to go with you, eh Bucko? But hey, that's OK, you're my brother. Always have been, always will be. We'll take care of each other, right Buck-germ?" He raised his long forefinger up in the air in his attempt to give me the thumbs up.

"You got it, brother," I said, as I gave him my "thumb's up." Actually, I used my forefinger so he wouldn't feel embarrassed by his attempt at a friendly Earth gesture. Maybe I could teach him a few things after all?

In a single thrust, we were off.

"I'll always be around you, remember that."

Then the thrust suddenly stopped.

I slowly lost focus and went into a hazy dreamstate, as I turned toward him for a last peek.

"Be careful. Many will try to stop you but none will have the force of God. Always remember the G-force and you will dissolve all matter that ain't good for you, bro. Remember your mission. Remember where you were once and remember where you'll be once again. The journey in between is that of selflessness and service to God. Most of all, my friendly brother, remember that you too are God."

"You're starting to sound like a Master, Lenahtal," I heard myself faintly think aloud.

"Yes, my friend. I think it's time to fully embrace my multidimensional being too. Take care, Buck-germ. I love you."

"I love you too, Lenahtal, and thank you."

"No, thank *you*, Bleakus."

Somehow I finally felt comfortable with that odd name of mine.

"God is all around you and in you," were the last words I heard from Lenahtal, my brother.

I took his words and love with me as I drifted off.

~ 35 ~

"Seven-thirty," I heard a mechanical voice say.

Oh no! Now I was in the land of robots.

I slowly and reluctantly opened my eyes. How much could one human take in a weekend? My weekends were usually reserved for sports, not meetings with God, never mind robots.

"Seven-thirty one," I heard shortly after.

Wait a minute, I know this voice. It's my alarm clock at home.

I bolted straight up and there I was, in my bed, at home in my condo. None of this had really happened! It was all a dream. It must have been. Surrender the nerf batter, Jack the Vampire, Merinda the Buddhist Vegan from work, the stuffed alien. Yeah, a dream.

I felt my head spinning and realized my body was feeling like lead. I put both of my hands to my face as though that would bring some kind of answer to what was going on.

"How are you feeling, Hon?" That voice was all too familiar.

That's weird, Sally never stays over weekends unless it's the rare time she doesn't go to her retreat. I'm sure I'd picked her up on Friday to go to her spiritual retreat, but how did I end up in my own bed? What's going on here?

Sally sat up beside me. "How do you feel, Sweetie?"

"Very confused."

"Surrender told me you would be dropped off here after your ceremony, which by the way, I heard was beautiful. I brought all your belongings and your car back."

I couldn't comprehend her nonchalance.

"What are you talking about?"

Sally looked at me as if she was confused by my confusion. I could see a little sadness cloud her face as she sank back into the pillows.

I looked at what I was wearing and realized it was the same white outfit that had been given to me by Surrender. I felt something around my neck and pulled out the pyramid crystal that had been given to Lenahtal and me.

But it *was* a dream. All of it. No?

Upon touching the crystal, I remembered. I remembered everything that had happened to me. I remembered everything as it rushed through my mind with blazing clarity.

My oh my.

I slowly lay back on my pillow. I held Sally's hand as we lay there together in silence. Her angelic presence was the only calming force in that room as my heart began racing at everything that had transpired this past weekend.

I turned toward Sally. The pictures of these past few days that flashed through my mind overwhelmed me.

"Did this, did I, did all this really happen?" I asked Sally, bracing myself for the real answer.

"Yes, Bleakus, it did."

My oh my. This was going to be hard to digest.

"How did I end up at the condo?" I wasn't sure I wanted to know.

"Your fun-loving little brother, Lenahtal, brought you here by his little ol' spaceship."

"And the crystal?" I needed confirmation.

"It was given to you as part of your initiation into being a Remembered One, not to mention being a hero of Atlantis and Lemuria." she said, smiling proudly.

"It's true then. Man oh man."

I laid there in stunned silence. The mechanical clock ticked on.

"But Surrender, Jack the Vampire, Merinda, the stuffed alien you gave me, I don't get it."

"You don't have to get it all. Some of it will do for now. You're just waking up."

I took a deep breath and stared at the ceiling, remembering my exasperating moments on the alter.

"So, then, did I really meet God?"

"Yes you did, Peter."

Her forefinger chased a tear making its way down my cheek.

"Are you really an angel, Sally?" I said, as I turned to her and began caressing her long blonde hair.

"Yes I am," she said in a soft tone.

I got up on my elbow and looked at the clock behind Sally's head on the end table.

I gasped.

"Tuesday?! Sally?! No, no, it just can't be. How could it-"

"Easy, Hon."

"Is it really Tuesday?" I asked, in shock at the time I couldn't account for.

"Yes. It's OK."

"But how? Why? What's going on? What's– "

"It's OK, calm down."

"This is too weird for me. This is just too weird."

Sally looked at me patiently as I squeezed my forehead, looking for a rational answer to pop out.

"First, I miss sleep on Friday because I'm walking in the fields with Surrender. Then Saturday night because I'm in Vienna exploring the nineteenth century with concertos and a vampire that looks like my boss. And now, I miss Sunday and Monday nights because I'm traveling around to lost continents in the oceans and to other planets in my alien brother's spaceship? Am I that bad at physics? *At reality?* What's going on, Sally?!" I screamed in panic.

"Peter! Peter! Please, calm down. You've got to realize that there is no clock in God's eyes. When we get out of our self-imposed limitations about time, we get into God's time. Which is no time. No time meaning the present time. *Now* time. Everything is happening right now, simultaneously. That's why they say 'live in the *now*.'

"I know you don't quite get it yet but when we get into God's time and not man-made time, we get everything happening simultaneously. Which means, since everything is happening *now*, wherever our thought is, that's what's happening. We can pick and choose our experience by our thought. That's part of being a multidimensional being. You chose specific thoughts to help you remember who you are and those new thoughts took you to those special places."

My face must have been as readable as a blank sheet of recycled paper.

I still don't remember choosing anything. This all just seemed to happen to me. The only thing I remember "choosing" is that I didn't want to live the life I was leading and called Sally. Whoa! All this happened because of that one choice? One bit of action I took by calling up Sally on a whim and this happens to me over a long weekend? Oy. I wonder what would happen if I made conscious choices.

"Surrender felt that you had had enough for one weekend, so he asked Lenahtal to return you to this very point in time."

I was beginning to get it, and that scared me.

I slowly leaned back onto the pillow again and could almost immediately feel my body begin to release the tension that it was holding.

I looked over to Sally, my newly discovered angel.

"I'm scared."

Sally moved over to snuggle and melt into my body.

"I think you'd better just stay home and rest today, Hon. I'll take care of you. I have some homeopathic remedies and medicines that will help you adjust to your new vibration."

I turned and gave her a soft little kiss on the cheek, and snuggled into her embrace.

Then I had a horrible realization. "Oh no! *The condom campaign!* I didn't even bring it home. Jack is going to kill me!"

I broke the embrace and tried to get up. Nothing doing. I was a lead weight.

Sally gave me a penetrating look.

"Forget your boss. You're your own boss now. You don't have to do anything you don't want to do anymore. It's time for you to rethink and rearrange your life here on Earth. There's a lot of us who are depending on you to help us ascend into the Fourth Dimension."

"That all sounds nicey-nice but how am I going to pay my bills? Whatever you say may sound hunky-dory to you and your New Age friends, and I mean no disrespect…"

"None taken."

"But the reality is, I have to make a certain sized nut a month in order to cover my expenses. Are *you* willing to support my lifestyle?"

Sally shot straight up. "Are *you* willing to support your lifestyle? Support the way you've been living? Especially now that you know what you know?"

She had me on that one.

How could I possibly go back to work and act as if nothing had ever happened? How could I honestly deal with myself when I wasn't honestly dealing with the public? How could I have this experience with God in one moment, then turn around and come up with a great slogan to sell chemically-ridden beef or chicken that's dead before they kill it, or big gas-guzzling SUV's, or aerosol cans of pollutants. Or air conditioners that leach our ozone layer, oil companies that have ruined millions of plants and animals, paper mills that have raped the forests for profit, et cetera And what about "green" products that aren't really green products but just a scam to rip off the consumer and jump on the "environmentally friendly" bandwagon? Lets not even talk about the recyclable condoms.

How could I? How could I when I knew it was all about making a dollar at the expense of other people's lives, livelihoods, and Mother Nature?

Sally was right. A new strategy was in order for my life. I could no longer sell myself short of who I Am and what I Am about. Something had to be done on this planet Earth. Mother Nature knew it. Now it was time for her children to not only know it, but to listen and do something about it.

I needed to make a major shift in my life. I needed to do it immediately. I needed to go in a completely different direction. There seemed to be so much to do in so little time. If what I had learned over the weekend and from Sally's past accounts of the predictions of the great prophets, teachers, and Native Americans was true, then something had to be done. I knew that I needed to be involved with those changes that would help us move into the Fourth Dimension as peacefully and as honorably as possible.

So if Law of Attraction *was* Action, what "action" did I need to take?

And did it really matter if this weekend was real to me? Not really. Not now. Because I *knew* that this planet *was* dying and a lot of issues needed to be addressed. Now. The choice was mine to play victim or healer. To quote a favorite truth of mine, if I'm not part of the solution, I'm part of the problem. I had to pick one, and I knew which one. I knew our future worlds were being affected by the choices that we were making now. More importantly, I knew that I had the courage to make a difference in my life and in others' lives.

I sat up with a burst of energy and turned toward my angel. My body felt lighter with these sudden realizations.

"That's what it all comes down to, doesn't it?"

"What's that, Sweetie?" she replied, in a soft whisper.

I looked deeply into her soulful blue eyes and said in full realization.

"Service to God. To others. To *us!*"

Sally squeezed my hand in silent joy as tears welled up in her eyes. They soon began their journey down her soft, red, rosy cheeks. I gently leaned over and kissed them away. Her angelic smile penetrated my heart.

I hugged her with all my love, as she did me.

I opened my eyes, looked at the mechanical alarm clock on the bedside table and realized that it was now my time to remember.

Oh dear.

PUBLISHERS CONTACT INFORMATION

Dreamstate Publishing Company
283 Danforth Ave., Suite 496
Toronto, Ontario
M4K 1N2

www.suitontherun.com

www.dreamstatepublishing.ca

www.dreamstatepublishingcompany.com

AUTHORS CONTACT INFORMATION

www.steveadams.tv

Printed in the United States
96090LV00005B/7-48/A

9 780978 335700